THE LATE ARRIVAL

Also by Jemima Hunt

NOTES FROM UTOPIA

THE LATE ARRIVAL

Jemima Hunt

FLAME
Hodder & Stoughton

First published in Great Britain in 2002 by Hodder and Stoughton
A division of Hodder Headline

A Flame Book

2 4 6 8 10 9 7 5 3 1

A CIP catalogue record for this title is available from the British Library

ISBN 0 340 75154 1

Typeset in Centaur by Palimpsest Book Production Limited,
Polmont, Stirlingshire
Printed and bound in Great Britain by
Mackays of Chatham plc, Chatham, Kent

Hodder and Stoughton
A division of Hodder Headline
338 Euston Road
London NW1 3BH

To GMPH and DHG

I have a long list of barristers to thank, without whom I could not have written this book. So, in chronological order, I'd like to thank Kaja Reiff-Musgrove, Grace Morden, Jess Gavron, Rosamund Horwood-Smart and Paul Michell for their assistance. A particularly big thank you to James Kirby and Mark Norman for taking me to court, to David Hacking for his shrewd advice and Louise Brooks for her invaluable editorial input.

I also want to thank Tony Miller for his adventuring exploits, Max Jourdan for letting me sit in on an edit and Andy Turner for his support.

And to my agents Stephanie Cabot and Eugenie Furniss.

Chapter One

It was one of those days when everything itched. Her ten denier tights, her woollen skirt with its bumpy lining, her horsehair wig, her wing collar, the stub of the label inside her bra. She cut out her labels because she'd had to at school. It had been a school rule. No labels, logos or brands allowed. Only the school motto, *Paulatim sed firmiter,* embroidered on the pocket of the blazer, gold on blue. Slowly but surely. She was a cautious person by nature. It had always made sense to her.

She arched her back and rocked gently from side to side. Court had been in session an hour, the minutes dragged, and already she ached. She slipped a finger beneath her wig and poked her scalp. Scrunching handfuls of gown, she gathered it on to her lap and watched it fall open both sides of her knees. The black cloth parted like curtains. She took a sip of water. She had learned through experience that water could clear not only the palate but also the mind. Nothing this morning could keep her thoughts on track. She had drunk her coffee too fast and now she had a blister. Exploring the roof of her mouth with her tongue, she teased the blister by pressing it flat. It popped and left her mouth moist as her thoughts drifted back to the man she had met on the plane.

It was his demerara hair, enough of it to run a hand through, his easy laugh and legs that wouldn't fold into the space in front she remembered. It was the way he had crunched his ice cubes, winced and shaken his head like a dog. It was his pronunciation of her name, Elinor, the third syllable long. It made her like him. They had spent eleven hours beside each other on the plane. Her only flight without Valium. A nervous flier, she would normally take a pill with the first offer of alcohol, fall asleep and wake without dreaming on the other side. This time, drugged by his presence, she had hardly slept a wink. At Heathrow they shared a taxi. They had been sitting in traffic in Soho when he decided to bolt.

'It's quicker for me to walk from here,' he said, then he leaned over and squeezed her arm. It was a short squeeze. The type of squeeze that didn't have to mean anything. It had sent electricity coursing through her.

'I salute you,' he said, paid the meter and was gone. And as she watched him disappear, she had felt bereft. His absence crushed her. She couldn't remove the feel of his hand from her arm or the ripple of his voice from her head. No one had ever saluted her before.

'Think of this analogy. If someone were to hand you a camera film and a magnifying glass and you were to look at it frame by frame you would have no idea of the story. You must look at the movement as a whole or you won't be able to follow the plot.'

Elinor looked up. She had been away for three weeks. She had missed the Pleas and Directions and Caroline, counsel for the prosecution, liked to win. All barristers liked to win, but Caroline was the type to get her name in the papers. She was a deputy head of chambers, sat on government committees and helped frame legislation. She was an energetic woman with fast-moving hands and a face beginning to lend itself to fleshiness. Her mouth was starting to droop so that soon she would look permanently unhappy.

'It is for you to listen to the evidence and understand how Frank Foster became so infatuated with Suzanne Price that when she said "I don't want to see you any more" he began a course of conduct intended to cause her maximum distress. Suzanne Price was bombarded with telephone calls and letters. She received foul parcels through her letterbox; blood, excrement and torn-up clothing. She feared for her personal safety. She lost her job, her freedom and her peace of mind, and this went on for fifteen long, painful months when all she wanted to do was put the past behind her and live beyond the reach of fear. But Frank Foster refused to allow this. Frank Foster wanted Miss Price to know that he was always there. Watching her. Following her. *Harassing* her.'

Caroline had found her tempo. Harassing was a hard word to spit at the jury to make them flinch. Caroline's words were familiar. All the best imagery had been used by some other barrister in some other case. Recycling was part of what they did. Phrases. Quotations. Allegories. The jury weren't to know. Most of the twelve looked stunned by where they had found themselves this morning. Arms were crossed and there were the usual squints, blinks and grins as they wondered where to look. Should they be looking at the judge, watching Caroline or inspecting their laps? Few would doubt a word of what Caroline was saying, which was why Elinor was here.

Elinor worked as a defence advocate, drugs mostly and domestic crimes. Her briefs took her out of London as often as they kept her in town. She was on the Western Circuit – Exeter, Southampton, Bristol and all the stops in between. Today she was in London. Her job was to convince the jury that the Crown had failed to make its case against Mr Foster beyond reasonable doubt. Mr Foster was charged with stalking under the Protection from Harassment Act. He was Elinor's first stalker. Firsts were by definition a headache, which was why most of last night had been spent in the bath, Silker Reconstructor on her hair as she untangled her curls and put together her defence.

She stole a glance behind her. Never betray what you're thinking in court was the rule, but her restlessness got the better of her. Her client was in the dock. He looked small. Good. He was meant to. He was staring glassy eyed into the distance. From their half-hour in conference she knew he felt hard done by. About what exactly? Life would be her guess.

She had found him in the lobby first thing this morning. He had been sitting next to Brian Henderson, her instructing solicitor whom she worked with a lot. Mr Foster had been hunched with his head in his hands. Brian, a bearded man from somewhere up north, had been speaking in a low voice into Mr Foster's ear. Going over to greet them, she had reached out her hand, but it was the clip of her heels that came first. This was important.

The sound of her shoes as she crossed the floor defined who she was or who she needed to be. Apprehensions that it was going to be a bad day, that she had not been properly briefed, that the judge was going to make it difficult for her, were masked by this sound. It was the sound of authority and the sound made her taller because the shoes made her taller. Five-five in heels. Heels were also proof of her femininity, which meant a great deal when the rest of what she wore kept her sex under wraps.

In this job armour was key. The gown was her weapon. It enabled her to point the finger, to accuse, because no one knew who she was. Her private self, her real self, was hidden beneath, along with last year's suit, the shirt that hadn't made it to the dry cleaner's and her bosom. She had a considerable bosom. Double D cup, sometimes bigger. She had learned early on that to be more than the sum of big bosoms it was essential to hide them away. Aged thirteen, she began to notice boys lose their train of thought as their eyes settled on her chest. Melons, they called out on the street. Breasts like hers could never passively be. They were seen to exist for sexual gratification. They were public property, she realised.

Joining the legal profession had done nothing to change

this. It was rife with unreconstructed men. Policemen breathed, 'Who's a big girl?' Barristers, remaining silent, undressed her with greedy eyes. In the early days she had panicked. Felt sick and flustered. No longer twenty-three, she was no longer subjected to the same frequent assault. She had learned to turn the other cheek. On days when she wanted to forget about her breasts entirely, however, she wore a minimiser bra and strapped them to her chest. They were merely a suggestion through her black gown, white shirt, black jacket.

Her gown she trusted.

She loathed her wig.

It made her feel like a man. It smelled of old age and slipped down her head, bringing on headaches on long days. Her own hair was too thick for the wig to sit comfortably on top. It bunched out at the back and ballooned at the sides. Only the male barristers took pride in wearing them, and this because it compensated for their own lack of hair. They thought they made them look younger when in fact they did the reverse. They added decades.

Mr Foster had shaken her hand without enthusiasm.

'I had a bloke last week.'

Depressed that her first greeting on her first day back was an insult, Elinor forced a smile.

'Now you've got me.'

Brian said nothing. He was funny like that. His unease around women manifested itself in a tendency to drink too much and say things he shouldn't. Things about her perfume and the whiteness of her skin. She didn't hold it against him. He put work her way. He specifically asked for her to defend his good clients, the ones in trouble who kept him in work, and for this she was grateful. For this his inevitable offer of a drink was occasionally accepted. She never agreed to a lift home. She had seen the way he looked at her. There were leg men and breasts men and Brian was a breasts man.

'Shall we find somewhere to talk?' she said.

She had led them to an interview room tiled like the ladies' room, as though it would be hosed down later on. She hit the lights and ushered them in, fanning the door to relieve the room of its' previous occupants and the damp smell of feet. She sat down on one side of the table. They took the other. Opening her notebook, she smoothed out a fresh page, peeled the lid off her cup and put it to her mouth. The best part of a cappuccino was licking the froth. Then she remembered where she was and put it down again.

'Mr Foster, I need to ask you a few supplementary questions to clarify what I've read in your statement regarding your relationship with Miss Price.'

No response.

'Why did your relationship end?'

They listened to the rain. A gutter somewhere began to overflow and they could hear the run-off hitting the ground. Sipping her coffee, she examined her client. His suit, too wide in the shoulders, was cut from a fibre that winked in the light. He had greased-back hair like pigeon feathers and the whites of his eyes weren't white but pink. He had a ruddy face, which was the legacy of a life outdoors. He ran a fruit-and-vegetable stall, she read in her brief. Forty-five. Divorced. Had a Bermondsey address.

He looked tired. Events had pushed him farther than he wanted to go.

'Did it have anything to do with the birth of your son?'

More rain outside. Coffee inside.

She paused. 'Mr Foster, you realise that to defend you I need all the facts, don't you?'

Her court voice rumbled in her ears. She hadn't used it while she was away. A decibel louder than she normally spoke, sweetened with concern, it was as unyielding as rock. She felt his eyes criss-cross her face. He planted both hands on the table, interwoven fingers to form a fist of gold. A collection of coins and pools of onyx. He blinked hard.

'You want to know what I think?'

He was hoarse.

'What do you think, Mr Foster?'

'This here's an f-ing joke.'

Her heart sank. The room was built to contain outbursts of emotions and she was used to this sort of thing – denial, counter-denial, referring to the charge as a joke. It didn't lessen her resolve. Still, it did nothing to brighten her day.

There was a rattle from above and she was reminded of where she was. Court eleven. His Honour Judge Green shielded his mouth with his hand. A tiny man, his head just visible above his red-and-purple robes, he was so high up in his leather throne that the room had an *Alice in Wonderland* feel. This was the jet-lag.

'The Crown says this is a very straightforward case. In

attempting to rekindle relations with the complainant, Mr Foster became a menace. All Miss Price wanted was to put the past behind her and move on.'

Caroline was playing to the jury. Reeling them in.

'On the evidence put before you today, there can be no doubt that Mr Foster pursued a course of conduct which amounted to the harassment of Miss Price. I suggest that it is your duty, as a jury, to return a verdict of *guilty*.'

Caroline sat down and the incriminating word lingered. No one dared breathe for fear of wrongdoing. The clerk was dispatched to summon the first witness and a low drizzle of voices filled the court. Elinor replaced the cartridge in her pen. Permanent black, never blue, never blue-black. Blue on paper looked watery and indecisive, she thought. When she looked up, Miss Price had taken the witness box.

Elinor tugged her cuffs. It was a nervous gesture. The same as tweaking her hair or kicking her shoes off and on. There was an instinctive sympathy in court for the victim, which she would have to overturn. Her job was to discredit Miss Price's story. Never easy, it was frequently unpleasant. Brian had specifically requested that she defend Mr Foster because she was a woman. They both knew this. The fact was the jury was more likely to find Mr Foster not guilty of a crime against a woman if defended by a woman.

She studied Miss Price. What had attracted Frank Foster to her? She was pretty in a girlish way. Wavy, light brown hair fell down one side of her face. She had high cheekbones and fondant eyes, a timid mouth. Her gold crucifix caught the light. Thin beneath her ill-fitting grey suit, she looked the type to skip meals. She seemed in need of looking after. That was the appeal.

'Is your full name Suzanne Mary Price?' Caroline began.

Her answer, a yes to those who could lip-read, was lost in the high-ceilinged room.

'Nice and loud,' boomed the judge.

'Yes.'

'Occupation?'

'Legal secretary.'

'Did you have a relationship with the defendant?'

'Yes.'

'How long did the relationship last?'

'A year and a half.'

'When did the relationship end?'

'January.'

'When did you next have contact with him?'

'February.'

'Where did this meeting take place?'

'At my flat.'

'What happened at this meeting?'

'I told him I couldn't see him any more. And we'd have to settle it through the courts for him to see Billy. Our son.'

'What was his reaction?'

'He got angry. He was shouting.' She took a deep breath. 'He punched a hole in my kitchen wall. He kicked over the chairs round the table and threw some of my crockery on the floor.'

There was tut-tutting from the jury.

'How did you feel?'

'Scared. He was drunk. He was going out of his mind. He got me by the arm.'

'What happened next?'

'I told him to get out else I'd call the police. He went. The next day I got a card from him.'

'Can you remember what was written on the card?'

She nodded.

'*My love for you will never die.*'

'Did you reply?'

'No.'

'Why not?'

'I didn't want to encourage him.'

'When did you next see Mr Foster?'

'He came round to the flat the following week. When I opened the door, he tried to grab me.'

'What did you do?'

'I told him not to touch me. Then I let him in. I had to.'

'What happened?'

'He was shouting and telling me not to listen to the lies. After I don't know how long, he went. The day after that I got another card, then I started getting them every day. I started getting messages on my mobile phone. Ten a day. Sometimes twenty a day. They all said the same thing. I'll die if I can't see you. I started getting hang-up calls at home. At work I got so upset that other girls had to answer the phone for me. My boss called me into his office and told me I had to answer it. That was my job. I told him I couldn't. A week later I got the sack.'

Her voice faltered.

'It's all right, Miss Price. Take your time,' said Caroline.

Miss Price took a sip of water. Caroline checked her notes.

'Going back, if we may. Can you tell the court what happened on the seventh of February?'

'I got home and all the flowerpots in my front garden had been smashed. The plants were everywhere. There was earth through my letterbox and graffiti on my door.'

'What did the graffiti say?'

She dropped her head.

'Slag.'

Caroline paused. Elinor shifted in her seat. She had inserted her tampon in a hurry. It was positioned incorrectly. She felt like a drug smuggler.

'I would like to submit as evidence Exhibit eight. One mutilated toy rabbit.'

The furry pink rabbit in a plastic bag was held aloft for the judge to see before being passed by the clerk to the jury. It travelled pass-the-parcel style along both rows before being handed back to Caroline.

'If I may describe it to Your Honour. The rabbit has been stabbed. Both eyes are missing and the incisions in the posterior would appear to indicate markings of a sexual nature.'

Caroline returned to Miss Price.

'In order that the jury can be made aware of the significance of the rabbit, would you like to tell them Mr Foster's pet name for you?'

She hesitated.

'Bunny.'

'Thank you. Did the rabbit and the cards come in the post?'

'No.'

'How, then?'

'They were hand delivered.'

'Did you ever see anyone deliver them?'

'A lot of nights I saw his van parked outside.'

'Whose van did you see parked outside?'

'Frank's van.'

'And what van would that be?'

'A white Ford Transit.'

'How do you know that this was Frank Foster's van?'

'We went driving in it.'

'Do you know the licence plate number of the van?'

'G449 FHF.'

'Thank you. Now, if I may, I'd like to move to the night of January the twelfth.'

'Can you tell us exactly what happened?'

Miss Price glanced at Frank Foster. Elinor caught her. It was the first time Elinor had seen this happen and she tried to identify the emotions involved. She couldn't. Instead she was left to feel that she had been prying and that she would never know all that had happened between them. Intimacy was a secret unto itself.

'I was home by myself,' said Miss Price. Her fingers looked skeletal dangling from the top of the witness box. 'The doorbell rang.' Her voice began to wobble. 'I opened it.' She breathed in and out. 'No one was there. Then I trod on it.'

'What did you tread on?' said Caroline.

'A rat.'

'Was it dead?'

'Yes.'

'What was attached to it?'

'A note.'

'Can you tell the courtroom what the note said?'

'Dead meat.'

Caroline faced the jury.

'In your jury bundle you will find transcripts of mobile-phone text messages and copies of cards that the Crown say were sent to Miss Price. On page ten you will find a copy of one of these cards. I'm going to ask Miss Price to read it.'

Elinor turned to the page. Standard threat, standard format in barely legible block capital letters as though written by a child. She had seen worse. It was the extra touch that was sickening. A lock of hair had been taped to the card. It was Miss Price's hair. Miss Price's face grew taut. Her voice scraped a whisper.

'*Dear Suzy . . .*'

Caroline intervened.

'Perhaps if I read the card for you. *I am watching and waiting. We have formed a soul union. I know what makes you tick.*'

Miss Price began shaking her head. Her shoulders heaved and now, in front of everyone, she began to cry. There were few things more harrowing than watching a person weep. The room temperature dropped. Judge Green, poker faced, tipped forward on to his elbows.

'I suggest we adjourn for a five-minute break. Do you suppose this will give you time to recover, Miss Price?'

'Yes, Your Honour.'

The usher led Miss Price down from the witness box. The rest of the room bolted. Any excuse for a break. Outside in the lobby Caroline inhaled deeply on a menthol cigarette.

'You know what they've got in next door, don't you?'

Elinor was kneading her calves, which were cramped with worry, while running through what she would need Miss Price to say.

'What?'

'The couple being done for bonking in a plane. They did it in the seats. She was meowing, apparently, and he was barking.'

Elinor laughed. They were summoned back in. Caroline had sat down. In see-saw style Elinor stood up. She could taste adrenaline dry on her tongue, liquid inside. She needed it there. Sometimes it made her dizzy but right now her head was clear. Her adrenaline took charge as soon as she entered the court building and was hit by the wall of smells. The cleaning fluid. Wood polish. Stale smoke. Canteen food. It was different from the blind adrenaline that flooded her body when she cycled home at night. This brought clarity, allowing her to think on her feet, retrieve facts from memory and fast-forward for a preview of where the next question should lead.

'Miss Price, I'd like to take you back to your first meeting with Mr Foster. How did you meet?'

'Through a friend. Steve Robson.'

'Where did you meet?'

'In the pub. The Barley Corn.'

'The following day, the day after your first meeting, what did you do?'

'I don't understand.'

Swivelling round to face the jury, Elinor felt the pinch in her calves, the flush of certainty in her blood.

'I'd like you to turn to page three of your jury bundles. There you will find a note on self-addressed paper sent by Miss Price to Mr Foster the day after that first meeting. I will read it for you. *You are the man I've been waiting for all my life. Don't ever leave me.*'

She turned back.

'Was this sentiment sincere, Miss Price?'

Elinor repeated the question.

'Was this how you genuinely felt?'

In the pause that followed, the life drained from Miss Price's face. Hugging her arms to her stomach, she doubled over in pain.

The judge sniffed.

'Yes. Well. This would seem to be an appropriate time to break for lunch,' he said.

Miss Price was led out.

Elinor sat down. Heart beating fast. She loved the courtroom. It was here she felt she performed her best. Here she could be convincing in a way she couldn't be elsewhere. Personal arguments were messy and convoluted. They ran overtime, were rarely resolved and somebody cried. All of which was true of court, she realised, only here she wasn't the one to cry. Her sympathies went out to Miss Price but there was no place for them here.

Caroline was mouthing something to her. Elinor read her lips. It was a survival skill. Tea and a pee. Tea and a pee, she was chanting.

'All rise,' ordered the clerk.

They rose like toy soldiers and waited for the door to close behind the judge's back.

'See you in the canteen.' Caroline scooted out from behind.

'Yes,' mumbled Elinor, vaguely.

Gathering her notebooks and brief, she switched on her mobile phone. '*You have no new messages in your mailbox.*' Swallowing her disappointment, she entered the stream in the hall. A group of teenage girls, their ears hooped with gold, were sharing a joke and a packet of crisps. One of the girls had two crisps between her lips like a beak. Flapping her arms, she was waddling like a duck.

'Quack, quack,' said her friends.

Elinor overtook them and stared through the window at a smear of grey. Waves of rain bounced off the glass. He didn't live far from here, she reflected, searching for a sign that he would call. She would never find one. But the secret to yearning was the determination not to give up. Not unlike the business of defending in court.

Chapter Two

They had met six days ago. Did it feel longer? Shorter? She couldn't tell. All she knew was that he had been in her thoughts ever since. She had been alone, the seat beside her empty, when he turned up.

'Thirty-one?'

Looking up from her in-flight magazine with nothing in it to read, Elinor found a man panting at her. He had a wild look in his eyes, pupils popping, and too many bags. Shoulder straps criss-crossed his body like the straps on a parachutist about to go down. The plane was about to take off. Everybody was on board and strapped in. They had their shoes off and eyes closed. The stewardesses had slammed shut the overhead compartments and were installed in their own special seats.

Elinor was doing the breathing exercise her friend Kendra had taught her. Long in-breath, long out-breath through the nostrils. It seemed to be working. She was on the verge of relaxing. Assisting her in this was the assumption she would have room to spread out. That 31A and B were hers. She had been silently celebrating her luck. For the first time ever she had been assigned a seat with no neighbour. But no, here he was to ruin her plan.

'I don't know,' she said.

It was a pointless lie but it flew from her mouth before she could stop it. He leaned in for a closer look before stretching to open the overhead locker.

'Sorry to bust in on you.'

No you're not, she thought, as she watched his torso grow. She was the only one who was sorry. He dropped a pile of magazines on to his chair and a book with pages so curled they looked unreadable. A smudgy photograph of a desert was featured on the cover. Somebody's account of a trip somewhere.

Struggling with his bags, he was murmuring to himself, as though sorting through shifting details in his head. His restlessness intrigued her. There were more hours ahead than she knew what to do with. This was the person she would knock knees with every time she got up to stretch her legs. The person whose leisurely sipping of his drink she would have to match so as not to appear greedy. Her irritation at landing a neighbour was short lived.

A navy skirt came bustling down the aisle. Her tights made a busy sound.

'Sir. Can I help?'

The stewardess put out her arms and removed one of his

bags as if it were a sleeping child. Elinor's neighbour removed his jacket. He was wearing a grey T-shirt baggy with age. He bowed his head and moved into the seat next to her. Elinor quickly looked away.

She had once read somewhere that the reaction time of one human being to another was a third of a second. It was the type of fact she enjoyed. Empirical and relevant. In this time humans, like animals, made a judgment based on whether the other person was a threat. If so, the instinct was to run. If not, the instinct was to take a closer look. There had been an instant when their eyes had met and something else could have been said. It had happened too fast. Their gaze had fallen into shadow and now they were strangers.

She wasn't good with strangers. She wasn't good at small talk. She knew how to ask questions. It was a skill she had been taught. Yet she would hold off making eye contact until sure of her company. It was probably why she had long hair. It offered protection. Besides, if the first rule of cross-examination was never ask a question unless you knew the answer, why shouldn't the same rule be applied to strangers?

She returned to her page. *Upon familiarising yourself with your nearest emergency exit, pull down your oxygen mask*. She had read this page before. Her neighbour was working out where to put his arms and legs. She heard his table bounce open on to his lap. There was a tremor as the row of seats in front shook.

'Is it me or are these seats even smaller than usual?'

His voice was pleasant and low. She looked around. He was handsome in a lived in sort of way. His skin was beaten by the sun, and when he squinted she saw laughter lines, a lighter shade of skin. He had fine features. Weak jaw. Firm chest. There was a faint smell of sweat. Groping for an answer, she felt herself blush. She never blushed. The courtroom had taught her how to control her colouring. Never allow anyone to discern your mood was the rule. This man had caught her out.

'Smaller,' she said.

'Yes.' He nodded. Then he unknotted the sweater from his waist and his head disappeared.

She stared out of the window. A boy was standing beneath the wing of a stationary Southwest plane. He was juggling with a pair of air traffic control batons that threaded the darkness with light. He dropped a baton. Stooping to scoop it up, he began to juggle again.

'Candy?'

A stewardess leaned in with a tray of mints. Elinor took one. Her neighbour declined the offer by shaking his head. He was wearing his headset and fiddling with the knobs on his armrest. She looked at his hands. He had slender, tapered fingers. She noticed his thumb. Swollen and bruised, it was wrapped in a bandage. Imagining a car door slamming, the impact of metal on bone, the zigzag of pain, she felt queasy.

No wedding ring.

This, of course, meant nothing. QC had worn his wedding ring throughout their time together, his wife's name inscribed on the inside of it. Her trick had been to use her tongue to try and suck it off. When she succeeded she would threaten to swallow it. There was nothing QC hated more than being made to feel vulnerable, so they would have an argument and he would accuse her of being unreasonable.

QC was a Queen's Counsel. His name was Peter Laslow, but after so many years of concealing his identity she had given up on Peter. He was QC. Her head of chambers and the man responsible for giving her a pupillage then a tenancy at the set of chambers where she worked. A well-preserved fifty-eight-year-old with a full head of hair, most of which was black, he had a wolfish smile and a boundless capacity for charm. He wore rimless glasses, cuff links engraved with his initials and a red silk hankie which flamed from his top pocket. Never had she imagined that within twelve hours of meeting him she would end up in his bed.

At his suggestion they had finished her interview over a glass of champagne at a wine bar around the corner. Then came a spot of supper at a bistro next door. It was only when they were in a taxi on the way to his Mayfair flat – he wanted to show her his first-edition Graham Greenes – that she accepted the inevitability of what lay ahead. She had never read a Graham Greene novel, not even *Brighton Rock.*

She had been seduced by his attentions and extremely drunk. She quickly became the woman he wanted her to be. He bought her clothing. Shimmery blouses. A dress with a sash. He scheduled when they would next see each other. Tuesdays, Thursdays, sometimes Fridays, never weekends. They would go for dinner, the theatre and were in bed before one. He paid for everything, made decisions and made her feel safe. It was a feeling she had craved for as long as she could remember.

In chambers she had found herself cast as the invisible woman everyone could see. It was common knowledge that when they left separately they were going home together. Even the clerks who traded in gossip lost interest in the end. Early on, the cloak-and-dagger stuff, the stolen fumblings, had been exciting. Then it became stressful. What did everyone think? What she could never have predicted was how long the affair would last. Five years.

Four months ago she had turned thirty-one. She had woken up beside him and studied his back. He had hairs on his back. Some were short, some were long and curly. She noticed that a few had faded to grey. One or two were white. These hairs were a mark of their years together, and suddenly, quite clearly, she saw that she was wasting her life. She had to give him up because she no longer liked the person she had become. A woman happy four mornings a week. I want a future, she said.

The parting had not been painless, though it was more an ache than a pain. Her orgy of sorrow had come years earlier when she had realised that she would never be the only woman, and certainly not the first woman, in his life. She had no regrets. She bought a white bikini, had her hair trimmed, booked three weeks off work and a ticket to LA to stay with a friend. An actress. Her first trip to America, it fulfilled all expectations. She had a ferociously good time driving down roads that didn't end, floating in swimming pools and having abstract conversations with good-looking men with surnames for first names. Presley and Walker and Hunter and Taylor. She was returning as an ex-mistress with a void in her life.

The boy juggler had vanished. The plane lurched and they journeyed down the runway. Pressing her face against the plastic window, she tried to remember the smell of heat before it was gone. The plane stopped.

'This is Captain Fleming, your pilot, taking this opportunity to welcome you on board United Airlines flight zero zero two flying non-stop from Los Angeles to London. I'm told there's a little back-up but we're third in line and it shouldn't be long before we're given clearance. So for now, folks, sit back, relax and enjoy the friendly skies of United . . .'

Her pulse raced. Her head throbbed. She was in an airless capsule. They were about to take off and there was no guarantee they would ever come down. Looking at her neighbour's hands, she considered that if anything happened they would be the last pair of hands she could ever hope to hold. She wondered what he would think if she took them now, slipping her fingers between his, as a precautionary measure? She clasped her hands together. Her palms were wet.

The fear of flying was the fear of death. When she thought about death, she began compiling a list. The result of being the so-called other woman for so long was that whenever she drew up guest lists, one of those sleep-chasing exercises, it was never a list of who would come to her wedding but who would attend her funeral. She looked out into blackness, comforted by the fuzz of chatter in the surrounding seats. Her neighbour was trying to be calm but found the confinement difficult. She could tell. He had a frantic air about him, as though fighting the constraints of being strapped in a chair. His left leg was jiggling up and down. He sighed repeatedly. Absorbing his energy, she shivered and sheltered her knees with her blanket.

They were up. Below, at a forty-five-degree angle, the city was a galaxy of twinkling lights. The pressure of lift-off forced her head against the chair. The sound of filtered air whistled above.

'Is your radio working?'

His voice startled her. It was gruff with fatigue. His face was pooled in light and his eyes, like blue marbles, peered at her from orbs of shadow. He looked exhausted.

'Do you want to use it?'

'I didn't mean . . .'

'I'm not using it.'

'Are you sure?'

'Yes.'

'My CD Walkman was stolen from the car. I've got some magazines here if you need something to read.'

'Thanks.' She accepted his offer, not remotely interested in his magazines. She was interested in his story. Did the theft from the car have anything to do with his thumb? She offered him the inside of her armrest and accepted his copy of *Newsweek*. He plugged in. She studied the cover. 'Killing in Congo.' She turned the page and tried to read. Her head was sore. Exhaustion. Emotion. Too many cocktails in a bar last night. She flicked aimlessly.

'You're missing the seventies hit parade.'

Holding his headset away from his ears, he had a half-smile on his lips. She smiled back. He removed his headset and left it slung around his neck.

'Have you been on holiday?'

'Yes,' she said, grateful to talk. 'A friend has moved here.'

'An actor?'

'Yes. You?'

'I've been in Arizona.'

The state where men used scrubland to practise moon-walking before going to the moon, she had read somewhere.

'On holiday?'

'Working. In a manner of speaking.'

'Are you an actor?'

He laughed as though she was trying to be funny. He had a good laugh, a kind of snorting chuckle. She saw no reason for him not to be an actor. He had a prominent nose but it fitted his face.

'No.'

'So you're a cowboy?' she said, tongue in cheek.

'I'm Gus,' he introduced himself quietly.

'Elinor Taylor.' Her last name slipped out automatically like shaking hands.

'I spotted you before we boarded. I noticed your hair. It sort of bounces.'

Instinctively she put both hands to her head and found that her hair had come loose. It was red and curly and she wore it in a bunch because there was so much of it. When she was younger it had been straight and had covered her back. When it rained it turned to frizz and there was nothing she could do. She was flattered he had noticed.

'My uncontrollable hair.'

'Is it?'

'Only . . .'

Napkins and miniature foil bags fell from above.

'What would you like to drink?'

A stewardess was looking expectantly at them, her eyelids arched blue. Her jaunty scarf puffed at her neck and her name badge said Kimberley. They clicked open their tables.

'Bloody Mary, please.'

'I'll have the same,' said Elinor.

'Ice and lemon?'

'Please.' They spoke in unison and pretended they hadn't. They sat in silence as the stewardess dipped down to open a tray at the bottom of the trolley. Her knees clicked and her heels rose out of the backs of her shoes. The trolley tried to roll away.

'Damn this thing. It's got a mind of its own,' she complained, standing up in a hurry. 'Here you go.'

Elinor's drink came first. Taking a sip, she felt the vodka ease her body into her chair as though its dimensions had grown. It tasted raw and male somehow. Gin and tonic was her preferred drink. It was a drink she had acquired an early taste for by stealing swallows from glasses littered around her aunt's house. When she was at boarding school, once-a-month weekends and holidays had been spent with her great-aunt. Her parents lived abroad.

Her aunt's name was Frida. She had worn her silver hair cut close like a pageboy's and ropes of tatty pearls. She lived in the south wing of a manor house that smelt of mildew and fermented fruit, where the warmest place to be was in the bath and there was never any food. Elinor had survived on doughnuts delivered by a baker on a bicycle and eggs laid by a brood of bantam hens. Frida liked things out of tins. Baked beans and peas and watery soups. And every night, when she came to kiss Elinor goodnight, they would say their prayers together and Frida's secrets would come out in gin-and-tonic whispers.

'Grant us the serenity to accept the things we cannot change,' she would say.

The stewardess went to park her trolley a foot farther down the aisle and Gus leaned towards her. He had a trace of red around his mouth. His ice cubes clattered where they would have clinked had they been in a glass.

'Don't you think the stewardesses look like extras from the seventies hit parade?' he said.

Elinor looked. He was right. Their figures spilled out of A-line skirts and were sealed into polyester shirts with floppy bows. Pill-box hats perched on top of bouffant hair. Amused, Elinor sucked through what she thought was the straw. It was the stirrer. A whistling came from her lips. She casually moved her mouth to the edge of the glass.

'Yes,' she agreed and hugged herself in her blanket. She

felt tipsy. Altitude and alcohol. It didn't take much. She wasn't sure whether it was the cramped confinement or lack of oxygen but either way she felt their closeness moving closer. They were sharing the same air. Their pillows nudged and her mouth felt tight. It was beginning to ache as she reined in her grin. From her sideways perspective, she caught freckles. An eyebrow stapled with a scar. A chipped tooth.

She broke the silence. 'You didn't answer my question about being a cowboy.' Realising that she sounded like a barrister, impatient, accusative, she regretted it. It had been his turn to talk and she knew better than to waste the confessional lure of silence.

Gus crunched an ice cube. His timing was good. She had noticed it already. He swallowed.

'Do I look like a cowboy?'

'You must know how to ride a horse.'

'It doesn't mean I trust them.'

Elinor thought he was joking, but a glance at him assured her otherwise. His voice was flinty. She didn't understand the fear of horses. Her earliest memory was of sitting in a saddle. Elevated above the world which jolted below, heady with Frida's honeysuckle perfume and salty hot horse, she had been three years old. Aged six, she was given a pony. Farthing was white, could wink and became her instant best friend. When she wasn't riding him or brushing him she would disappear to the stable and straddle him. Stretched across his mane, she would tell him how much she loved him, and he understood because she spoke his language.

Gus was rubbing his eyes. When he uncovered them they were bloodshot.

'I was making a documentary.'

'About what?'

'Border life. People on the run.'

'Criminals?'

'And people looking for work. UDAs.'

'Undocumented aliens.'

'Yes.' The jump in his voice revealed his surprise.

'Mexicans?'

He nodded.

'Salvadoreans, Guatemalans, Panamanians. We were in a town called Juarez for a while. It's run by the drug cartels. The thieves cut your ankles to stop you running. The Mexican knife trick, they call it.'

'You must be a fast runner.'

'I am,' he said seriously, but she liked his seriousness. She saw it as his courage and an assessment of himself. She watched him lean sideways and tug his blanket out from beneath him. His headset was still slung around his neck, the wire fastened to her armrest. He moved and the wire snapped tight, like a leash. He jerked backward. His sweater caught on his safety belt and slid up. His jeans, loose, slid down, and she caught sight of a band of skin. It was lighter than his face and hands but brown against the whiteness of his underwear. She felt aroused and surprised by herself in equal measure. It had been a long time since she had been ambushed by desire. Their hands collided as they set the wire free.

'I'm losing my mind.' He rubbed his neck. 'Thanks.'

The touch of his hand on hers lingered. She lodged her hands between her knees.

'Chicken or beef?'

It was the stewardess again. Chicken, said Gus. This was interpreted as a joint request and two trays were passed over. Removing the silver foil, Gus was presented with a dish of dirty green string beans, powdery mashed potato, and a moat of gravy. He speared the chicken with his fork and hacked it with his knife.

'Not hungry?'

He noticed Elinor wasn't eating.

'No.'

Drinking her wine, she watched him eat. He wasn't a messy eater nor was he fastidiously polite. He was thorough. Large mouthfuls. Not too fast. QC ate as if winning a race, complained of indigestion and sucked chalky pills all afternoon. He was a greedy man.

'Do you travel a lot?' she wanted to know.

'Too much.'

His mouth was full.

'How much?'

'Eight, nine months of the year.'

'How many countries have you been to?'

She watched him wipe his finger along the edge of his knife and lick the potato off. She imagined he must eat on planes all the time. She imagined he must do this all the time, lick food off his fingers, or perhaps he usually ate with his hands.

'Fifty?'

He registered her amazement.

'It gets depressing. I'll wake up before it's light and have to spend the first twenty seconds working out where I am.'

She couldn't tell whether he was being sincere. She imagined him able to talk himself in or out of any situation with his mannish confidence and boyish air.

'I was born in Baghdad,' she told him. It wasn't a fact she often revealed. There wasn't the occasion.

'So you are a world traveller.'

'Not really. I was sent to boarding school when I was seven. My parents have always lived abroad. I prefer England. I used to hate the "unaccompanied minor" label I had to wear on planes. I'd purposely lose it. I don't really like flying.'

He ripped open his bread roll. Her imagination forged ahead. Greedy for his experience, she wanted it all.

'I suppose you've been in all sorts of trouble.'

He didn't say no.

'Have you ever . . . I don't know . . .' She hesitated. 'been held at gunpoint?'

He laughed, mirthlessly.

'Yes-or-no questions now, is it?'

'Yes.'

'Well yes,' he admitted, as she had known he might. 'In Burma.' He spoke slowly. 'I think the soldier was as scared as I was. He was shaking so hard, I could hear his teeth rattling.'

'Kidnapped?'

He laughed again.

'No. Stoned by a mob, yes.'

Elinor felt excited. He ran straggly fingers through straggly hair.

'Where?'

'Mustang.'

'What happened?'

He stopped eating.

'We'd been there too long. They wanted us out so they accused me of stealing a Buddhist statue. Well, what they did was wake us up – me and my cameraman – in the middle of the night and drag us through the streets. I had my nose broken. They set up a kangaroo court, rather like a medieval execution trial. The King and Queen were sitting in stripy deckchairs and our bodyguard, an ex-policeman from Kahtmandu who turned out to be a useless drunk, ran away. Next thing we knew we were being sentenced to death. It was surreal and frightening. We were supposed to be thrown from the battlements but they couldn't find the third burial man. Two men couldn't officially do it. In the end we paid two thousand dollars and rode out of town on horseback.'

He made a weary 'ha-ha' sound and Elinor sensed a detachment from his past. Picking up his empty coffee cup, he sat it in the palm of his hand and spun it like a top. Elinor dragged her blanket up to her chin.

'No such thing as a typical day, then.'

He met her eyes.

'What's your typical day?'

'It depends. If I'm out of London on a trial . . .'

'Hang on. I thought you were an actress.'

She laughed a tight laugh. Flattery mingled with disbelief.

'No.' She wondered whether he was disappointed.

'You're a journalist.'

'Keep going.'

He hesitated, brain working slowly.

'Solicitor?'

'Barrister.'

Something in his response to her changed. A sharpening of the senses.

'When was the last time you broke the law?'

It was a good question.

'I stole a lipstick.' It was as much as she was prepared to admit. 'I was twelve. It was a dare. I don't think I've ever worn red lipstick since.'

He gave the trays away to the stewardess.

'What was your first big case?'

'Burglary. He was seventeen.'

'Did you get him off?'

'He was sent down for six months.'

On Christmas Eve. He wept and later so did she was what Elinor didn't tell him.

'Do you enjoy what you do?'

'Sometimes I hate it. I suppose what I love is the quirky stuff.'

She watched his face light up. It was as though she had said something important. Something profound. They looked at each other for a moment that seemed to last much longer, and then he looked away. His eyelids fluttered and closed. Thumbing the button on his armrest, he eased his chair back.

'I hate to do this to you.' His voice was fading fast. 'But I'm falling asleep.'

That they could have been in bed was her very next thought. He was out like a light. Even with him asleep she was aware of his proximity. Listening to him breathe, a measure of his being, something in her went out to him.

'Can you close your blind properly?'

It was the stewardess. Elinor did as she was told. Readjusting her pillow, she gave in to the soporific drone of the engine. The plane was drowsy in the cavernous dark. There was a shudder and a groan as Gus flip-flopped and fell back into sleep on the other side. Must be having a bad dream.

'Hi. Hello. Can you open your blind? We're serving breakfast.'

Elinor opened her eyes. They had slipped into dawn. Her mouth was sour. Blinking to see clearly, she took the tray that was thrust at her and tried to prise her head from her shoulder. Everything ached. Gus was awake. He had a laptop computer open on his table and his fingers were furiously hitting the keys. She ripped the seal off her orange juice and drank.

'Unlawful. Unlawful.'

Uncertain why he was repeating this word or how long he had been awake, she amused herself with his dishevelled appearance. His hair was piled up on one side of his head and his sweater, inside out and back to front, swung from his neck but his arms were bare.

'Another word?'

Was this a trick question?

'Illegal.'

'Yes,' he said, and went back to whatever it was he was typing.

The Tannoy crackled.

'This is Captain Fleming from the flight deck. We should be arriving at London Heathrow in approximately thirty minutes where the temperature is ten degrees Centigrade with low cloud cover and light rain.'

Rain. Elinor felt instantly morose, a sentiment she had avoided for weeks. She was back in London, and for what? Ten months ago, fed up with London, her friend the actress had announced that she was moving to LA. The following week she was gone. The actress had arrived at the airport to meet Elinor in a station wagon with a dog in the boot. She had cut her hair and taken up yoga. Her arms were roped with shiny muscles. She looked younger and lively and full of promise. Elinor had envied her newness.

'I'm dog-sitting for the weekend,' she said, a sun visor cupping her face. 'You haven't changed a bit.'

Quite so. When Elinor examined what it was she was going back for, the best she could come up with was work. She was going back to chambers and court and making decisions about other people's lives. To Derek the senior clerk, Kendra who shared her room and QC who she had sworn not to see. She was also going back to a flat that she had been given two months' notice to leave. The landlord was selling. That this was the extent of her life scared her. For the first time ever she wanted to know what it was to choose something else, to live somewhere else. She wanted to know whether she had any dreams and if so what they were. Looking out of the window at banks of cloud, she discovered that all the colour had gone. It was back to her monochrome world.

'Do you always sigh like that?'

She looked around surprised.

'Like what?'

'A horse.'

She stared at Gus's chapped lips and scratchy stubble and realised he was flirting with her.

'So do you.'

He laughed.

'That's when I'm not grinding my teeth.'

He resumed typing, then he stopped.

'Do you want to share a taxi?'

'No one's picking you up then?'

It was what she had wanted to say but she hadn't intended saying it.

'No. And I can expense it.'

'Oh . . .'

'Good. I've got to finish this. You'd better finish your breakfast.'

She tore open the top of her cereal box and began eating her cornflakes one by one, mildly infuriated that she liked this man.

Chapter Three

'Are you all right?'

Elinor had arrived at Caroline's table and set down her tray. On it were a bowl of minestrone and a roll.

'Fine.'

'I thought perhaps you were sickening for something.'

'Jet-lag.'

'Oh, I say. The life of Riley.'

Elinor ignored this last remark. Caroline organised her life as though running for election. She could never concede time out and was exhausting company. Buttering her roll, Elinor warmed her face in the sun. The windows in the court canteen touched the ceiling and shafts of light fell across the tables. Barristers with their wigs off and Archbolds (the criminal manual) at their elbows were eating eggs and chips and gulping coffee. At the far end of their table was a man with his wig on who was smoking a cigar, which wasn't allowed. His eyes were thin and cruel. He looked the type to go hunting, thought Elinor.

A tall man with a copy of *The Times* beneath his arm stopped at their table.

'Reggie. I say. You're not still here?' said Caroline.

'Afraid so. Mountain of evidence to wade through. Going over telephone logs. "The CID just drove round the carpark." Bloody awful waste of time.'

'Have you met Elinor Taylor?'

'Girls together. What fun, eh?'

He clicked his heels and moved on as Caroline rattled her jewellery and waved him goodbye. She turned back.

'Is this really your first stalker?'

'Yes.'

It was the cab-rank principle. Next in line, Elinor took what she was given. Or rather she took what Derek gave her.

'I've lost count of how many I've done. You remember that first husband to be found guilty of stalking his wife, of course?'

'Yes,' Elinor lied.

'That was me. Beastly man. Car salesman. Terrorised his wife with death threats. Tried to run her over. Got off with a fine. Then there was the navy officer who stole pants from the woman's washing line?'

Elinor nodded. This one she remembered.

'He got three years. Horrible business. And you know what the worst thing is?'

'That the victim ends up as obsessed with the stalker as the stalker is with the victim.'

'Bingo,' said Caroline, biting down on a piece of chocolate with a strong set of teeth. 'Now I still say he should plead. You can't get around the DNA evidence.'

'I know.' Elinor put down her spoon. Her soup was tasteless and her head felt thick. 'He won't plead.'

'It's his funeral.'

Elinor looked at her watch.

'I think I'll pop out for a coffee.'

Caroline pursed her lips.

'Don't be late.'

Late.

The word was still ringing in her ears as Elinor stood on the island in the middle of the road and waited for the buses to pass. She resented it. She was never late. She crossed the road. The Court Café was the most popular café for miles. The windows dripped with condensation and the only view in was through a hand print smeared inside. She pushed open the door. On it was a handwritten notice. JesusTeksis were looking for night drivers. *Must have one vehekal.* She was met by a wall of wet heat and noise.

'*Buon giorno,*' said the man behind the counter.

His name was Tony. An affable chap. Big girth. Big smile. Streaks of hair carefully forked across his crown. On the wall behind were photographs of him with his arm around a notable selection of criminals, lawyers and police officers. His allegiances ran both ways. Elinor often thought that it was with Tony that the real power lay. He rolled his head and wiped his hands on his apron.

'What you going to have, my lovely?'

'Cappuccino – strong, please.'

'Nothing to eat?'

She gazed at the sticky buns.

'Not today, thanks.'

'No need to watch your figure, good-looking girl like you.'

She thought of the bits behind her thighs and smiled. He turned his back. His elbows dipped as he slid the silver jug up and down the nozzle and puffed the milk. The radio was on. The DJ was asking callers to suggest top ten ways to dump their lovers. Text-message-dumping came in at number one.

'What you got over there today, then?'

'Stalker.'

Tony never shied from asking questions. Elinor didn't hesitate to answer. Tony had a knack of extracting information painlessly. He nodded.

'My daughter had one of them. Is what all the men want to do, right?'

Elinor toyed with the sugar spoon.

'She don't love you no more? You wait outside her house. You want to break her legs. Chocolate?'

'Please.'

'Is a bad man. Okay, my darling. Ninety pence.'

Elinor paid and left and crossed the street. Tony was right. Infatuation led to obsession, which in turn inspired acts of gross stupidity. Insanity even. One Valentine's Day she had photocopied the definition of 'Affair' and sent it to QC. *Liaison. Entanglement. Intrigue. Flirtation. Hanky-panky. Triangle. Forbidden love. Adulterous love. Cuckoldry.*

'How marvellous it should end with the c-word,' QC had remarked and, folding it up, had slipped it into his wallet. He thought it rather clever of her and wonderfully risqué to have evidence of their affair courtesy of *Roget's Thesaurus.* She cringed to think of it now. Even so, what she hadn't done in these months since their split was change her mind and attempt to win him back by leaving threatening messages, and arriving at his flat at odd hours with a tear-streaked face. She hadn't, in other words, behaved like a grieving ex-lover. She had forced herself to let go.

At the entrance to the court building was a revolving glass door. Elinor stepped inside and pushed with her free hand to rotate it. In her other hand was her cup. Without warning, a wall of bulky clothing pressed against her from behind. She tripped and nearly lost her balance. A groin impressed itself in the small of her back. Hot breath in her hair. Denied room to turn and see who was there, she was tossed into the lobby trailed by hoots of laughter as the boy who had ambushed her space was given a round of applause.

'Oi, you lot. I've told you before. Over here,' barked the security guard with a serpent tattooed up his arm.

Four boys in coats that looked like sleeping bags, hoods up, formed an untidy file before her. They loped beneath the security gate, arms swinging to attest to their manhood. Mindless of their surroundings and their futures, they were evidently in and out of court all the time. Their white trainers squelched along the floor. They activated the security alarm as if on purpose, with more laughter, as Elinor passed silently behind, powerless to protest. No one did or said anything.

She spotted her client Frank Foster sitting by himself underneath the clock. The lobby was a miserable place. It housed a mood like a bad hangover. A mixture of inertia and self-loathing. This was where you ended up when your luck ran out. The clock indicated two o'clock.

'All parties in the case of Frank Foster please make their way to Court eleven.'

Elinor arrived by his side.

'Mr Foster. That's us.'

He coughed. His eyes were rheumy. He didn't look well.

'Don't worry. You won't get called this afternoon. I'll see you in there.'

Standing up, he tucked himself in.

'All rise for the judge.'

Here they were, back again. The only light in the room was artificial and gave everyone a touch of jaundice. The jurors looked more relaxed. They usually did by the afternoon with a bite of lunch inside them. A few had picked up their pens and were chewing the ends. They might even take notes. Elinor took a sip of water as Caroline began.

'Your Honour, the complainant is too unwell to give further evidence this afternoon. Instead I call Steve Robson.'

The room waited for the witness to appear. There was hush, but no witness. The silence, growing louder, was underscored by a collective clearing of throats. Caroline stood rigid as the clerk scampered to the front of the court, stood on tiptoe and passed on a message to the court manager, who, in turn, stood up and whispered into the judge's ear. Judge Green peered over his glasses. His brow furrowed and his black mood darkened the room.

'Does the Crown know of the whereabouts of Mr Robson?'

'Yes, Your Honour. I call Steve Robson.'

Caroline repeated his name as if it were abracadabra. It was a ploy Elinor knew well. She had been here herself. All the same, she couldn't help but enjoy a frisson of pleasure at Caroline's expense. It was so rare that Caroline wasn't entirely in control. She flicked the nib of her pen with her forefinger to assist the flow of ink and gave him a title. *Prosecution witness.* Somebody sneezed. Someone in the public gallery dropped a glass. It rolled but didn't smash.

'I will not have my courtroom turned into a public house,' stormed the judge.

Relief spread like sunshine across Caroline's face.

'Your Honour. Steve Robson.'

His Honour Judge Green sat back in his chair as all eyes in the room settled on the man in the witness stand. Wearing a well-pressed pin-stripe suit and an expression of studied self-assurance, Steve Robson gave the impression that he was used to making people wait for him. His tie was cut from a silky fabric with the sheen of smoked salmon. Plainclothes DSs wore cheap imitations from tie shops in train stations. His looked like the real thing. His hair was nutty and cut close to his head. He had a healthy glow and a brow with a ridge. Elinor didn't need to be any closer to know that he was scented. She watched him grip the stand with both hands. People who were nervous tucked their hands away. He pressed one hand on the Bible and the clerk swore him in.

'Mr Robson,' Caroline addressed him. 'Am I correct in saying you're an estate agent with Brook & Brook Estates?'

'Yes.'

'And how long have you known Mr Foster?'

'Three years.'

'Can you see him in this courtroom today?'

'Yes.'

'Can you point him out?'

He pointed at a man who, from where she was sitting, Elinor couldn't see. He did so without hesitation, the confident gesture of a confident man.

'Was Mr Foster a close friend?'

'No.'

'How would you describe him?'

'An acquaintance. A contact in the area.'

'How would you describe your relationship with Miss Price?'

'Close.'

'Can you be a little more precise?'

'We went to the same school. We were brought up on the same street. I've known her since I was a kid. We see each other most days, otherwise we speak. You could say we're like brother and sister. I always know where to find her.'

'Did you introduce Miss Price to Mr Foster?'

'Yes. Not on purpose, mind. I was in the pub with Suzy, Miss Price, when Frank came in.'

He had a London accent, the rougher edges smoothed away, decided Elinor.

'When did you first see the cards and parcels that Miss Price was sent?'

'A week after she started getting them. I was round there one morning when the post came.'

'On this particular occasion, what did Miss Price receive in the post?'

'A card.'

'If you could turn to page ten of your bundle. Do you recognise the card?'

Steve Robson rifled through the pages. Elinor read it too. More childish scrawl. *I know what makes you tick.*

'Yes.'

'How did Miss Price react to this card?'

'She got upset. She said she couldn't go to work so I took her down the doctor's. He gave her something for her nerves.'

'Thank you. No more questions, Your Honour.'

Elinor stood up. Tilting forward then back, she moored her position, a habit as unconscious as using her voice to propel her, her uncertainty to guide her.

'Mr Robson . . .'

'Hello.' He smiled, fleetingly, but she caught it. It wasn't improbable that he was enjoying himself. Individuals partial to an audience were known to enjoy the theatre of the courtroom. It was a prime place in which to show off.

'You've known Mr Foster for two years but he isn't a friend. Is that right?'

'Well, there are friends and there are friends, aren't there?'

'Yes or no is all that's required,' interrupted the judge.

Steve Robson dropped the smirk.

'No, Your Honour.'

'I suggest you've never liked Mr Foster,' she resumed. 'I suggest you used his friendship for your own professional gain. Mr Foster has worked on the market for thirty years. He is well known to the trustees of the market. You thought that by winning his friendship you could secure property deals in the area. Isn't that right?'

He recoiled from her insinuation.

'No.'

'Were you pleased for Miss Price when she began her relationship with Mr Foster?'

'Er, yes.'

'You didn't try to dissuade her from seeing Mr Foster?'

'Why should I?'

'Do I have to remind you that it is for Miss Taylor to ask the questions?' said the judge.

Elinor took a breath.

'I suggest it was you who persuaded Miss Price to stop seeing Mr Foster. You didn't think he was good enough for her, did you?'

'No.' He paused. 'I didn't tell her what to do.'

He reached for his glass and took a sip of water, dabbing his lips with his forefinger.

'After Miss Price finished the relationship with Mr Foster and began to receive cards and packages, she came to you. What advice did you offer?'

'I told her not to see him.'

'But she didn't take your advice, did she? You saw Miss Price with Mr Foster again in the pub only two days later, being perfectly amicable with each other. Behaving, in fact, like a couple in love. Is this not true?'

'Er . . . Yes.'

The judge sighed.

'Miss Taylor, I do hope we are going to arrive at the point you are trying to make.'

Elinor smiled at the judge.

'Your Honour, I'm simply trying to ascertain the nature of the relationship between the complainant and Mr Robson in order to show how this reflects upon my client.'

'Yes, yes, all right. But do let's get on.'

He had thrown her. The volley had been leading up to something. What was it?

'Mr Robson. Did you ever threaten Mr Foster?'

She watched him squirm.

'I . . .'

The ring of a mobile phone ripped through the room like a scream. Elinor dropped her arms to her side. People began to whisper and turn their heads and shuffle in their seats. The judge's eyes grew small and mean. To lose control of your courtroom was the ultimate ignominy.

'Will the person responsible stop this immediately,' he roared.

But the bleeps continued to detonate in the room. No one took responsibility, nor were they answered. The judge glared at the tourists, court-hopping regulars, law students and loners seeking refuge from the cold, crowded into the public gallery. He fumed at the jury. Someone was sabotaging proceedings on purpose. Elinor joined the judge in scrutinising the room. She wanted to resurrect her cross-examination before it was too late.

Caroline caught her eye.

Rolling her eyes to the floor, Caroline indicated that Elinor should do the same thing. She was moving her lips as though blowing kisses, her lips forming a long O. Elinor's heart missed a beat. A shiver snaked down her spin. She felt very hot, very cold and extremely foolish. The word Caroline was mouthing was 'you'.

Elinor didn't dare move. One of the clerks in chambers had changed the ring on her mobile phone for a laugh, he said. She hadn't recognised it because it was no longer a tidy two-note but a head-splitting flurry of electronic sound. Looking straight ahead, she slipped off her shoe. She felt for her phone on the floor. When she found it she trod down on it hard. The ringing stopped. The room held its breath.

'If it happens again, I'll have the public gallery cleared,' threatened the judge. 'Now, if you would like to finish your cross-examination, Miss Taylor.'

'Yes, Your Honour.'

Wobbling as she retrieved her shoe, she composed herself and looked up at her witness. Her relief at being able to proceed was rudely cut short. Mr Robson met her gaze with a cool, level stare. A smile creased the corner of his mouth. He tapped his fingers against the stand and then he winked. He had seen it all. Elinor's mind went into free-fall before going blank. She tried to resurrect her final question. Don't do this to me, she pleaded in vain, but there was nothing there. Only a tightness in her throat, an elastic band around her head. Bubbles of nausea.

The judge's patience was gone. He was bored.

'Miss Taylor . . .'

She watched her cross-examination ebb away.

'I have no further questions for this witness, Your Honour.'

She sat down. Mr Robson was led from the dock and out of the courtroom. It was all she could do not to pick at her hem. She had taped it up this morning and it was falling down. She found a ladder in her tights she hadn't known was there and stroked her skin. She had squandered a vital cross-examination and had no one to blame but herself.

'Don't encourage him. He's being foul enough as it is,' hissed Caroline.

Elinor jumped to her feet. She had missed the clerk's summons for all to rise. Everyone in the room was standing but her. Judge Green exited through the door at the back. She and Caroline slid out of the bench together.

'Why haven't you got a silent vibrate option?' Caroline looked disapprovingly at her.

'I have,' said Elinor, dismally. 'It was a mistake.'

* * *

Outside in the hall Mr Foster was waiting for her. He was slouched with his hands in his pockets and was kicking at the floor like a boy with a can.

'He's a liar.' He spat out the words before she had time to say hello.

Elinor walked on. He would follow her, she knew, and they would lose the crowd as they went. He produced an inhaler and sucked to keep up. His lungs rattled as she slowed her pace.

She lowered her voice. 'What did he lie about?'

'Us.'

'Who?'

'Me and Suzy. He hated us being together.'

Elinor stopped. Without the clatter of her heels against the scuffed stone floor, she felt acutely alone with Mr Foster and the row of faded photographs of judges who had once presided over these courts. They looked severe and all knowing and she felt tired and angry with herself for screwing up the cross-examination, and frustrated with Mr Foster for not facing facts.

Last night she had taken home a stack of *The Journal of Psychiatry* to read in bed. The statistics were alarming. One in five women would at some stage in their lives find themselves being stalked. The duration of stalking incidents ranged from one month to twenty-eight years. Forty-eight per cent of stalking incidents involved ex-partners. Ninety-six per cent of victims knew their stalkers. Thirty-seven per cent suffered post-traumatic stress disorder. She didn't have much with which to defend this man.

'Mr Foster. I think I should remind you that the DNA tests came back positive.'

Crevices corrugated the bridge of his nose. Sweat began to collect in them.

'What?'

'The stamps taken from the letters sent to Miss Price were tested. The DNA matched the saliva on the swab you gave to the police.'

His body began twitching. Jewellery jangled beneath his clothes.

'What's wrong with sending her letters?' He coughed. 'It's not against the law.'

Elinor hugged her notebook to her chest and swung her weight to her other hip. She was wearing her wig and her scalp was prickly. Did she have to spell it out?

'It's the quantity of correspondence, Mr Foster, and the content. Taken with the packages, the calls and the unwanted house visits, it is construed as harassment. On two occasions Miss Price has also stated that she feared violence would be used against her.'

'I never sent nothing but cards. I'd never touch her.'

'That's not what she says, Mr Foster.'

She was about to say goodbye when Frank Foster grabbed his head between his hands. He squeezed so hard that his cheeks changed colour. His fingers were like breadsticks, his face a boiled ham.

'Cunt.'

That was it. Elinor had had enough. Excusing herself from him and the c-word, she took to the hallway fast. She heard a noise. It could have been the impact of fist against plaster or forehead on wall. She didn't look around. She made it to the Ladies' Robing Room and flopped into a seat. The room was lined with lockers, littered with bags and gowns and crammed with chairs.

She removed her wig and massaged her scalp. There were few certainties in this job besides the guilt of most of those charged. What she could never predict was her response to a client. It was different every time. Some she was repulsed by, with their clammy skin and their absence of remorse. Then there were the charming rogues. 'You a barrister? Na. You're too young.' was a line she had heard so many times that she was disappointed when it failed to come.

What she could never admit to was feeling sentimental, because sentiment smacked of partiality and partiality was unprofessional. Feelings were uncontrollable. Feelings weren't influenced by whether she believed the client or not. As a human being she had an emotional response to every person she met. Where did that leave Mr Foster? Something about his despair made her believe that love had once prevailed. Before it turned ugly.

'You planning on spending the night here?'

The cleaner had arrived to do the floor. Flinging the mop from side to side, she was singing a song in Portuguese. Only now did Elinor remember the call. Ducking down, she extracted her mobile phone from her pile of belongings on the floor. She had one new message. There was his voice, as sweet, as clear as honey. The intimacy of it was paralysing. She couldn't move from her chair. She sat crossing and uncrossing her legs, her stomach turning somersaults, her breath fast in her throat, until she had to do something. She stood up.

In the Ladies' mirror, tarnished with age, she inspected her face. Her features might have been poured on as opposed to planted there. Alabaster skin covered a high forehead. Her eyes, like murky lakes, sat within a storm of freckles. It was a face that needed a frame of hair. Trying to see what he had seen, she unfastened her ponytail and shook out her hair. Only now did she recognise the person Gus had called, because now she was a woman not a cunt in a suit.

Chapter Four

The driver ran the red and cut up the car in the lane beside them.

'Careful.'

Elinor's head bounced off the seat as a trickle of brandy ran down her chin.

'Learn to fucking drive,' yelled her driver at whoever he had nearly hit.

They flew over the bridge. She looked out of the window at a city she didn't know. Magnificent buildings were reflected in the river like castles of light. It wasn't the same city she inhabited by day. Wiping her chin with the back of her wrist, she licked off the brandy. She had been looking for her lipstick when her hand had fixed on something else in her bag. Smooth and silver, it fitted her palm. It was a hip flask and a present from QC. She had come to depend on it for solace on train journeys back from unhappy towns when she felt chilled and out of sorts. It left her uncluttered and inevitably made her think of him, as he must have known.

She wound down the window to freshen her face. She wanted the rush of air to instil a sense of normalcy. She felt a little out of control. The actress would call it having a wobble. She was on her way to meet Gus – she didn't know his surname – and under normal circumstances she would have said no. No one called in the afternoon to say let's meet this evening. It didn't work like that. There were rules about dates, as Kendra had reminded her. Wednesday was no strings attached. Thursday was pregnant with possibility, while Fridays didn't fool anyone. Today was Tuesday.

'Foolish or desperate,' said Kendra.

Elinor thought perhaps both. She was wary of last minute-decisions. She had lost count of the number of clients she had defended who had got into the car *at the last minute*. Spontaneity was a short cut to disaster. I'd love to meet, she'd said.

She had dreamed about him last night. In her dream they were sitting around a table with others she didn't know. She had been wearing his clothes. The dirty grey T-shirt. The jacket with the pockets. They had been at opposite ends of the table and she had wanted to reach out and touch him but had to pretend they were strangers. She had woken to the sensation of being adrift in a bed as big as the sea. It was a mood she had been unable to shake all day.

She felt anxious. She was trying to remember what it was, besides sitting next to one another on the plane, which had brought them together. A sense of what? She understood the men in her world by the jokes they told, the suits they wore and where they suggested going for dinner. They had a predictable line-up of questions. Where did you go to school? When were you called to the Bar? Their motives never changed. What they wanted was to win; every line was the punch line and their gags were always funny. They thought so, anyway. With Gus, she remembered thinking she had missed the punch line but was in on the end of the joke.

She sucked her teeth. They hummed with brandy. Digging around for a mint, she found one in her pocket and put it, lint free, in her mouth. She reapplied lipstick and rubbed it off again. Staring out of the window at rows of alms-houses and crumbling walls, she realised that they were south of the river. This side was different. The land lay lower. The streets were empty. The night was oily.

The cab flung itself around a corner and rolled down a side street. An open-fronted hangar loomed to their right fenced in behind a grille. She had never been here before yet knew immediately where they were. This was the market where Frank Foster worked. Ahead a convoy of lorries was blocking the road. Brake lights were flashing. Someone was sitting with his hand on the horn and a male voice was shouting directions, 'Over here, mate', as a fork-lift truck piled with boxes began reversing towards them. It was picking up speed.

'For fuck's sake.' Her driver tossed his arm around the passenger seat, reversed fast and braked. 'That's twelve.'

She paid and got out and the taxi shot off, leaving her with the sound of the engine's acceleration ringing in her ears. She stood on the corner of the street and stared at a row of terrace houses dwarfed by one or two miscellaneous buildings. The only indication that anyone lived here was the flush of red geraniums in a box on a wall. She heard rumbling overhead. Looking up, she saw a procession of faces as a train passed by level with the roofs. Behind it the sky was like blotting paper marbled with ink and a chink of moon.

She began searching for where she should be. He had said he lived in a former granary with a drug dealer's door. She was standing in front of a grey stone building with a heavy wooden door pockmarked and gouged. Missing a number, it was next-door to number 7. He lived at number 9. Last chance to walk away? She slapped the door with her palm. It stung and the wood absorbed the sound. She tried again with her knuckles this time before stepping back to wait for the sound of footsteps growing louder. A shout. *Hang on. I'm coming.* Nothing. She looked up and down the street. A car was parked on the other side. It was the only car parked on that side of the street. Someone was sitting in the passenger seat. He looked to be asleep. Perhaps she had the wrong address.

She knocked again. Without warning the door swung wide and she tripped and fell. There was a collision of elbows and arms and she was reminded of the hands that she had liked. The softness of his skin.

'Perfect timing,' he said.

'Where's your number?'

She sounded like a policewoman.

'It was stolen.'

'Oh.'

Both hesitated, as though waiting to be reminded of why they were here. But here he was. The man who had occupied her thoughts so vividly day and night. She opened her mouth to help her breathe. Her heart was trapped like a bird in her chest. Gus was as she remembered him. Better. He had lost the exhaustion beneath his eyes. They weren't frenzied but had the vitality she remembered she liked. His skin was paler, cleaner perhaps. His hair was wet and pushed back behind his ears, and there was a lick of foam on his upper right cheek. He struck her as a man who didn't shave very often but he had shaved for her. It was nice.

'The music was on. Have you been out here long?'

He had a remote control in his hand.

'No.'

It only felt like hours.

'It's good to see you.'

Leaning forward, he kissed her. She had thought the moment had been lost, crushed by their awkwardness. His cheek was damp and left hers tingling with toothpaste and soap.

'Do you mind coming up?'

Unable to speak she shook her head while he waited for her to come inside.

'I should warn you. It's an obstacle course getting to my place.'

He took the stairs in easy strides. She had to raise her knees quite high. Her legs were short where his were long.

The steps were roughly half a foot deep and cut from stone. She could feel their chill through the soles of her shoes. His jeans were frayed and scraped the floor. Watching his calves grow taut through the backs of them, she saw that his feet were bare and his heels cracked with fine lines which made her think of sandy beaches. She was glad that she had wiped off her lipstick.

They stopped at the top of the stairs. There was another door, which he pushed with both arms. It moaned. He went first and she joined him, stepping into blackness as if stepping into space. For a moment she thought that she had made a terrible mistake. She hated surprises. She wasn't supposed to be here. Then she understood. Her raincoat rustled against her legs; there was a brackish smell of water and a breeze in her hair. The shadows below weren't buses and cars. That was the river. She could see the spire of the cathedral and traffic crawling across the bridge. They were standing on a roof.

'Party trick.' He said.

Elinor gazed up at a sky fizzing with stars. She picked out constellations and found the Plough.

'Which one's that?' She pointed at a number Three.

'Cassiopeia. Watch out. There's a chair.'

She was confronted by a drop. He went first, ignoring the chair and landing on the roof with his knees bent like an athlete or someone who did this a lot. He turned and held out his hand. She couldn't see his face but fell into his disembodied grip all the same. His hand swallowed hers, her skirt rode up and her heel jammed in a hole in the back of the chair. Jerking her foot to wrench her leg free, she arrived with one shoe.

'Is this a temporary thing?' she asked, breathlessly, unravelling her fingers so as not to be the last one to let go.

He laughed.

'You don't approve?'

'I didn't mean that.'

Although subconsciously she probably had. He went ahead. She wiggled into her shoe and joined him beyond glass doors through which warm light beckoned. His feet brushed against the trunk-sized floorboards and tingly music drifted from the stereo. She surveyed the room as though waiting for her eyes to adjust to the light. It was a very long room with bare brick walls and timber beams. A pyramid of bags sat by the door, which made her think he must be off again soon and made her feel sorry. Next to the bags was a stack of newspapers and a crate of empty bottles. He was going to recycle. He liked to entertain.

No sign of a female presence. This pleased her. It was a male lair with an air of neglect about it, as though everything was covered in a film of dust. Nevertheless, it felt lived in. She could recognise the home of someone who lived alone and equated solitude with misery. A home used exclusively for sleeping, where the sheets were never changed, there was never any milk and with soap so old it wouldn't lather. It was a description of her own home more often than she would care to admit.

She took a look around. On the desk was a computer, on it was a screensaver. *There's nothing permanent except change.* The words glided by. She thought it probably said quite a lot. On the desk was a hoard of unpaid bills addressed to *Gus Cox.*

So now she knew his surname. There was a kitchen counter with a row of oils in bottles flavoured with twigs, and a sink clogged with dirty dishes. A sofa lay buried beneath books. On the wall were photographs of two boys in a sailing boat with flared trousers and bushy hair. One of the boys was recognisably Gus.

'Who's the other boy?'

'My brother.'

She had guessed as much.

'How long have you lived here?'

'Three years. More off than on.'

Then she saw the window at the far end. Floor-to-ceiling, it was vast and from where she was standing, she was granted the same view she had seen from the roof. The same colours bleeding into blackness, the glint of water, the city unfolding beyond. Walking towards it in the dim light, mesmerised by the view, she was mid-way there when something grabbed at her navel. She bounced off it like a ball. Looking down she discovered a tent, waist height, dome-shaped and pillar-box red.

'You're supposed to be able to put it up in five minutes.'

Gus was perched on a chair tugging on socks. He made no apologies about getting dressed in front of her or having a tent up in his flat.

'You've been practising?'

He had to be joking.

'I only got it today.'

'You've been timing yourself?'

'Six minutes thirty seconds.'

Uncertain as to whether she was reading his matter-of-factness correctly, Elinor studied his face for a sign that he was pulling her leg. His expression didn't change. He stared doggedly back, and she was reminded of the moment when their eyes first met. The flash of recognition. The certainty that there would be more to come. Fluttery, she looked away.

'Show me,' she said.

'What?'

'Put it up.'

He stood up in his shoes.

'You don't believe me?'

'No.'

He plunged his hands in his pockets and narrowed his eyes.

'You take it down. I'll put it up.'

Sensing a challenge, she felt a thrill.

'I can tell you're a lapsed camper.'

He was right. She suddenly remembered how much she had loved camping. At school, one weekend every summer they would set up camp in the meadow by the river and there in the darkness they would scare each other with tales of ghosts. The fireflies were the eyes of vampires. The wind in the bushes was the whoosh of their flapping capes.

Elinor circled the tent. Eight tent pegs gripped by fat rubber bands had been hammered directly into the floor. There were two bendy poles. There was a porch, a groundsheet and an inner tent too. She would rather not do something than do it badly or fail. She hated being unprepared. She felt herself softening. Calculated risk was a persuasive thing.

'You're on,' she said.

He was smoking a cigarette.

'When was the last time you slept in a tent?'

'That would be telling.'

He laughed.

'Ready?'

'Yes.'

'On your marks. Get set. Go.'

This was ridiculous. Down on her knees, she had four pegs out with four to go. She jerked the base of the poles. The tent collapsed. She pushed the poles through to the other side and they slithered across the floor. She wrenched them apart, picked up the tent, grappled inside for hooks and eyes and detached the inner sheet. It fell on the floor in a swirl of netting. She rolled the tent sheets up separately, ironing out the air, and stuffed them into a bag. The pegs and poles went in too. Sitting back with her legs beneath her, she smiled slowly.

'You've done this before,' he protested.

'I've never even been in a tent like this.' She watched him pace. Rubbing his hands. Limbering up.

'So you're a fast learner. Have you got a second hand?'

She wore a slim, gold watch with a rectangular face. It was a duty-free present from QC to commemorate a weekend away. She flashed it at Gus.

'Go,' she said

He dragged the tents out of the bag and laid them flat on the ground. He crawled inside and she watched him, a travelling hump, peg the inner tent to the outer tent. He came out backward, had the poles out and was feeding one into the next. He propelled them through the loop in the fabric and bent them to give the tent shape. It was up. He flew around the tent, knocking pegs through rubber rings with a brick in his hand. Pulling strings, he fastened them tight. The porch shot up and he looked up at her with an expression of such exuberance on his face that she forgot everything. She glanced at her watch.

'Six minutes and . . .'

'You forgot to time me.'

Disbelief deepened his voice.

'No. Yes.'

He raised himself to his feet. She didn't know what to say. How could she explain that she had been marvelling at his body form right angles, at the way he moved? That she had been reminded of the pleasure gained from a task as simple as putting up a tent. That it made her feel carefree in a way she had forgotten.

'I believe you. That's the main thing, isn't it?' she said.

Lifting a jacket from the back of a chair, he untangled his collar to expose a neck still dark from the sun and began to laugh.

'Come on. Let's go and get a drink.'

Relieved they wouldn't be competing all night, she smiled. She had been impressed by his dexterity and she would tell him that. She was also as good as him, which meant he hadn't won.

The pub was empty save for a solitary drinker at the end of the bar. It was a tiny room with a long wooden pew and a handful of tables. Pictures of foxes and badgers cluttered the walls. The smell of beer and hot glasses hung in the air. They were standing side by side at the bar. Elinor leaned in, touching shoulders. He didn't lean away and it took a feat of concentration to maintain the semblance of a person waiting for a drink at a bar. Not someone whose entire body felt as though it were being yanked towards the other person's with gravitational pull.

'Nice perm.'

Elinor didn't look round. She didn't have to. She was the only person in there with curly hair. She had also heard it before from clever dick clients. It was one of the more benign comments she had been on the receiving end of. *You are the ugliest woman I've ever met* being perhaps the most offensive. Ignoring it, she watched a boy who looked too young to buy alcohol sidle round behind the bar. Gus ordered their drinks before nodding at the man.

'You all right?'

'Been better.'

Zipped into a white track suit, the man bit the head off a cigar, torched it with a long flame and tapped it against the ashtray. Elinor couldn't see his eyes. Squiggles behind thick lenses. Catching a whiff of his smoke, she found it unsettling.

People laid claim to smells and this one belonged to QC. She would always know when he was in chambers because his smoke would come and find her.

'Heard about Frankie?'

'I heard.' Gus stood with a glass in each hand.

'Un-fucking-believable.' The man sucked his cigar. 'Makes you sick. I mean, what did he do?'

Gus nodded. 'It's tough.'

Elinor said nothing. They were discussing her client. Given her whereabouts, it was perhaps not entirely surprising. All the same she felt as though she had stumbled across confidential information. She didn't know where to look. Studying her shoes, she waited for Gus to lead the way.

'He likes your hair.'

'I heard.' She sat on a pew facing the room and slid out of her coat. She was wearing a cashmere jumper. If he said nice sweater it would be a euphemism for something else. The thought was unfair. It was the fault of the man at the bar. He had put her on edge and left her feeling defensive.

'I apologise.' Gus pulled his stool closer.

'How do you know him?'

'He's a market man.'

Like Frank Foster. She fingered her glass.

'How's your film?'

Gus lit a cigarette and squeezed his eyes as if she had asked him a difficult question.

'I don't know. I've stolen from so many people's lives that I've forgotten why I ever decided to make it.'

'Do you have a story?'

'A few.' He hesitated. 'Do you really want to hear this?'

'Yes.'

'Okay. There's the sheriff who runs the border patrols. Shoots illegals – they're called wetbacks – on sight. Not that he knows we know. The church groups who set up water stands at crossing points told us about it. There's Ernesto. Great guy. He's a coyote, which means he guides wetbacks across the border at night. A lot of times, they find themselves abandoned by coyotes who take their money and run. Ernesto's saved the lives of quite a few men. There's also a tunnel between Arizona and Mexico used for drug smuggling.' He paused. 'But that's another story.'

Gus adopted the downward smile of a bashful man. Elinor knew him well enough to know he wasn't bashful but he appeared reluctant to give too much away.

'I was in court when you phoned.' She tried to make it sound interesting. 'My phone was on. It rang. In court.'

Gus lit another cigarette. The flame wobbled and he snuffed out the match with smoky breath.

'I was in the middle of cross-examining,' she tried again.

He exhaled because now he understood.

'What happened?'

'The judge threatened to clear the court.'

He raised his glass.

'Contempt of court. Can we drink to that? I hope I didn't get you into trouble.'

'The judge didn't know it was mine.'

He spread his fingers round his glass.

'I suppose you have to be good at deceit.'

Elinor tried not to let this comment spoil her mood.

'In court I mean.'

She knew what he was getting at. Still, she couldn't help but feel judged for being someone she was not.

'Have you ever been married?'

He coughed.

'No. Though I feel like I've been through a divorce. I gave her everything, which is why you may have noticed there's nothing in the flat.'

Her face relaxed.

'How long were you together?'

'Ten years.'

'What happened?'

'Irreconcilable differences. We were apart too much.' Ash scattered messily across the table. 'I never did the washing up.'

'You didn't buy a dishwasher?'

She was testing him.

'It was too late for that.'

A Frank Sinatra song came on the juke-box. He was singing about the good times and Elinor thought of the actress in LA and why she was here. Crunching an ice cube, she made her teeth hurt.

'My last relationship was with a married man.'

As soon as she said this she wished she hadn't. He looked embarrassed. His shoulders tensed, he had troubled eyes, and she wanted to be giving him the version of the person he could see. She hadn't intended to sound sorry for herself.

'Did he lie about it?'

'I was stupid.'

'It's not a crime.'

She smiled weakly.

'Another drink?' he said

She could drink a vat of gin and tonic.

'Yes, please.'

He stood up and reached for the glasses.

'What happened to your thumb?'

'Car door,' he murmured as he left her.

Following him with her eyes, she watched him lean over the bar and was struck by the desire to slip her hands into his pockets and fold herself across his back. He felt her gaze. He looked over his shoulder and smiled. She smiled too, blushing inside. Someone was playing a fruit machine. There was the wrench of a handle and the flutter of lucky fruits lining up. He arrived back with drinks.

'There's something I want to tell you.'

Everything came grinding to a halt. Misgivings of every sort ran through her mind. He was going to ask her a legal favour. He was some sort of weirdo. He sat down.

'I have been shot.'

Elinor stared at the shamrock traced in the head of foam on his pint. It was perfect.

'I told you I was held at gunpoint. I didn't tell you I was shot.'

She extracted the wedge of lemon from her glass and sucked it until her eyes watered.

'In my leg. The bullet chipped my femur. Nothing fatal. Well, obviously.'

He drank thirstily. She drank to understand what it was he was telling her and why he was telling her now.

'What did it feel like?'

'Like walking into a darkened room is the only way I can think of to describe it. One minute I was walking away from the soldier and it was light. Next thing I was on my back and looking up at the stars and thinking what a beautiful night it was. It was hot and I remember feeling as though I was lying in snow. And I thought about my girlfriend. I thought, she'll leave me when she finds out I've been shot.' He wiped his mouth. 'And she did.'

'Does it hurt?'

'It aches.'

'Do you have a scar?'

'An ugly one. I was in hospital for a week. When I got out, she moved out.'

Elinor nodded. She didn't want to talk about exes. She wanted to see his scar. She wanted to press her hands flat against his chest and feel his strength and the fragile movement beneath. Too many conflicting desires crowded her brain. If it happened tonight, it wouldn't be honest. It would be to purge herself of QC and him of stray ghosts. It wasn't what she wanted.

'I've got a very early start,' she said.

He nodded. 'Me too.'

She appreciated his dishonesty.

'Shall we go?' he said.

The door jerked shut and they were greeted by the empty hangar and a confetti of lettuce leaves and no-good oranges turning to squelch on the ground. A poster on the wall announced service times at the cathedral. *SUNDAYS ARE FUNDAYS.*

He pointed. 'This way.'

There was a nip in the air. Heads down, they marched side by side, walking not talking. The distance between them seemed to grow with each step. Turning a corner, they were met by the fumes from the traffic and a man walking slowly ahead.

'It's Frank. Frank!' he called.

She turned around quickly.

'Don't.'

'What?'

'Please.'

They watched him disappear. A nervous silence tailed them down the street. They stopped at a Zebra Crossing. Gus jabbed the button.

'I know him.'

'So do I,' she said. 'I'm defending him.'

The beacons began flashing. Gus's face pulsed in yellow light. It made him look angry. She was saved from further explanation by an orange glow that came bobbing through the gloom. They saw the taxi at the same time, hailed it and watched it glide to a standstill beside the kerb. She wanted to jump in and speed away and do this moment later on by herself. She felt confused. She hated goodbyes.

'So . . .'

'Well . . .' he said, and kept on talking. She could see his lips moving but couldn't hear what he had to say. Then he stopped mid-sentence and kissed her. His mouth was warm and as persuasive as his voice. The voice that had told her this would happen right from the start. The taxi-driver revved the engine. She had to decide what to do. Breaking away, she reached for the door.

'I'll call you.' He slammed it shut behind her.

She fell back against the seat.

'Soon,' she said so that only she could hear.

Chapter Five

She wore her arms folded across her chest as a kind of test. Try me, they said. It was 9.45a.m. and she was sitting in an interview room with a strip light that flickered and a radiator that belched dirty water at regular intervals. A puddle was beginning to collect on the floor. On the other side of the hard yellow table sat Mr Foster. He had a black eye swollen like a putrid fruit. Purple and orange and green.

'What happened?' She uncrossed her arms and poured the second sachet of sugar into her coffee. Punctuating her speech with the movement of her hand, she stirred, round and round, making the granules dissolve. It was the only movement in the room, and the eyes of the room followed her hand. She picked up her cup and blew on her coffee, rippling the surface, enjoying the ripple.

Frank Foster was rubbing his hands up and down his thighs. Admittedly the room was cold. A problem with the thermostat, said security, none of whom were qualified to fix it.

'Steve Robson.' His hands locked on his knees.

Elinor stared.

'Steve Robson punched you?'

'That's what I said.'

'What were you doing with him?'

She watched Frank Foster's mouth compress. He didn't want to be having this conversation; nor did she. His appearance certainly wasn't going to win him any favours in court. He hadn't shaved and was wearing the same suit as yesterday, only it was shabbier. Crumpled. She couldn't be sure he hadn't slept in it too. Scuff marks strayed at the elbows and there was a stain of something, possibly blood, on the lapel. He had managed to keep hold of the tie. Beige and brown checks.

'He came looking for me down the pub.'

Elinor could smell his breath. Ill health floated off his tongue. It smelt livery.

'Why?'

'To tell me to keep away from her.'

They were startled by a drum roll. White stones bounced off the window and gathered on the sill.

'Hail,' said Brian, helpfully.

Elinor turned back.

'Why?'

Frank Foster laughed like an unblocked drain.

'He can't stand it.'

Elinor curled her hands around her cup for warmth.

'What?'

'Billy.'

Elinor looked at her watch. Two minutes to go.

'Why didn't you walk away when he became aggressive?'

'I did.'

'Hence the black eye.'

Frank Foster fell back in his seat, and Brian cleared his throat as a way of expressing support for his client. *Back off.* Which was what she would do. As a servant of the court it was her duty to report anything that might amount to attempted interference with the course of justice to the judge. She would not, however, be taking this matter up with the judge. No need. Steve Robson was no longer a witness. What she couldn't ignore was Mr Foster's previous conviction for fighting. A previous conviction meant she would not be able to describe him as being of good character. Those who understood would know why.

'Mr Foster.' She put down her cup. 'Your relationship with Mr Robson still bothers me.'

'All parties in the case of Frank Foster please make their way to Court eleven.'

'Oh dear. That's us.' She glanced up at the Tannoy.

Scraping their chairs, they stood up and filed out one by one.

Miss Price was wearing a different suit today. It was black and neatly waisted. A pointy white collar trimmed her neck. She wore her hair pinned back and her lips were pearly pink. She had the same frightened eyes. Elinor set down her highlighter pen and got to her feet.

'Miss Price. You were involved in a relationship with Mr Foster for eighteen months, is that correct?'

'Yes.'

'In what capacity,' interrupted Judge Green. 'Just so we are all clear.'

Miss Price stared at him. 'I don't understand.'

'Was it romantic?'

Judges liked to be pedantic.

'Yes, Your Honour.'

'Thank you. You may continue.'

'Were you living together?'

'Er . . . well, in the end.'

'Is that a yes?'

'Yes. Only for two months.'

'Whose idea was it that the two of you move in together?'

Elinor saw her hesitate.

'Mine.'

'Can you repeat that for the jury to hear?'

'It was my idea.'

'Why did your relationship with Mr Foster end?'

'He wanted too much from me.'

'Can you be more specific?'

'He wanted to marry me.'

Elinor allowed the jury to grasp what was being said. These were important points that Miss Price was making.

'To clarify, Miss Price. Mr Foster asked for your hand in marriage and you spurned him, is that correct?'

'Yes. I said no,' she said softly.

'I suggest, Miss Price that by rejecting Mr Foster's offer of marriage, you broke his heart. It was a cold-hearted move on your part. You were playing with his emotions. You had encouraged the relationship. In fact you asked him to move into your flat much earlier on in the relationship, did you not?'

'Yes.'

'Mr Foster wasn't convinced it was a good idea to move in with you but you pleaded with him until eventually he said yes. Isn't that right?'

'Yes.'

'When Mr Foster asked you to marry him, you turned around and said no. You went farther. You asked him to move out of your flat. And all this two months after he'd given up his home, packed up his belongings and moved into your flat. Why did you ask him to leave?'

Miss Price looked bewildered. Elinor repeated the question.

'I couldn't go through with it. I was scared.'

'Scared of what?'

'Everything.'

'You are going to have to be more specific. What were you scared of, Miss Price?'

'I don't know.' She shook her head.

'Well, let's try and work it out, shall we? Let me refresh your memory and go back to February the twenty-fifth when

Mr Foster arrived at your flat. You could have spoken to him there on the doorstep but you didn't. You asked him to come inside. Didn't you?'

Elinor shot the jury an emphatic look. She wheeled back again.

'I didn't know what else to do.'

'What you could have done.' Elinor challenged her. 'was say, "I don't want to see you. Go away." But you didn't do that, did you?'

'No.'

'You invited Mr Foster into your home, didn't you?'

'It was cold. I was catching my death.'

'You invited him into your home, didn't you?'

Never sound shrill, Elinor reminded herself. Keep control. Above all, be persuasive.

'Yes.'

'What you said was come inside and have a drink, didn't you?'

'He was already drunk.'

'Which was why, when Mr Foster came inside, you poured him a glass of whisky?'

'It was all I had in.'

'What happened next?'

'I don't know what you mean.'

'I think you do, Miss Price. What happened next was that you invited Mr Foster upstairs to your bedroom, didn't you?'

Anticipation hollowed the room. It was the silence that preceded a confession. Or a public execution.

'Can I have a minute, please?' said Miss Price.

The court usher refilled her glass of water and Elinor was haunted by a memory she had hoped to lose. A woman she didn't know once spat at her in the Ladies'. Whore, she said. The woman's sister had been on the stand. She had broken down during Elinor's cross-examination. Elinor hadn't felt proud of the emotional distress she caused, nor did she feel shame. It was a lawyer's job to be shameless. Only when she got home and sank into a bath did she allow her feelings to surface. She had scrubbed off the dirt.

'Are you ready to continue?' asked the judge.

'I think so.'

Elinor took up where she had let off.

'On the night in question, February the twenty-fifth, Mr Foster spent the night with you in your flat. Correct me if I'm wrong.'

'Yes.'

'And in allowing this to happen, you effectively re-established your relationship with Mr Foster, did you not?'

'No.'

'You deliberately misled Mr Foster into believing that the relationship was back on again, didn't you?'

The right question flushed out the facts. The wrong answer would incriminate her defendant further.

'No.'

'You asked him to stay, didn't you?'

'It was a mistake.'

'You're going to have to be more specific. What was a mistake?'

'Getting pregnant.'

Hysteria choked her speech.

'And after what he's done, I don't want him near us. You have to keep him away from us.'

That was it. Elinor had lost her cross-examination and there was nothing she could do but stand by and allow a wave of emotion to flood the room. Miss Price crumpled and the room swallowed as though with one throat.

'This would seem to be an appropriate time to break for lunch,' concluded the judge.

Unable to stomach the prospect of Caroline's cheery post-mortem, Elinor shrugged on her coat over her gown and made a dash across the street. The sky was thundery and the expected showers had begun. Raindrops pelted her face. She opened the café door to a sea of steaming shoulders.

'*Principessa.*' Tony slapped his hands on the counter. 'What can I do you for today?'

'Ham and cheese on brown, please.'

She sat by herself and ate her sandwich too fast as she considered QC's response to her situation. He would quote his favourite World War I commander whose name she could never remember. Firstly grasp the essence of the situation. In court, as in war, readiness is all. The jury know when counsel has taken his eye off the ball, he would add. They can smell a mistake just as they can smell fear. Downing her tea, Elinor hurried back.

* * *

The man passing through the security gate had a familiar shuffle. She caught up with him on the other side. Sopping wet he didn't seem to care.

'Mr Foster.'

Startled – he must have been dreaming – he shielded his face with his arm in a gesture of self-defence. When he realised who it was he shamefacedly let it drop. Elinor paused, allowing them both to recover before she confronted him about what she didn't know.

'We need to talk about your child.'

'What's to talk about?'

Elinor planted her fists on her hips. She was smaller than him. She had sawing indigestion and needed to burp.

'You have a child with Miss Price. That's what we need to talk about. So far I haven't been able to use this in your defence. The prosecution are about to jump on this fact because as far as they're concerned you have threatened a woman who is in an extremely vulnerable position. A woman with a baby.'

His eyebrows drew in sharply at the corners. Locking her out.

'No one can take him away from me.'

'That's not the point,' she said, fed up, because right now she failed to see what the point was.

* * *

The next witness was up. He was young, mono-browed and tormented by a shaving rash. His ears glowed as he fumbled with the words. Jurors were impressed by a uniform. Their faces were chiselled with concentration.

'PC Mitchell,' said Caroline. 'Can you take us back to the night of January the twelfth.'

He cleared his throat.

'Myself and PC Hatchett were parading for duty when we were told on the radio to report to 5A Woodstock Terrace.'

'When you arrived, what did you find?'

'We found Miss Price in a state of distress.'

'Was she able to tell you why she was so distressed?'

'Yes. Her telephone had been ringing all night but the caller hung up every time she answered it. She had also been subjected to repeated ringing on her doorbell. When she opened the door, no one was there. At approximately ten past twelve, when she opened her front door, she found a dead rat on her doorstep.'

'Was the dead rat still there when you arrived at Miss Price's flat?'

'Yes, ma'am, it was.'

'And what time would that have been?'

'Approximately twelve-forty.'

'What did you do?'

'We proceeded to drive twice around the neighbourhood and we advised Miss Price to keep all her lights on.'

Elinor buried her smile. The police were full of good advice. Their life truisms were equally as edifying. *Flashers come out in the heat like mosquitoes,* was a personal favourite.

'Did Miss Price mention any names?'

'Frank Foster was the name mentioned, ma'am.'

'Do you know why she mentioned the name of Mr Foster?'

'Earlier on that same evening, she had seen Mr Foster's van parked outside her flat.'

'Thank you. No more questions.'

It was Elinor's turn. She felt nothing except her fingertips pressed against the wooden shelf in front. Every inch of her was taut with purpose.

'PC Mitchell. May I have a look at your notebook?'

The clerk went to fetch the notebook from the policeman. He handed it over to Elinor. Elinor examined it. She took her time.

'PC Mitchell, am I correct in saying that this record is your record?'

'It is.'

'We have just heard you tell the court how on the twelfth of January you went to Miss Price's flat at twelve-forty p.m. In your notebook, at the top in the box where the time should be noted, I see no record of the time.'

He frowned. 'No.'

'In truth you cannot be sure at precisely what time you arrived at Miss Price's flat, can you?'

'I know it was after midnight. Earlier on, when PC Hatchett asked me for the time, I looked at my watch and I remember telling him it was midnight.'

'And you are certain that PC Hatchett asked you for the time before you visited Miss Price and not after?'

'Yes.'

'I suggest there is a discrepancy between your recollections and your notes, PC Mitchell. The fact remains that you have no record of the exact time at which you arrived at Miss Price's home. I suggest it took place much earlier at an hour when children are still playing on the streets. Miss Price's flat backs on to the Cranwell Estate. It is well known to your station, is it not?'

'Yes.'

'Can you tell the courtroom why this is?'

'Because of the high incident rate of acts of vandalism and petty crime that are committed on the estate.'

'Thank you, PC Mitchell. In view of this, I suggest that Miss Price had been the victim of this type of harassment on many occasions prior to this one. I suggest that the ringing on her bell happened once, possibly twice, and that it was the action of local children playing a prank. I suggest the dead rat on her doorstep was part of this prank. However, on this particular night, she was feeling emotional and distraught so she called the police. Ashamed to give the real reason for calling you out, she used another, quite delusional reason. A pretence.'

'I can only say what the victim told us, ma'am.'

Elinor sat down. One – nil.

That evening she went to the theatre. QC had booked the tickets months ago.

'They're jolly good tickets. It would be a shame to waste

them,' he had said when he called. 'That Hollywood actor's in it. The one who got the award.'

They sat in the darkness, knees touching. Elinor felt nothing. It was the story of an older man who falls in love with a colleague's younger wife. The characters' age difference mirrored their age difference. The man was a lawyer. Only a few months ago this symmetry would have meant something. Tonight it didn't. Instead she thought about Gus and their kiss. A first kiss was instructive. It had told her everything she needed to know about what to expect next. The anticipation was killing her.

At the interval they went to find their drinks. Two glasses of prepaid champagne on a hand-written note that read *Laslow*. They elbowed their way to a corner and held their glasses close to their chests.

'Perhaps not quite what we had expected,' QC remarked, looking up from his programme. In the basement light his skin was sallow, his jowls saggy. He pecked her with a salty mouth.

'You must be starving. Have a nut.'

She polished off her glass. Afterwards they went for supper at a fish restaurant in the city where QC knew the maître d'. He ordered bream. She had the Dover sole. She sliced the flesh along the spine and picked it slowly off the bones.

'You haven't asked about today's ruling.'

'Tell me.' She continued filleting.

'Substantial damages.'

He had been fighting a libel case.

'How much?'

'Six figures.'

He was good.

'Well done.'

They shared a lemon tart. Licking the spoon, he leaned across the table and stroked her arm.

'What do you want?'

His voice was silky. 'My bed.'

He tapped his spoon on his espresso cup.

'You're not coming back, then?'

She looked at him.

'Do you realise that, when we met, I was the youngest member of chambers? Now you're the oldest.'

'Oh, don't be like that.'

'Like what?'

'Resentful.'

He waved impatiently at the waiter to bring the bill, and she thought what a long time it was since he had been tender. She had known it was over last summer when they had had sex in a hurry with him in his cricket whites still sweaty from the game. She had listened to him panting. She hadn't enjoyed it. They were no longer on the same team, she remembered thinking. He was out to beat her. Their passion was frustration. Frustration that they couldn't give each other up. They had been in competition to see who needed the other less for a very long time.

He put her in a taxi and planted a kiss on her head.

'Thanks for dinner,' she said.

Guilt accompanied her all the way home. At the flat she found three messages and her guilt faded quickly.

'What happened?'

It was Kendra with glee in her voice chasing news of last night's date with Gus.

'Any sign of my bike pump?'

Upstairs neighbour Nigel. Dumped two weeks before his fortieth birthday, he had been playing the same record over and over again ever since. Steely Dan's *Greatest Hits.* He used any excuse he could to call.

'Elinor.'

What was it about her name from his mouth that meant so much? Surrendering to the sofa, she drowned in his voice.

'It's Gus. I want to apologise for boring you with my terrible stories. It was very nice to see you. But you're not there. I'll try again.'

As his words lingered, the stale taste of her evening left her and was replaced by the sky they had flown through at night. The sensation of being sucked into vastness as they spiralled through space. The golden light on the wings in the morning and the terror of turbulence as they rode through the bumps. And all the while his words had been her comfort as he told her beginnings of stories, the endings of which she could only guess at. She couldn't wait to see him again.

Chapter Six

Morning seeped beneath her eyelids, and she knew that she had been grinding her teeth. There was the familiar ball of pain at each temple and the aching jaw. She stuffed both pillows behind her head and stared at the stripes of shadow that criss-crossed the windows. The scaffolding had been up for six months. It made her feel claustrophobic.

It was a rented flat, two bedrooms, one of which had been occupied by the actress until she moved to LA. It was on the second floor of a three-storey house on a street lined with cherry trees. She considered it centrally located. QC had not. He refused to stay there. He owned a pied-à-terre in Mayfair, which was where they used to meet.

It was early. Hugging her knees to her chest, Elinor cocooned herself inside her nightgown, which was white, paper thin and embroidered with daisies hand stitched by ladies in India. It was a treasured possession, because as a child she had seen Frida's toes protrude from beneath it. Also inherited from Frida were the sapphire ring she wore on her forefinger, the mahogany desk by the window, and a group photograph of Frida and Uncle Ted with thirty Indian civil servants on the wall in her hall.

Madras, India, 1936. Uncle Ted was in a white suit. The Indian men were sporting ties and lungis and sitting with their legs crossed and serious faces as they blinked in the sun. Frida was wearing a garland of flowers and a slim-fitting dress with mutton-chop sleeves. She wasn't smiling. It hadn't been a happy marriage. There had been no children. Uncle Ted didn't have a gravestone. A stocky man with trombone-player's cheeks, he had been a district officer. His first love had been for gambling, his second for horses. Frida had been a scandalously beautiful woman with an impressive command of Tamil and a taste for stronger men. She suffered from depression, boasted a formidable knowledge of the spices essential to Indian cooking, and had an affair that lasted eight years. She never had an orgasm with Uncle Ted.

Elinor never discovered apropos of what this fact had been revealed. It had been during a particularly bleak Christmas holiday. They had been in the kitchen preparing supper. Rather, Elinor had been peeling potatoes and frying mince while Frida had been casually finishing off a bottle of gin and railing at the television screen. It was a programme about the near-extinction of the Indian tiger.

'Selfish bloody man,' she exclaimed. 'Of course I had to look elsewhere.'

'Look for what?'

'Sexual satisfaction. He had absolutely zero interest.'

Elinor remembered staring at her aunt's haughty neck and earlobes trailing jewels and wondering what to do with this piece of information. She had nowhere for it to go. Frida had introduced her to the mysteries of life and done her best to see that they remained that way. When Elinor had been much younger, nine or ten years of age, Frida had announced that there were only two matters of consequence. Sex and death. What about horses? Elinor had ventured. It's the same for horses, replied Frida. Sex and death.

Never an easy woman, Frida resented the loss of her youth. Her features like hot wax dripping down her face. Her lashes, too fine for mascara, depositing black clots like soot around her eyes. Elizabeth Arden Balmy Coral lipstick leaking into the cracks around her lips, making her look a clown. I can't look in the mirror today, she would despair. She had possessed a glacial reserve that thawed in the company of few, a cutting tongue and sharper views. Never wear diamonds before eleven. Every woman needs a husband, although what she does with him is up to her. An old-fashioned woman with modern tastes, she wore a denim shirt over everything, loathed the telephone but believed in the supremacy of power tools. The electric drill was a constant companion.

Elinor had never met Uncle Ted. He died of a massive coronary as he stepped off a plane, before she was born.

The snooze alarm went off. Six-forty-five. Elinor got out of bed, put on socks and padded downstairs. She picked up the newspaper, made a cup of tea and tore back the curtains.

The sky was pink as if it were a secret she had suddenly been let in on. It seemed auspicious. She spread open the paper, skimmed the front and back before steering her way through the pages in between. Certain stories leapt off the page. Fallen royals and random acts of fate were not to be missed.

Princess runs off with circus trainer. Hostage talks end in temple storming. Ice bombs – frozen effluent falling from airplanes – will reach record levels this year.

Turning to the crossword, she found a pen.

1 Across: Shifted blame to another (6, 3, 4). PASSEDTHEBUCK. Something QC accused her of doing.

11 Across: Boxer leading with right hand (8). SOUTHPAW. She once defended a boxer. Dusty Dick. Shaved his chest with a Lady Shave. This fact had been crucial in his defence.

14 Across: Aztec name for Avocado (8). TESTICLE. Wild guess. It fitted.

Running out of time, she went to run a bath.

Frank Foster was in the witness box. He didn't look good. He had developed a shut eye, which was veiny and blue, and above it was the beginning of a nasty haematoma. He had an unhelpful habit of blowing air into one cheek and transferring it into the other. There was also the matter of his darting eyes. It made him look shifty. Elinor could sense the jury's disapproval, and he hadn't even been sworn in.

'Don't look so guilty,' she muttered beneath her breath.

Her examination-in-chief was about to begin. It was always a risk putting a client on the stand, anything could happen, and today was no different. Her half-hour in conference with him this morning had been bloody. The first rule of client relations was to know which approach to take. Whether to paint it black or slightly less black. There had been no point telling him she was cautiously optimistic or quietly confident. She wasn't. They're still talking about pleading, she said. Your chances of conviction are extremely high. You must be fucking joking, he told her. Appraising his strengths – paternal duty – and weaknesses – anger – she told him where she needed him to go. It was the best she could do.

Elinor stood up.

'Can you tell the court your full name?'

'Frank Henry Foster.'

'You are going to have to speak up,' said the judge.

Elinor recognised the symptoms of a dry tongue. Her own voice had deserted her on a number of occasions. Once she had fainted. She had been passed a photograph of a naked body, blue flesh slashed with deep purple wounds left by a metal ruler. In fact it was skipping breakfast and standing for too long in shoes that cut off her circulation which had sent her crashing to the ground. Her tumble hadn't impressed the judge or her client.

'How long were you involved in a relationship with Miss Price?'

He drank some water.

'A year and a half.'

'Mr Foster, did you love Miss Price?'

'Yes.'

'Did you believe that you were going to make a life together?'

'Yes.'

'How did you feel when Miss Price rejected your proposal of marriage and asked you to move out of her flat?'

'I was gutted. Totally devastated.'

'What explanation did she give?'

'She didn't give one.'

'What did she say?'

'That's the thing. Nothing. It was like something happened but she wouldn't tell me what.'

'Which is why you tried to see her? To talk to her?'

'Yes.'

'When you say that you tried to see her, what did you do?'

'I rang her, like, to ask her to see me. She said no. I kept ringing, and first off we'd speak. Then something happened. She stopped answering so I'd leave messages. I told her I wanted us to be happy. To make a life together.'

'When did you find out that she was the mother of your child?'

'When she was four months gone.'

'Did Miss Price break the news to you?'

'No.'

'Who broke the news to you?'

'Steve Robson. I bumped into him in the pub and he told me to keep away from her.'

'What did you do?'

'Like I said, I kept ringing. I'm Billy's dad. I wanted to look after her and the baby. I went round to her flat to try and talk to her.'

'And you sent cards?'

'Yes.'

'Approximately how many cards did you send?'

'Twenty. Twenty-five tops.'

She turned to the jury.

'If you could turn to page thirty-one in the jury bundle. Mr Foster, perhaps if you could read this card.'

Sentiment infused his words.

'*In the morning, when I see your face, I know I'm alive. Your smile gives me hope to carry on. You are my sunshine when you walk through the door. What can I do to make it better?*'

'Thank you. Now if you could turn back to page ten you will find a copy of another card. A card with a very different message. Could you read this card for the benefit of the jury, Mr Foster?'

'*I am watching and waiting. We have formed a soul union. I know what makes you tick.*'

'Did you send this card, Mr Foster?'

'No, I did not.'

'Have you ever seen this card before now?'

'No.'

'Do you know who might have sent this card?'

'No.'

'Thank you, Mr Foster. Now, if you would, I'd like you to tell the court what happened on November the twenty-first.'

'That's the day my son was born.'

'Did you see your son on the day he was born?'

'No.'

'When did you first see your son?'

'I went round to the flat the day after he was born. They wouldn't let me in.'

'Who wouldn't let you in?'

'Steve Robson and his mate. A foreign bloke . . .'

'If you could stick to answering the questions, thank you, Mr Foster,' said the judge.

'What did you do when they wouldn't let you in?' Elinor resumed.

'I left the flowers and the present for my son on the doorstep.'

'What was the present?'

'A cuddly toy. A rabbit.'

'Would that happen to be the same rabbit as this?' said Elinor, holding up Exhibit eight.

The clerk passed it to Mr Foster.

'Can you describe the rabbit for the jury, please.'

The jury had already examined the rabbit. She wanted them to see Frank Foster's reaction to it. He grimaced.

'It's disgusting. It's been butchered. The eyes and the ears have been pulled off. It looks like it's been stabbed with a knife.'

'But this is the same rabbit that you gave to your son?'

'Not like this it isn't.'

'Can you explain?'

'The rabbit was brand new when I gave it to my son.'

'You weren't responsible for mutilating it?'

'No.'

'Do you know who did?'

'Someone who wanted to give the wrong idea to Suzy and my son.'

'Thank you. No more questions.'

Caroline was up.

'When Miss Price said that she no longer wanted to see you, Mr Foster, what did you do?'

'I tried to see her. To talk about it.'

'But she didn't want to see you, did she?'

'No.'

'You couldn't accept her decision, could you?'

'No.'

'Why not?'

'It didn't make sense.'

'But it made plenty of sense to Miss Price. Why couldn't you respect her wishes, Mr Foster?'

Frank Foster frowned.

'I couldn't.'

'You mean you chose not to. Instead, filled with rage, you left a dead rat and a mutilated toy on Miss Price's doorstep to intimidate her. Isn't that right?'

'No.'

Caroline turned to the jury.

'I'd like you to turn to page fourteen of your jury bundle.'

They rifled through their pages.

'Eighty-nine cards and letters in total were received by Miss Price. This particular card is postmarked April the sixteenth. *Where ever you are I'll find you. Leave me and you'll die.* What did you mean by this, Mr Foster?'

He gulped his water.

'I never sent it.'

'Mr Foster, where do you say you were on the night of January the twelfth?'

'In the Barley Corn.'

'Who were you with?'

'Jim Jones.'

'When you left the pub where do you say you went?'

'Home.'

'You went straight home, is that right?'

'No. We went to get my van. But the van had been nicked.'

He sounded impatient. This was Caroline's intention. Wind him up. Make him say things he didn't want to say.

'Thank you, Mr Foster, for bringing me to the point at which I was hoping to arrive. It does sound suspiciously convenient that your van should have been stolen on the night in question. Did you report this theft to the police?'

'No.'

'Why not?'

'The van was knackered. I'd been driving it for fifteen years. It was cheaper to buy another one than go to the police and have the hassle of the insurance . . .'

'Mr Foster,' she interrupted him. 'To clarify. What you're

telling the court is that on the night of January the twelfth, a night during which Miss Price was subjected to repeated hang-up calls and knocking on her door, and at the end of which she found a dead rat on her doorstep, a night during which your white van was seen parked outside her flat, you were outside the Barley Corn looking at an empty parking place. Is that correct?'

Mr Foster's eyes glazed over.

'Is that correct?'

'No. I was walking home.'

'Accompanied by anyone? You don't have a witness to this, do you?'

'No.'

Caroline shook her head, a gesture matched by a rise in her voice.

'I suggest it is *not* correct, Mr Foster. I suggest that at midnight, when you left the Barley Corn having drunk several pints of beer, you got into your van and drove to Miss Price's flat. There you parked. Determined to make Miss Price aware of your presence, you proceeded to make a series of hang-up calls from your mobile phone. At approximately twelve-ten p.m., you deposited a dead rat on Miss Price's doorstep before you drove away.'

'No.'

'No what, Mr Foster?'

'None of it's right. I didn't have my van. I didn't have my mobile. It was in the van when the van got nicked.'

'Doesn't that rather defeat the object of having a mobile phone, Mr Foster? Indeed I suggest, Mr Foster, that your story falls negligibly short of the truth. You are not, Mr Foster, telling the truth. No more questions, Your Honour.'

Caroline drew breath. Smoothing her gown beneath her, she sat down. When Elinor looked over, she smiled.

* * *

She took the Tube home. She didn't deserve a taxi. She hadn't done well today. At Euston a very small man got on. He made it just before the doors shut. Wearing a wide-brimmed fedora and a child's duffel coat, he perched in the seat next to hers with his feet dangling. He caught her eye, smiled, and said hello. 'Hello.' Elinor returned the courtesy before returning to her evening newspaper. *Peace talks end in acrimony*. The Tube braked in a tunnel, making the sound of a swarm of angry bees, and they were left to sit in semi-darkness. No one complained.

'I'm reminded of a séance,' said the man. He could have been an actor.

'I've never been to one,' said Elinor.

'Oh, I'd highly recommend it.'

The Tube rattled and moved on.

'Upon arrival the last set of doors will not open.'

It was her stop. When she got off, he waved her goodbye.

* * *

At home, she checked her messages. Two hang-ups and a wrong number. 'Pick up, pick up,' blundered a heavy foreign voice followed by an eerie silence. She erased it, poured herself a medicinal gin and tonic and slumped on the sofa. When the window was open she could rest her glass on the scaffolding plank as though it were a coffee table. She wasn't alone in realising the potential of the scaffolding. Cans and bottles and a used condom had appeared out there. Someone had been having a party. Checking that the window was locked, she closed the curtains. She wanted to speak to Gus but made do with Kendra instead. Kendra was in a wine bar.

'It's going terribly badly,' Elinor shouted over the din.

'Have a drink.'

'I have.'

'Have three. Tomorrow you'll be fine.'

'You don't think . . .'

'Don't be stupid.'

It's because I can't discuss everything with QC was what she was going to say. Up until four months ago she had been sleeping with QC and on top of her work. Since then she had been slipping. The timing fitted.

'You win some, you lose some.'

'Lose them all,' said Elinor miserably.

Why do we do this job? was a question they occasionally put to one another. Because we like to win, was the answer.

'You'll never guess my client's name today.' Kendra chuckled. 'Kevin Cowmeadow, one word. Fake Es. Poor love. Looks like my shout. Better go. See you in chambers.'

Elinor went to take a shower. She would always shower in the darkness when she didn't want to think. Closing her eyes, she stood with her spine like marbles against the tiles and let the shower-head do the crying for her. The rushing water stroked her body back to life. Cupping her breasts in her hands, she waited until a dam had formed in her cleavage. She released them and felt the water flow between her breasts and slide down her stomach and sluice between her legs. The moistness made her yearn for what she missed. She silently howled.

Chapter Seven

The Ladies' Robing Room offered sanctuary. Steeling herself with three cups of coffee, Elinor experimented with two lipstick shades. Reds and pinks clashed with her hair. She had the same problem with clothes. Applying a smudge of orange to a layer of plum, she achieved a successful claret which made her feel feminine and brave. It was her closing speech today.

Time, said the Tannoy. Spraying her neck and wrists, she added a final slick of lipstick and shoved her hair beneath her wig. In the corridor, she took deep breaths and thought unexpectedly of Gus. He would enjoy seeing her now. His appearance in her thoughts deepened her stride.

* * *

'Your Honour, I'd like to call Jim Jones.'

'The Alliteration Association,' chortled Caroline from below.

Elinor had thought the same thing but she couldn't afford to snigger. The man on the stand was Mr Foster's alibi witness, and drinking partner. He had an inflamed nose and raddled cheeks. His bewildered eyes and visible discomfort at being buttoned up in a suit did however appear to indicate an unfamiliarity with his surroundings. Men in and out of court all the time postured like peacocks and wore expressions of contempt. Mr Jones uncurled his hand against the Bible.

'I swear by Almighty God that what I say will be the truth, the whole truth and nothing but the truth.'

'Mr Jones,' said Elinor. 'Can you tell the court your occupation?'

'Market man. Same as Frank. Fruit and veg.'

His voice was jittery.

'How long have you known the defendant?'

'Ten years.'

'Where were you on the night of January the twelfth?'

'In the Barley Corn.'

'That would be yourself and the defendant, Mr Foster?'

'Yes.'

'What time did you leave the Barley Corn?'

'Midnight.'

'Where did you go?'

'We went to get Frank's van. He'd left it parked in the market. I was getting a lift back with him.'

'What happened when you went to find his van?'

'It weren't there.'

'Can you explain what exactly you mean by this?'

'The van had been nicked.'

'It had been stolen?'

'Yes.'

'What did you do when you discovered that the van had been stolen?'

'Frank couldn't believe it. Everyone knows his van. He's had it forever. His number plate is FHF. Frank Henry Foster. He bought the van because of that plate.'

'Did you call the police to report the theft?'

'Er, no. Frank said he'd do it in the morning.'

'What did you do?'

'We went back to the Barley. They hadn't stopped serving so we had another pint as I remember. Later we called us a taxi and went home.'

'This would have been at approximately what time?'

'Half past one.'

'Thank you, Mr Jones. No more questions.'

Caroline bounced up like a jack-in-the-box.

'Mr Jones. You say that you've known Mr Foster for ten years. In what capacity? What do you do when you get together?'

'Drink, mostly.'

'How much do you drink?'

'Depends who's paying. Depends what time we get down there.'

'How much would you drink, say, over the course of an average evening?'

'I don't know. Six, seven pints.'

'How much did you drink on the night of January the twelfth?'

He shrugged.

'I wasn't counting.'

'Approximately how many pints did you drink on the night of the twelfth of January, Mr Jones?'

He was perspiring.

'Five. Could have been six.'

'By which point you must have been fairly inebriated. Your visibility must have been impaired. Let's see, six pints of beer is four times the legal limit for getting behind the wheel of a vehicle.'

'I know what I saw. Frank's van wasn't there.'

'Which brings me to my next question. Correct me if I'm wrong but isn't your nickname Driver?'

He coughed nervously.

'Would you like to tell the court how you came to acquire this nickname?'

More coughing.

'Perhaps you'd like to take a drink of water, Mr Jones.'

He did as he was told.

'I've always had it,' he said, recovered.

Elinor flicked through her witness statements prepared by a pupil in chambers while she was away. There was no record of a nickname. One step forward. Ten steps back. This was becoming painful and tedious.

'Mr Jones, from your records it is as plain as daylight that you acquired this name because of your ability to hot-wire and steal cars. Isn't this so?'

Mr Jones fidgeted uncomfortably.

'Mr Jones,' said the judge in a pernickety tone. 'If you would please answer the question.'

Elinor made a silent wish. Tell me its not true.

'Yes.'

Her heart sank. Mr Jones was a man with a criminal record. He was not to be believed.

'I suggest that on the night of January the twelfth, you and Mr Foster got into Mr Foster's van. He dropped you at home. He then drove onto Miss Price's flat where he parked and began to terrorise Miss Price with a series of harassing phone calls before depositing a dead rat on her doorstep.'

'No. That's not what happened.'

'I suggest that it's precisely what happened. No more questions, Your Honour.'

Caroline sat down and Elinor felt her sinking feeling turn to lead. Humiliated by Caroline's unrelenting projection of authority, she envied her winning streak. Until four months ago, she had been able to go three months minimum without losing a case. Her hope of winning this one was less than slim. She didn't know what had happened to her. Nor could she remember ever having received instructions as poor as these. Brian should have picked up Mr Jones's criminal past. It was his job to check for previous convictions. Instead she was left with a witness who had been discredited and a defence marred with distrust.

Mr Jones left the witness box.

Elinor stood up. Hands clasped before her, her face long, she turned to the jury. Caroline had presented the jury with one motive for Frank Foster's actions. Her job was to convince them of another.

'Members of the jury.' She found her tone. Measured. Compassionate. 'What I am asking you to do here is to put yourself in Mr Foster's position. Here is a man who lost his chance, perhaps his only chance, of true happiness. A man who found himself not only robbed of the woman he loved, but the mother of his son. A boy he wanted to watch grow up, day by day. Being no different from any other man, he was angry and upset, understandably so, and was not prepared to give up without a fight. He tried to contact Miss Price by every means available to him. He called her at home and at work. He sent cards and love letters. You have heard him say that he sent twenty, at most twenty-five, cards and letters. Love letters. What he did not do, and I repeat, did not do, is send eight-nine cards, nor did he send cards that sought to threaten her or wish her harm.'

Elinor leaned forward, using her body, her eyes, to beseech them. The jury listened with impassive faces.

'You heard Mr Foster tell this courtroom how on the night of January the twelfth, the night when Miss Price found a dead rat on her doorstep, Mr Foster was stranded at the market where he works, looking for his stolen vehicle. It wasn't possible for him to have driven to Miss Price's flat and deposited a dead rat on her doorstep because he didn't have his van. You have heard Mr Jones corroborate the testimony of Mr Foster. There is also no evidence to prove that the hang-up calls, graffiti or threatening correspondence that Miss Price was subjected to were in any way connected to Mr Foster. Indeed, the evidence against Mr Foster hangs by the merest of threads. The prosecution have attempted to erect an evidential edifice based upon presumption and circumstance.

'Members of the jury.' She paused. 'You have heard Mr Foster speak today. He is not an aggressive man. You have seen him. He is not a threatening man. He is a man in pain. A man with a broken heart. What I'm doing here is not asking for your sympathy, absolutely *not,* what I'm doing is asking you to consider this evidence. We know nothing of Miss Price's past. It is not for us to speculate upon who might have wanted to threaten her with hang-up calls and hate mail and graffiti. All we know is what we've heard in this courtroom and what we've heard is the evidence which proves that Mr Foster tried to win back the heart of the woman he loved, the mother of his son, by sending twenty five love letters and attempting to see her five or six times. And that, members of the jury, is all he did.

'Before you can convict Mr Foster, whatever your feelings, you must be sure beyond reasonable doubt of his guilt. That is the law. It's my job and yours to apply the law. What I'm asking you to do is to go to the jury room and come back with the only possible verdict. That Frank Foster is *not* guilty.'

With soggy knees, it took a force of will for Elinor to sit down and not come crashing down. Had she done a reasonable job? She didn't think she had left anything out. She had made the case understandable to the jury and had applied the barest sentiment to highlight the facts. The eyes of the room left her as she regained her breath and His Honour

Judge Green began his summing up. He would conclude it the following day at which point the jury would retire to reach their verdict. He finished with his usual request that the jury not discuss the case with anyone. They were dismissed and filed out. He exited and the public gallery emptied.

'Well done,' said Caroline.

'And to you.'

'Verdict tomorrow. What do you think?'

She wasn't giving Caroline the satisfaction of agreeing to agree. Brian was waiting for her outside the courtroom, flapping his briefcase like an apron.

'Why wasn't I told about his convictions?' Elinor couldn't hide her exasperation. Walking fast, she was feeling fraught.

Brian tugged at his beard.

'Must have slipped through.'

'Listen.' She ripped off her wig. It was a mistake to vent her anger on Brian. He kept her in work. 'I'm not blaming anyone. But if I don't get the instructions I need, I've got nothing to work with.'

Brian nodded. 'I thought maybe a quick one?'

'I can't.' She ruffled her hair. 'Thanks anyway.'

Chapter Eight

She was saved by her bicycle, and not for the first time. Out of the gates, she cycled on the pavement to avoid the one-way, apologising to pedestrians who dodged to avoid being knocked down. The burn in her muscles, the pollution on her tongue, purged her of the courtroom and the person she had been up until half an hour ago. She had taken off her wig and placed it in its tin. Her gown, folded up, had been squashed in her bag. Her heels swapped for trainers. She had tied back her hair and twisted her skirt so that the slit at the back met the front of her saddle. She stopped at a zebra crossing for a confused woman in a leopard skin coat to cross.

'Four in a bed. Four in a bed,' shouted the woman, stabbing the air.

It was an uphill slog to reach the bridge. The approach to the river was heralded by cool air that slipped beneath her helmet. Crossing the water, she gazed down at the metallic olive sludge. A barge chugged by, barely making a ripple. At the intersection she balanced with a foot on the kerb.

'Lucky saddle,' hissed a voice.

She turned to find a man who wasn't young sitting in an open-top sports car wearing a shirt unbuttoned to the waist and a grin. He could have been an ex-client only he wasn't, because she never forgot a face or a haircut. A tail of hair, going grey, strayed at the nape of his neck. She overtook him, mac flapping. He caught up with her and leaned over the passenger seat.

'Why are you in such a hurry?'

'Oh, grow up.'

'Bitch,' he snarled, and flooded her with exhaust as he gunned the engine and shot off.

The next left was hers. She took it. The U-turn from flattery to vitriol was so depressingly predictable that it failed to arouse even the mildest of reactions. Across the street, sandwiched between a pub and a terraced house, was a building with a blue plaque – a code-breaker once resided here – and a list of names beside the door. QC's name was at the top. Chambers.

'If it isn't the film star.'

Derek was tapping numbers into a calculator.

'You by yourself?' She unbuckled her helmet.

'They saw you coming and hid under their desks.'

She released a spray of hair.

'That's what I thought.'

The fax machine hummed and deposited a length of paper on the floor.

'About bloody time,' he grumbled.

Getting up from his desk, he went to retrieve it.

The clerks' room was cramped. There were three of them – Derek, Derek's nephew Norman, and Norm's chum Lee. They sat behind three desks crammed together to form an untidy L. Each desk had a computer, an in-tray, an out-tray and a jumble of executive toys inherited from barristers whose desks were full. Derek wore V-neck sweaters on dress-down Fridays and sharp suits the rest of the week. He was a short man with beady eyes, hair like steel wool, a diamond on his pinkie finger, and a tendency to speak from the side of his mouth. A professional cynic, he pretended to be impressed by nothing when actually most things delighted him. His bark was worse than his bite, and Elinor was always pleased to see him. It was a bit like coming home. She was trying to remember why she had come in.

'What's that noise?'

Derek looked up from reading his fax.

'What noise?'

'That ticking.'

'It's the radiator. What's wrong with you, anyway? You look all hot and bothered.'

'I am.'

'If it's got anything to do with your fancy man who's been bothering us all day, do us a favour, miss, and tell him to call you out of office hours.'

Her heart missed a beat.

'Who?'

'Some bloody joker who won't leave his name. I told him to ring your mobile.'

'I'll check my messages.'

'I got you a possession with intent to supply. Isleworth.'

'Thanks.' She paused. 'Is he here?'

'Sports day. Went at lunch.'

QC's youngest daughter was still at school. Elinor was relieved he wasn't here. If he had been, she would have pretended that he wasn't.

Her room smelt of Kendra's lunch. Something fishy. It was a boxy room with wooden panelling painted white. The carpet was grey and brown with coffee spills. The ceiling sloped and the shelves were bowed with briefs gathering dust. There was no sign of Kendra. Post-divorce she kept her diary full. She had an engagement or activity every night of the week. Squash. Dinner. Theatre. Therapy.

Elinor opened her laptop and checked her e-mails. Twelve of them, ten of which were work related. There was one from the actress in LA. *Woke up to swimming pool lapping against bedroom window. First earthquake. Miss you.* There was one from her father. A civil engineer based in Saudi, he was overseeing the construction of a pipeline through the desert. Elinor got past hello to find mention of OPEC price wars. She would read the rest later.

Outside her window the light turned violet. The evening stretched before her like eternity, and she wanted to know why Gus hadn't left a message if he had gone to the trouble of tracking her down to chambers. Consumed by a longing to hear his voice, she stared at her computer screen. She looked at her sad indoor plant, out of the window and back at her screen. It was bad form to pursue men. Bad luck. It wasn't what good girls did. But her head was spinning too fast to let go. Finding his number, she dialled it before she had time to reconsider. Someone at the other end answered too fast.

'Gus?'

'Hang on.'

The phone was passed over.

'Yup?'

He was in the middle of something.

'It's Elinor.'

'Elinor.'

'Have I caught you at a bad time?'

'No. I'm stuck in a room with a man on the verge of dementia, that's all.'

She had no idea what he was talking about.

'Where are you? Are you wearing your wig?'

She heard laughter in the background.

'No,' she told him, wanting to hang up and forget that she had called. It wasn't her day. It was pointless trying to remedy it now. She made her excuses.

'I'll let you get back to work.'

'No. Don't do that. What are you up to?'

'Now?'

'Yes.'

'I'm . . .'

'Come and have a drink. If you've got nothing better to do.'

'No. Really. Don't worry.'

'Sorry. That wasn't much of an invitation. If I give you the address, will you come?'

'Well . . .'

'Good. It's number four . . .'

The air was moody. The calm threatened rain. She walked her bicycle through the Temple past Daimlers and Bentleys and shiny Jaguars. Union Jacks were flying three in a row. She emerged on Fleet Street and straddled her seat. A bike courier overtook her so swiftly that he made no sound. Arriving in Soho, she was confronted by people everywhere. The lost ones lingered on corners and looked the wrong way while the rest ran her down. The address Gus had given her was a cul-de-sac. She locked her bicycle to a lamp, pressed the buzzer and rearranged her skirt. Nervous, she felt out of place. She was wearing a black suit and the residue of this morning's make-up. She didn't look her best.

No one asked who she was and she was buzzed in. At the reception desk a boy was drinking a beer and battling a computer game with a frenetic thumb.

'I'm looking for Gus.'

He didn't bother lifting his head.

'Third door.'

She proceeded along the hallway, knocked on the third door and ran a hand across her hair.

'It's open,' came a shout.

The room she entered was warm like a cave. It smelt of men and ashtrays and hours passed. She was greeted by two backs hunched over a table with a set of monitors ahead of them.

'Cut to the wide shot. Unless you want to cut it.'

That was Gus. The other man was tapping keys on a keyboard.

'I can't stand trees. You can't see where you're going. You can't see where you've been. I can't stand trees ...' said a helium voice at high speed.

Elinor remained standing.

'Hello.'

The spine in the blue shirt flexed. He swivelled round. When he saw her he smiled. It made her heart sing.

'Elinor. I'm sorry. I thought it was that bloody boy again. This is Connor. My editor. Take a seat.'

'Hey,' Connor called over his shoulder in a Scottish brogue.

Elinor fell into the sofa.

'Can we blow it up? The logic's fine.' Gus was talking to Connor. Without warning, he whipped back in his chair, thrust a glass in her hand, flew back to the table and returned with a bottle. He poured her some wine.

'You've got some catching up to do.'

She sat back. A stranger in his world, she tried to work it out. It was important to see a man at work. A mark of respect, it gained their respect and talent like success was seductive. This was a Frida-ism she had learned to be true.

The room was blank except for the images on the screens. There were three of them. The left one displayed a blur of unintelligible text, the middle one was split into four images, while the right one showed the picture in full. On the table were empty take-out cartons, mugs and a stack of videotapes. There were two speakers, papers and pens. The equipment hummed. Blinds kept out the light.

'That's the one,' said Gus.

Elinor looked. On the monitor was a street in a small town lined with shops and houses and cars. As she watched, hundreds of horses, some with riders, most without, galloped down the street. It was as surreal and beautiful as a lost dream.

'Cowboys and Indians.' She let slip her thought.

Connor laughed.

'No prizes for guessing who's the cowboy.'

Gus spun round. 'Don't believe a word he says.'

In that instant Elinor knew it would happen tonight, and it would happen because she had come here to make it happen. Emotions raged. Giddy with pleasure, she felt confident and free. The possibilities were endless.

The two men continued to operate as one. There were mutterings, prolonged silences and hand signals to indicate direction. The horses ran faster and loomed larger as if about to leap from the screen. With a sigh, Connor threw his hands in the air and flopped back in his chair.

'That's it. I've had enough of your shagging Indians . . .'

'Mexicans.'

'. . . for one shagging day.'

He stood up, whipped his jacket off the back of door and shoved his arms into it.

'I'm out of here.'

''Bye,' they called after him.

His departure left a hole in the room. They drank some more but tension lurked uneasily in the corners and they slumped into silence. Elinor could think of nothing interesting to say; when she did she didn't want to say it. Every gesture felt exaggerated. The physical distance between them unnatural. Her knees looked bony and her brain felt tired.

'So you're on a bike?' said Gus.

'Yes.' She rattled her helmet. Fed up with words.

'Me too. I don't know about you but what I'd like to do is get out of here.'

'Yes,' she almost shouted.

'Good.' He smiled and began switching things off. 'Let's go.'

The rain had gone and now came mist that was thick and milky and not of this world. Gus didn't wear a helmet.

'I have a talent for survival,' he joked, winding her up, although by virtue of saying it he must have thought it was true. 'I wear a Walkman.'

'If you cycle every day you're going to get hurt.'

'I know.' He shot ahead.

Cycling alone was about reaching the final destination. Cycling as two involved competition. Speeds crescendoed, wheels brushed and threatened to tangle. They overtook, braked and cycled side by side again. Elinor led the way. Arriving at Regents Park, they found the gates open. The Georgian terraces were so white that they offered light. They churned the mist through fast-moving spokes. The road was straight. The streetlights painted orange smudges in the distance and her breasts jogged up and down, jolts of pain, as a reminder that she needed to invest in a new set of bras. Hers wore out faster than those of anyone she knew. Her bosom was expensive.

Gus came alongside.

'Do you know where we're going?'

'Don't you trust me?'

'Should I?'

She watched him go. Without a plan, just a hunch, she was feeling reckless and brave and a little bit anxious. The shish-shish of tyres on tarmac provided a rush of something like freedom, and she caught an echo of the happiness she felt in the saddle. Shedding her day, she sensed that he was doing the same thing. They passed the zoo. At night it had a brooding stillness. Shadows fluttered through the aviary that crowned the trees. Once she had heard a lion roar and had visions of someone falling into the pit. It had thrilled and frightened her. A big cat so close.

His back light spotted red in the distance. She changed gear, gaining ground. With one wheel in front, she pushed hard and swept ahead. She stretched out her arms and threw back her head. He caught up quickly, breath pouring from his mouth.

'I had no idea you were so competitive. You'll be doing tricks next.'

She raised both arms, showing off, and hit a sleeping policeman. Lurching violently forward, she lost control of her bike. He threw out an arm and seized her handlebars and they wobbled together like a circus act.

'I was joking,' he chortled.

She felt embarrassed.

'That's my repertoire all used up.'

Then he let go and she felt a rush of so many things that it was hard to know what to do. Drizzle began to leak from the sky. He reached inside his collar and pulled out a hood. They had entered the night.

'We could stop,' she suggested, but he didn't reply and they crossed an invisible line. Both now knew where they were headed.

The secret to cycling in the city was to stick to back streets and parks. The smell of damp earth rose through the mist as he followed her behind a tall privet hedge beyond which tennis courts lay empty, nets drooping. NO CYCLES, read the sign.

'Are we going up?'

They had arrived at a path that dissolved into blackness. They were at the base of a hill, the summit of which was obscured by nightfall and weather. Around them lay emptiness. They were enveloped in silence, their senses heightened as they felt their way ahead.

'Go on,' she said.

The incline was steady but it became steeper as they rode. She followed, zigzagging, twisting her handlebars hard. Left. Right. Her skirt rode higher. Rain soaked her tights, nylon stuck to her skin, and she wondered whose idea this had been. It seemed absurd, and yet when they had set out together, she had known that this cycle ride would be the one by which she would come to measure all the rest.

'Go, go, go,' he said in her ear.

Their lights wove in and out of each other's paths. They stole deep lungfuls of air where the path flattened, then pressed on in earnest. Her body and bicycle worked in tandem, each willing the other not to quit. She couldn't quit now. She had the impression of leaving everything behind. At the top it would all be new. Her thighs shook. Her shoulders ached and she heard her knees, or was it her ankles, pop. Then they were there.

'Mother.' Gus doubled up over his handlebars, fighting for breath.

Laughing deliriously, Elinor felt her calf muscles spasm. Her hair was a bush and her shoes were buckets. Beneath them lay London's hazy lights, a distant place in another time zone, as they sucked oxygen on a hill high above. His panting subsided.

'Are you cold?'

She was hot.

'Yes,' she said.

She knew what was coming next. He leaned towards her. Their bicycles fell together and jammed. Handlebars snarled.

He managed to get to her, his face becoming bigger, and their mouths met as the bicycles smashed to the ground. His face was moist with exertion. His fingers gripped hers and they clenched palms, pressing harder and harder until their elbows locked. The current that flowed between them felt important. More important than words or gestures, more important than the rain down her neck or her desire to sneeze. She curved into him as far as she could go. Engulfed by the present, the past slipped away.

'Shall we go home?' she said. It was the first time she had ever asked a man home.

Chapter Nine

'Where's your cat?'

'I don't have one.'

'I thought all women who lived alone had cats.'

It was an annoying cliché but he wasn't altogether wrong.

'The actress had one. She gave him to her parents when she moved to LA. I'm a dog person.'

'Without a dog.'

She gave him a look. They were in her flat. They were removing layers of wet clothes. She had given him a towel and he was towelling his hair. He stopped rubbing and she saw him eyeing the room and laughing as though she weren't there.

'I've got it. Your flat reminds me of . . .'

She was pouring whisky. It was all she had. She was pouring large ones. He had another look around.

'A flat I used to visit.'

She took a sip of whisky. It burned. She tingled and now she wanted to take off her tights.

'Where?'

'Warsaw.'

She passed him a glass.

'Oh right. Well, it couldn't be in London, could it?'

He took her point and sat down on the sofa.

'It's rented,' she said.

'I got that.'

The flat had been decorated decades ago and hadn't been touched since. The landlord didn't care. He didn't live in London, and she hadn't intended staying here five years. Until recently she was spending four nights a week with QC, and the legacy of being a boarding-school girl meant that home was wherever she unpacked her bag. Blind to the bowl-of-fruit wallpaper, bamboo shelving and orange linoleum floor, she saw only her contribution to the flat. The books, inherited pieces of furniture, photographs and paintings. And now the landlord was selling up. Been offered a price I'd be a nut to refuse, he said.

'Do you mind if I take off my tights?'

Gus widened his eyes in mock surprise.

'Why should I mind?'

Elinor had imagined that when they got to the flat and their faces became visible to one another in the light, the spell would break. It hadn't happened. She didn't want to leave the room for fear of losing his face. She rarely brought people back here. It was her sanctuary away from the world. And yet she had wanted to bring him here away from the world.

Remaining where she was, she reached beneath her skirt and peeled off her tights. As she did so, she experienced a sharp sense of déjà vu. They were enacting a scene she had known would happen. His bemused eyes, his head in his hand, his arm propped on the arm of the sofa as he drank whisky, weren't so much familiar as unsurprising. She looked down at her legs. They were damp and sausage pink. Bending over, she slipped each heel out of her tights and freed her feet.

'That's better.' She balled them up and threw them in the bin.

'That was lovely.'

She laughed and joined him on the sofa, landing at the opposite end, leaving a hundred miles between them. She felt shy.

'I have a can of beer.'

She stood up again.

'To go with our whisky?'

'Or headachy holiday drinks. Retsina. Ouzo.'

She was waffling. His presence dominated the room and all of a sudden she didn't know what to do.

'Beer would be nice.'

She went to the kitchen and brought back the can. It had been in the fridge for ever. She brought two glasses and poured the beer down the sides of the glasses as she had seen others do to prevent frothing. It was cold and as delicious as anything would be right now.

'What were you doing in Warsaw?' She sat down. Closer this time.

'A lot of drinking. I was a student. At night, to get a drink, you'd hail a taxi and say, "Please take me to some vodka," and the taxi-driver would take you to one of his friend's flats in a tower block somewhere.'

'And the flat looked like this?'

He nodded. 'I'm not insulting your flat.'

'Yes you are.'

He laughed. 'How long have you lived here?'

He was trying to be serious.

She was tempted to lie. 'Too long.'

'Can I have a look around?'

'Yes.' She jumped up before thinking how ridiculous it was that he should want to look around. There was nothing to see.

'I've never been in a barrister's flat.'

Their conversation was dying. She led him out of the room.

'Bathroom.' She slid open a door with a frosted glass panel, She pulled a string that made a ping pong sound and revealed a bath that was thin and plastic and achingly turquoise.

'Fantastic.' He nodded his head. 'I really am in Warsaw.'

The floor was cracking up beneath plastic tiles. The curtains, glazed cotton, were printed with a boxy beige design. There was a bar heater on the wall that smelt of fire even when it wasn't on.

'Enough?'

'Yes.'

She ping-ponged the light and continued the tour.

'Kitchen.'

'I'm having flashbacks.'

The kitchen was orange Formica. All of it. There was a free-standing gas hob and a whistling kettle that sat on a ring. There was a clock with an Alpine scene and a row of brown cups on hooks on the wall. They stood motionless, staring at the kitchen as though it were of some intangible significance. Turning suddenly, she brushed against him. He caught her hand and didn't let go.

'It gets the sun in the morning.' She winced as she heard herself becoming an estate agent.

Gus didn't say anything. They were stalling for time. He had seen the living room. There were two rooms to go. Her heart was speeding and she almost wished that they could remain in suspension for ever, drifting from room to room propelled by woozy, nervous tension. They passed the actress's empty room. Its door was ajar and cardboard boxes were visible, stacked inside. Now came her door. She leant against the frame.

'Bedroom.'

She gripped his hand more tightly as though standing on the edge, about to jump in. She couldn't remember ever having felt so completely aware of herself in relation to a man. She turned to check his reaction. He removed his hand from hers. She watched him unbutton her shirt. She was wearing her favourite bra. It was red.

'I love your freckles.' He kissed her cleavage. She buried

her face in his hair. It was wet and smelt of smoke and hidden places.

'Come here.'

They walked to the bed. There was just enough light for them to see. She lifted his shirt over his head and pressed her hands against his chest. He unhooked her bra. Skin on skin. They fell on the bed. The mattress groaned. It was a very old bed, and they rolled into the dip in the middle. She lay on her back and watched him unzip her skirt. There was her hip bone. I love this man for his hands and mouth, she thought. He was gentle but he was firm.

'I hate this bed,' he said.

They moved to the floor. She watched him get undressed. Finding his scar, a smooth round of puckered skin, she touched it with her finger and made him wince.

'Does it hurt?'

'Yes.' He didn't lie.

'It's your distinguishing mark.'

'Where's yours?'

She showed him the scar that wormed down her arm.

'I fell off my horse.'

'It's pretty.' He kissed her hungrily, his fingers buried in her hair. The carpet was scratchy but she didn't care. They crashed into something and a stack of box files tumbled around them.

'Cases,' she said.

He pushed them away.

'Your skin's so white.'

Then everything went white. Flashing eyes. White noise.

White horses thundered through her head. His tenderness overwhelmed her. It scared her. Their bodies fitted. I'm going to cry, she thought, and he's going to think I'm the type of tragic woman who weeps during sex. She wanted to explain that she didn't usually weep but it didn't seem to matter. She wanted him to unlock every part of her. Raising herself to meet him, she wiped her tears on his face and said his name. Gus.

She woke to the sound of rushing water. He wasn't there. She couldn't remember falling asleep. She remembered their final conversation word for word.

'Who shares your bed?' he said.

'I sleep with my books.'

It was true. Preparing for court in bed, she would end up with a wedge of books beside her. During the night, when she rolled against them, she would imagine their weight to be the weight of another person. Reaching out to embrace them, she would jab her face on their stiff corners and wake herself up.

'Who was the last person you slept with?' she asked, because suddenly it was important she know.

'A holiday romance.' He shrugged it off, and she had tried not to feel jealous of his past.

She liked to think she wasn't a jealous person. How else could she have survived so many years with a married man? By containing it. Jealousy was the spur to love. Later, lying beside Gus, she had observed him, his arm crooked above his head, as she had on the plane. More awake than she had ever felt before, she wanted to absorb every part of him, every second spent together, because already she missed him. Already she was scared she wouldn't see him again. It was ironic that she had never felt this way about QC, she remembered thinking. The fact was that despite QC's familial duties, she had never doubted his motives or the strength of his desire. He was a faithful adulterer.

She rolled over. Her breasts came too. She hunted her pillows for his scent and found a hair.

'Scrambled eggs?'

Gus was waving a box of eggs. He was wearing her dressing gown and her bath hat, lilac with turquoise rubber flowers. She was speechless.

'I was looking for your wig.'

He sneezed and the rubber flowers danced. She smiled.

'It suits you.'

He yanked it off.

'I'm running a bath.'

'For me?'

'For us.'

'Oh.'

She wrapped the sheet across her chest. Bathing together was more intimate than sex, and she wasn't sure they had reached the daylight stage. He held out his hand. She took the sheet with her. The mirror in the bathroom was misty with steam and only a corner was clear. Letting the sheet drop to the floor, she caught sight of her collarbone and breast and imagined they belonged to someone else. She dipped her foot in the water. She liked her water hot. Climbing in, she slid up and down, wetting her shoulders.

'It's scalding.' He looked on in horror.

'Baths at school were freezing. We were allowed ten minutes twice a week. Don't you like hot water?'

'I'm fine with cold. I used to go surfing every day after school.'

She knew nothing about his childhood.

'Where?'

'Cornwall.'

'Do you ever go back?'

'Once a year.'

He was standing with his shoulders squared against the wall, as though posing for a mug shot.

'My mother still lives there. I got out as soon as I could. After my brother drowned.'

He jerked the light string on and off. Sitting in the bath in the stormy light, Elinor watched him talk in black and white.

'How old was he?'

'Seventeen.'

He breathed in and out as if blowing out candles.

'He was my elder brother. Thomas. He bunked off school to go fishing. I didn't want to go. There were some rocks near where we lived, where we used to go to fish and smoke. A wave got him. He was knocked unconscious. It took them two days to find his body.'

'I'm sorry.'

'Yes.' He released the string. It swung for a while before hanging still.

Elinor watched him remove her dressing gown. She was attracted to his nakedness in an uncomplicated way. She liked his stomach, its curve, and the height of his stomach button. She admired the dents like dimples in his deltoid muscles and the same in his thighs, in his gluteal muscles. Muscles had names. She knew their names because she had learned them when defending her boxer.

She made room for Gus to get in. He draped his thumb over the side of the bath. The bandage was peeling off and his head was wedged between the taps. He looked more comfortable than she knew he could be. Their legs slid into place and she studied his face.

'When did you last have a shave?'

'I hate shaving.'

She wanted to lather his face, to hear the rasp of stubble against the blade. QC had never let her do it. *It's not that I don't trust you but I would rather do it myself.* He used an attachable blade. Weightier. It lay closer to the skin. Less likely to nick. She had disposables.

'Can I shave you? I've got foam.'

Gus didn't look convinced but he didn't say no. She climbed out of the bath, found a blade and her foam and slid in behind him. He took an uneasy breath and she felt his ribcage expand against her breasts.

'Relax,' she said.

She wasn't comfortable and nor was he. She had to

concentrate hard. Moving slowly from left to right, she shaved in a downward motion from ear to chin. She reached his mouth. He looked in pain.

'I haven't cut you,' she pleaded.

Moving beneath his chin, she travelled down his neck. Using more delicate strokes, she shaved him to the ridge of his Adam's apple and allowed him to swallow. She felt guilty. It was a lousy blade. She continued around his neck and he arched his head to stretch the skin. She moved to his right cheek, feeling with her knuckles the smoothness left behind. Then she nicked him. A drop of red flecked the water and she felt deflated for having failed. For having hurt him. He leaned forward and rinsed his face.

'Best shave I've ever had.' He stole a watery kiss.

'Liar.'

She tossed the razor away. He pulled her round. She sank backwards to listen to her heart beat underwater, and speared up again. Water sluiced over the side of the bath as she scrambled to manoeuvre her legs round his waist. Slippery skin. Easing herself on to him, she fantasised that they were back on the plane. That she had straddled him in his seat and they were doing it midair. The snooze alarm in the bedroom went off. She wanted the whole world to go away. I want to stay here doing this all day. I don't ever want to lose this happiness, she thought.

They said their goodbyes outside the flat. The day was cheerless, the sky like spit. Grey skies were the great leveller, she reflected, observing the humourless faces and pasty complexions. It felt strange to be clothed and outside and forced to return to their own separate lives.

'Good luck.'

'With what?'

'The verdict.'

'Oh, that. Yes.'

He made a cage of his arms and she stepped in. They embraced. Grazing her nose on his jacket zip, she pulled away. She wanted him to go. It was unbearable to have to look at him when he was no longer hers. She sensed a hardness in his cheeriness. An ability to cut off and move on. He swung a leg across his crossbar.

'Thank you,' he said.

She watched him go. From everything to nothing. She climbed on her bike. The saddle between her legs made her wince. Gingerly she joined the traffic.

Chapter Ten

She sat in the canteen and tried to eat a piece of toast. It was impossible to gauge how long a jury would be out, and waiting for the verdict never failed to unnerve her. Today's butterflies were particularly active, roused by memories of last night. Hungry flashbacks stole across her mind as she tracked the course of his hands across her body and looked at the parts of herself that she could see. Wrists. Ankles. Thighs. It all looked different. Celebrated. Redefined. She bought another cup of tea.

She read the newspaper from cover to cover. The Mode of Trial bill had failed again. The House of Lords had killed it. Pleased about this, she believed in the right to a jury trial. Turning to foreign news, she tested herself on the names of the American cabinet. Attorney-General. Secretary of State. National Security Adviser. Two-thirds she got right. Taking out her mobile phone, she composed text messages that she didn't send. *I want to see you again and again and again and again, I want to do it again and again and again and again.* She saved them.

She tried not to worry needlessly over which way the verdict would go. It had been hardly worth offering sweepstakes. The verdict wasn't difficult to predict given her performance in court. The jury took less than three hours to consider. At 11.45 they were summoned in.

The court clerk asked the foreman of the jury to stand and Elinor knew instantly which way the verdict had gone. If jurors looked at the defendant, he or she would walk. They never made eye contact with those found guilty. She observed them purposefully avert their eyes.

'Have you arrived at your verdict?' asked the clerk.

'Yes,' said the man with the paunch.

'Do you find the accused, Frank Foster, guilty or not guilty?'

'Guilty.'

'That is the verdict of you all?'

'Yes.'

Judge Green shifted forward in his chair.

'Would there be a pre-sentence report?' he demanded. 'Were there any grounds for mitigation?'

Elinor rose.

'Your Honour, my client is not someone who has done this before. He took leave of his senses and never intended any harm. He would, however, prefer to be sentenced today.'

Frank Foster stood up in the dock and the judge wasted no more time in announcing his sentence.

'I have taken into account everything your counsel has said on your behalf, Mr Foster, and that you have never done this before. The court, however, takes this conduct very seriously indeed. I am satisfied that you set out to intimidate Miss Price for no good reason. In so doing you have caused her considerable mental and physical anguish. In my judgment there is no alternative to a custodial sentence. I would be failing in my duty if I did anything but sentence you to a term of immediate imprisonment. You will go to prison for six months.' He paused. 'Take him down.'

Elinor experienced a familiar twinge of guilt. Having your client detained at Her Majesty's pleasure was never good for self-esteem. Caroline had won and she had lost. The hush that followed the sentence was disrupted by the noise of scraping feet. Glancing up at the public gallery, Elinor caught the eye of the person getting up to go. He smiled and she smiled too, thinking that he must be someone she knew. Then she realised who he was. It was Steve Robson, the prosecution witness. The man who had winked. He briskly absented himself, leaving her with a dim sense of shame. When she turned back to the courtroom, Mr Foster had gone too.

She went to visit him in the cells. Given a choice, she would not have done so but it was expected of her. Brian was going. He wasn't pleased with her job. He hadn't said as much, but he would have said 'Good fight', as he customarily did, if he thought otherwise. Not that Brian had grounds for complaint. His instructions had been abysmal.

The cells were located in the bowels of the building. In order to pass through the X-ray machine, Elinor removed her jacket. Her armpits were moist and there was a tear in the seam of her shirt at the arm.

'Your shirt's ripped,' said Brian right behind her.

'Yes. Thanks.'

Her nostrils reacted to the stench of unwashed skin and airless confinement, smells she would never get used to, and she tried not to breathe. The walls were rubbished with graffiti. Names and dates. Protestations of innocence. Beyond the grate was an iron door. On the other side of the door sat a broad-shouldered man at a desk. Securicor.

'Frank Foster,' said Brian.

'Frank Foster.' The man shouted his name down the hall.

They heard clanking and footsteps. Frank Foster was in the cell at the end. He arrived handcuffed to a custody officer, their movements shadowed by the officer's rattling, bunch of keys. Elinor and Brian followed them into an interview room.

'What are you doing here?' demanded Frank Foster, as soon as the handcuffs had been removed. The custody officer gone. 'I'm going to prison because you let the jury believe all them lies.' He pointed a finger at Elinor. 'It was your job to sort it out.'

Elinor imagined being bludgeoned to death by his irate finger. She didn't know where to look. Frank Foster's face was pale. His eyes on fire. She had anticipated hostility. It did nothing to cushion the blow.

'The problem was they didn't believe our case.' She tried and failed to appease him.

'That isn't my fault. What I told is the truth. All I ever did was tell her not to believe the lies.' Paranoia crept into his speech. 'I want to appeal.'

Elinor twisted the stone in her earlobe. A diamond. Fake.

'There are no grounds for appeal, Mr Foster. You could have got more. You'll be out after three.'

'You're all the fucking same. I said I should have had a bloke.'

There was silence as the three of them stood apart as though there was some rule about distance. Mr Foster flicked his wrist at her.

'Go home before I tell you what I really think of you. Honest to God, I've had enough of your face.'

Elinor shuffled her feet. With an uneasy smile she nodded her goodbye and banged on the door. Get me out.

She bought a tandoori chicken sandwich from the man in the hut near chambers.

'Isleworth's off. He wanted a bloke so I gave it to Kendra. I'm joking. I gave it to Esmond,' said Derek when she entered the clerks' room.

'Lucky Esmond.'

'Stalker got six months, then?'

'Yes.'

Derek knew of most things before they happened. He was

a bloodhound. The television above the door was on. The one o'clock news featured a triple murder, weapon missing, father suspected of slaying family, somewhere provincial. Norm, whose unformed face gave him the appearance of a child when he was in fact twenty-one, was watching it with his mouth open.

'I hate fly-catchers,' said Derek. Loudly.

Norm's mouth shut like a trap. He blinked and began hastily organising a pile of rubber bands.

'That's better. And next time get the phone before it stops ringing as opposed to after. Got it?'

Derek had a copy of the *Racing Post* under his arm. He liked to have a flutter at lunch. He handed Elinor a brief tied up in a pink ribbon.

'PDH. You'll like this. Assault. Girl beats up man. Says "See him off" to pit bull. Dog bites man somewhere salty. She says man abused her first. Self-defence.'

Elinor took it.

'Thanks.'

Upstairs in their room, Kendra was at her desk. She had a cup of tea and a packet of biscuits and was dipping and munching and shedding crumbs.

'Why don't you water the plants?' she sang from behind her computer screen as Elinor shimmied behind her desk and sat down.

'I do. I bought them.'

Kendra poked her head out.

'So why do they cry out for water every time I enter the room?'

'Because you speak their language.'

Kendra had a heart-shaped face and sticky black hair and a sense of the ridiculous that surpassed what was needed even to survive in this job. She wore iridescent eyeshadow, moons of pink and purple, and dangly earrings. She was gutsy. She said things like, 'Isn't it bloody brilliant to be alive?' Elinor would never say this, even if she thought it. They had shared a room forever.

'What did he get?'

'Six months. I went to see him. He told me to bugger off.'

'And?'

'He spent the night.'

'Congratulations.'

Elinor grinned and sat down.

'Well, my good news' – Kendra shoved her papers aside with pointy elbows – 'is I've finally got myself a fetishist. Better still, a plastic mac fetishist.'

Elinor laughed. Where her laugh was low and steady, pebbles splashing water, Kendra's was high and shrill. A bray.

'What's the charge?'

'Come on, it's obvious how a plastic mac fetishist gets his kicks. He buys a van, paints yellow stripes all over it and poses as a breakdown man. Off he goes around the country picking up women whose cars have broken down. "Hello, Miss Scrumptious, if you'd just like to put on this plastic mac I'll have your car up and running in a jiffy." I'll read you a bit of statement. *He forced me to put on a see-through pink mac with a hood with a string that he fastened around my face, he said, to keep me warm. He made me sit down by the side of the road and expose my legs. He wrapped my legs in clingfilm. He asked if he could cover my car in polythene. I said no . . .'*

'What sort of car?'

'A Mini.'

'What's his name?'

'You won't be disappointed. Crispin Roach.'

They laughed some more, then Kendra got back to work and Elinor flopped her head on the desk. She meant to do it gently but her forehead hit the surface with a head-splitting crack.

Kendra looked up. 'Tired?'

'Shattered.'

'Go home.'

Elinor rubbed her eyes. She still had her coat on. She waved at Norm on her way out.

'They found the weapon,' he called after her. 'It was in the shed.'

Chapter Eleven

There was a jam of mail on her mat when she opened the door. She kicked it away before bending down and shovelling it up. Take-out menus from the local Indian restaurant, the new Chinese, the pizza parlour, where boys who didn't speak English delivered on bikes. Massage services offered by a lady called Shanti and a slew of estate agents' property lists. She threw them in her bag and went upstairs.

Unbuttoning her shirt, she tossed it on to her pile of dirty laundry. She unfastened her skirt and hung it up. She found a bruise on her thigh. Shadowy fingerprints circled her upper arm. Fitting her hand around them, she tried them for size. They were her trophies. She liked them there. When she thought about the welt she had left on his cheek, she wondered whether he thought of her when he felt it sting.

The flat felt empty without him. She drifted around it, tracing the moves Gus had made last night. Where he sat on the sofa. The cushions knocked on the floor. The empty glass where his feet had been. Where he stood in each doorway as he inspected the rooms. Her body felt altered by the events of last night, and so did her view of the flat. It had amused him and it wasn't hard to see why. She and the actress had originally taken it because it was spacious and cheap. They had convinced each other that the faded décor was glamorous. They had been younger, poorer, looking for excuses. It belonged to a life she had left behind, a life lived for QC when her own didn't matter. Now it did.

In the kitchen, she switched on the radio. The afternoon discussion was of *Macbeth*. He lost the milk of human kindness, that was his flaw, said a man in a solemn tone. Could a man be a hero yet not be kind? simpered a female panellist. Weren't ego and kindness mutually exclusive?

'Please,' said Elinor, and switched it off.

There were men on the roof. She could hear their whistling and banging as they exchanged new slates for old. The old ones were sent spinning to the street where they shattered in mini-explosions. They were going to decapitate someone, thought Elinor, as she considered going outside to complain. She hadn't the stamina. Her mobile rang. It was Derek. She didn't pick up. She had a job to do.

She had six weeks left to find somewhere else to live. She had spent too long as a tenant. Her days of rented accommodation were over. Positioning herself at the table, she spread out her collection of property lists, estate agents' names at the top, gathered over the past few months. Some names she knew. Men who called themselves negotiators had taken her to view dismal properties on forgettable streets.

She had been shown a dingy hole, which had reeked of cannabis and where the tenant had been asleep. I'm not fucking getting up, he shouted from his bed. Don't trip over the chainsaw, quipped the estate agent. There had been a flat with a bathroom in the basement with a ceiling so low they had been forced to duck their heads. You could make this a second bedroom and sleep down here, he said. As opposed to in a coffin? She had listened to stories of broken marriages and fixed pipes and ever-so-helpful neighbours and bus routes that skirted the end of the road. She had become quickly disenchanted. Having viewed twenty-two flats, not one of which she had been able to imagine living in had it been the last dwelling on earth, she gave up looking.

One of the estate agents' names rang a bell. She had no idea why but she had to start somewhere.

'My name's Elinor Taylor,' she introduced herself to the man who answered the telephone. 'I believe you showed me a number of two-bedroom flats before Christmas.'

'Really?'

'I've been away.'

'It might have been my colleague.'

'I'm back on the market.'

'Glad to hear it.'

'I was wondering if you might have anything suitable. Two bedroom. In the same sort of area. Ideally with a garden, or some kind of outdoor space.'

He paused.

'Instructions come in waves. But you could be in luck. Something new has just come on. I could do you this arvo, as it happens.'

His language was ludicrous. Her body said no but her head said yes.

'What's the address?' she said.

'Got a pen?'

Hulking storm clouds patrolled the sky. She took the bus and alighted just as the clouds exploded. Lashing rain obscured her view, forcing her to walk sideways beneath her large black umbrella. The road in the street-finder was hidden beneath the staple in the page and she lost her way. After several wrong turns, she came across the street by accident, by approaching from the wrong direction. It was situated in a soon-to-be-desirable neighbourhood, a location that she hadn't been sure about until she arrived. It had not been a wasted journey.

It was as though she had visited before, although not for some time. The houses were painted seaside pastels. Pinks and blues. One or two had magnolia trees in early bloom, and there was a pub with tables outside. The houses at the bottom of the street had been gentrified with silver dustbins, tended gardens and security alarms. The houses at the top end, the end where she was headed were in a state of disrepair. Paths lay under a siege of black bin-bags. Gardens were rank with weeds. Each house was divided into as many flats as there were bells beside doors, and net curtains curdled behind grimy panes of glass.

Ahead, with his back to her, a man was waiting in front of a house. Dressed in a dark suit, a zip-up wallet slotted beneath his arm, he was sheltering beneath a golfing umbrella. Red and white stripes. Elinor was about to call out his name when she realised she didn't know it. Hearing her footsteps, he wheeled round.

'Elinor.'

Holding her umbrella in a vice-like grip, she felt her breath desert her. The crocodile eyes, the bulk of head and shoulders, the confident speech, were unmistakable.

'Steve Robson,' he introduced himself, as if formalities were necessary, sauntering down the path to meet her with his hand outstretched.

There was nothing for it but to take it and shake it, which was what Elinor did. His palm was smooth. His shake was firm and she absorbed his strength, imagining the flexor muscles in his hands, his forearms, stiffening. She knew about his strength because she knew about him punching Frank Foster. This fact she kept to herself.

'I had no idea.'

'Who doesn't like a surprise? My turn to return the favour, I thought. After you got him . . .' He broke off. 'You're a professional woman. I wouldn't want to compromise your integrity.'

He spun a bunch of keys around his index finger. The smell of his cologne seeped through the rain.

'So. Like I said on the phone. This property has just come on. Perhaps not quite what we had in mind but finding the right home is about a process of elimination. This, I feel, is something special and lightning doesn't strike in the same place twice.'

Elinor fell silent. Not only was their meeting like this highly unexpected – he was a prosecution witness whom she had last seen in court – but he had known who she was when they spoke on the phone. She hadn't. This arrangement bothered her. She considered walking away. She didn't like him or his flip manner. She didn't like his use of 'we' or the assumption that she would comply with his plan, any more than she liked coincidences.

She watched him unlock the door. Security locks top and bottom. He pushed it open with a shove.

'My rule of thumb is start in the lounge. Mind the step. Twenty by fifteen. Bay. Fireplace to be restored. Original fittings. Needs work.' He was reading from a piece of paper.

She followed him in. He was the salesman with the perfect pitch. The man from whom she couldn't get away because it was as though he had his palm in the small of her back. In the hall she ran her fingers across heavily embossed wallpaper. Garlands of flowers were visible in the thin light. The stairs ahead were covered with a plastic runner. Something spiky crunched underfoot. She quickly stepped off it. Looking down, she found a collapsed umbrella like a fallen crow. She arrived in the lounge.

'Lots of character.' He placed his emphasis on lots.

Two armchairs with doilies as headrests faced each other across a gas fire. On the tiled mantelpiece stood a Bo-Peep figurine holding up her skirt. A glass ashtray, *Blackpool Lights 1964*, sat next to it.

'Year I was born.' He pointed at it.

Elinor nodded. It felt rude to talk. It was as though they had broken into somebody's house.

'Has someone died?' she whispered.

He coughed into his fist.

'Every property of this period has witnessed on average between two and five deaths.'

'That's official, is it?'

Suspicious of statistics, she watched him work out what to say. She was reminded of their moment in court. Already it seemed mildly irrelevant. Now that she was here, she wanted to have a look around. The house was special. It felt precious. Like a gift.

'The owner passed away,' he confirmed. 'His son's selling the house.'

'How did he die?'

'Peacefully. He was eighty-two. Dining room's next door.'

The dining room's furniture was similarly intact. There was an oval dining table and a sideboard on top of which sat stacks of plates and bowls. There was a painting of a horse in a cheap gilt frame. She liked the picture.

'My advice? Knock it through and create a modern living space,' he said.

Elinor liked the idea of a modern living space but she was smitten with the house because of its associations with the past. The scent of hair oil, bath salts and cups of metallic-tasting tea were embedded in its fabric, and she had an overwhelming physical sense of being back in Frida's home. She would be buying the house with the inheritance left to her by Frida. The pieces were beginning to fall into place.

'Did I say it's a three-bed?'

He led her upstairs and she felt the house come alive. Every step led to further discovery and the whiff of something good. The banisters rattled in her hand. Upstairs there was a skinny landing and three rooms. Big. Medium. Small. The front room would be her room she decided as soon as she entered it. It was empty but for a pile of yellowing newspapers, twisted coat hangers, damp patches on the walls, and a spindly chair in the corner.

'Nice view.'

The back two rooms overlooked an overgrown garden. Only when they were back downstairs again did she realise what was missing.

'Where's the bathroom?'

They were standing in the kitchen. It was a gloomy little room. Virtually bare with a slimy sink and a window through which you couldn't see for dust and mould.

'Outdoor toilet. No bathroom.' Disgust was etched across his face. 'Don't touch anything. Whole place wants gutting. Filth like this I hate.'

Unperturbed by the squalor, Elinor saw beyond it. She dragged a fingertip across the draining board and it came away black.

'Keen gardener, are you?' he said.

The back door threatened to come apart in his hands. He forced it, snapping the creepers that covered it, but even then it would only go so far. Elinor eased herself sideways through the crack.

'You're on your own.'

Beyond the door lay a jungle. The grass was knee high and ran down to a shed. There was a nice mix of trees. Two apples, a willow-leafed pear and what looked like a plum. Mauve tendrils of wisteria dripped from the side of the house. Clematis with snail-ravaged leaves climbed the fence.

Elinor arched her umbrella, hiked up her skirt and waded in. Her heels slipped into the wet earth and she ran the risk of laddering her tights as thistles and brambles clawed at her legs. Sticky burrs beaded her skirt and a sunflower nodded its ragged head. Reaching the shed, she pushed open the door and went inside. The air was cool and mossy. It smelt of creosote and rust. There was a collection of flowerpots, a handleless spade, nails and screws in jam jars, cloudy pint glasses and two faded deckchairs. This had been his secret place.

'You all right?'

She jumped.

'Coming,' she called.

Never more certain of anything in her life, she ran all the way back to the kitchen door and squeezed in through the crack.

'Steve' – She used his first name, her eyes very bright – 'I have to have it.'

'How did I know you were going to say that?'

'Because you're a mind-reader.' She felt giddy. Whatever reservations there might have been about striking up a rapport with this man were long forgotten.

'Car's outside.' He wrapped up the viewing and they reverted back to their original roles. Prospective buyer. Negotiator.

He drove a BMW. It was red. He zapped the alarm with his key-ring, opened the passenger door and she folded herself in. The seats were cream leather. Everything hummed. There was a car phone, glow-in-the-dark dials, stereo, smoke-tinted windows and places to put things. A gym bag lay on the back seat with a squash racket jutting out. Elinor watched a sheet of water slide down the windscreen. Her taste buds reacted to his musk as he joined her on the driver's side. Leaning over, he clicked open the glove compartment and his wrist brushed against her knee but it seemed impolite to move it so she didn't. He clamped his hand around a stack of papers, clicked the compartment closed and sat back in his seat. Flicking through sheets of paper, he licked his forefinger to separate each page. Elinor stared at the gadget attached to the dashboard.

'Does it work?'

He looked up.

'My satellite navigator? How do you think I got here?'

'Can I test it?'

Handing over what looked like a remote control, he showed her how to tap in her home address. She thought about tapping in a false one. Why would she want to do that? A black-and-white flag fluttered on the screen.

'That's your destination,' said Steve Robson, handing

her a piece of paper. 'Price of the property is on the top.'

Elinor hardly dared look. She looked. It was horrible but she would swing it. She had to.

'If I put in an offer and it's accepted, will the owner take it off the market?'

She knew this wasn't how it worked but it did no harm to try. Faux-naïveté was a secret weapon not to be underestimated. Steve Robson turned the key in the ignition.

'Let's me and you go back to the office, you put in an offer and we'll take it from there, shall we?'

'Turn right two hundred metres ahead,' bleated the dashboard

Elinor stared.

'Voice synthesiser.' Steve eased the steering wheel through sturdy hands.

He drove too fast, came too close to the car in front and braked too hard. The office wasn't far. It occupied a single room with Brook & Brook Estates stencilled on the top half of the front window in a curly black typeface. It was furnished with a coatstand, a water cooler, a fish tank containing a day-glow castle and a guppy swimming round and round. Tea-bag stains marked the journey from the wall to the bin. A map of London dotted with drawing pins hung slightly askew. Three desks were positioned in a row.

'Maureen went early. Kevin's in Ibiza.' He showed her to a metal chair with a canvas seat.

Elinor noticed a sticker on the filing cabinet. *I am the beast.*

'Who's the beast?'

'Sons of Satan, we get called. I thought everyone knew that.'

She didn't, although she wasn't surprised. He took a seat at his desk. Behind his head was a whiteboard with a list of addresses along the top, the status of sales in red marker pen below. Some were starred, others question-marked, and they were ranked according to price. Top of the range was a property for over half a million. She watched him arrange his stapler, his box of staples and his box of paper clips in a neat row side by side so that their edges were parallel with the edge of the desk. He picked up papers and set them down again.

She felt nervous. She wished she had someone with her, although she didn't know who.

'What's your advice?' She studied his chin. Closely shaved. 'On the sort of offer I should put in.'

He held her gaze.

'Higher?' she tried. 'Or lower?'

Lacing his fingers behind his head, he hooked his foot beneath the desk. He began to rock backwards and forwards. This he did for a while. When he had had enough he pitched forward, catching himself at the desk with one hand.

'Lower. Marginally.'

Elinor waited for further explanation. It didn't look forthcoming. She found it hard to believe that this was how property deals were normally transacted. Though now wasn't the time to query procedure. Steve Robson's face was stern. He had a way of keeping the musculature rigid, on guard, as though holding something back. He was pushing a notepad towards her, and here came the pen. The pen felt heavy. Her arm felt light. She wrote down a number. The line-up of zeros appeared abstract but her racing heart told her that they were very real. She slid the notepad back to him and watched him rotate it. This he did slowly.

'Very nice,' he said after a moment's delay. 'It's a pleasure to be doing business with you, Miss Taylor.'

Chapter Twelve

Days had passed. Five. She was counting. Days that were as empty as her life had become. She felt savaged. Slightly sick. Gus hadn't called and she didn't know why not. She couldn't understand how his life was continuing when hers' was not. She had fallen into slow-moving, flashback time. She was drowning in his silence, holding her breath, until she couldn't breathe any more. His silence was killing her.

There were different types of silence, like different types of love. This was her theory. Some gave you strength and you could feed on what you had. Others left you lonelier than you had ever been before. She had lost sight of who she was before she met Gus, and this scared her because she didn't know how it could have happened so fast. Her mind was running away with her. She wanted to know what it was she was being excluded from. She was jealous of what she didn't know.

She forced herself to focus on the girl sitting before her.

She had a girl in her room. The girl whose pit bull had bitten the man. The dog's name was Raj. Lucy was the girl's name. She had a triple-barrelled surname, which ended with Frisbee, and an air of mystery, a sort of residual sadness, about her.

'They were taking up the whole pavement,' she said.

Not the pedigree of girl thought typically to own a pit bull, Lucy cut a trim figure. She had feathery blond hair and a coat with a fake fur trim that she said she would rather not take off. She had a fashionable handbag and cut-glass vowels. She worked 'in art'.

'When you asked the men to move, what did they say?' Elinor moved forward in her chair.

'Get a life.'

'At which point you told Raj to "see them off"?'

'No. I asked if anyone had a smoke.'

'Did they?'

'Yes.'

'Which of them gave you a cigarette?'

'None of them. That's the whole point. They were smoking but they wouldn't give me one. It was intolerable. I was dying for a cigarette. You don't have one, do you?'

'No. Sorry.' Elinor had begun doodling in her notebook. She was remembering the texture of his hair. Downy. His mouth on her breasts. Smooth. It made her want to say things, inappropriate things, out loud. Sober sex had been a revelation. She could remember everything. It was how she had wanted it.

Returning to Lucy's liquid grey eyes, Elinor found the

girl looking at her as though she had all the answers. She wished she did.

'Who head-butted who first?' she said. Taking control.

'He had me in a headlock.'

There was a step missing here.

'Why did he get you in a headlock?'

'Because I'd pushed the other one and he fell over. Like I said. They were Irish.'

Elinor noticed that Lucy's hands were shaking. Her nails were chewed to the quick and she was picking the cuticles on her thumb with a worried forefinger.

'It was when you were in the headlock that you set Raj on him?'

'Yes.' Lucy nodded emphatically. 'I shouted, "Kill, kill, kill".'

'At which point Raj bit the man's testicle?'

'Yes.'

Kendra was in the library. Elinor went to find her and made her take a break for lunch. They went to the local Italian where men in bow ties and braces were telling stories and ordering more wine. Puddings came round on a trolley that squeaked. Elinor sat down.

'Do you think pit bull owners get a fair trial?'

'They don't deserve one. Vicious creatures, they should all be put down. The dogs, I mean. Red or white?'

'White. Did I tell you I've found a house?'

'I thought you were looking for a flat.'

'It's in a terrible state. I'm using my inheritance and crippling myself with a massive loan.'

'Congratulations.'

'There is something rather odd about it.'

'About the house?'

'No. The estate agent. He was a witness in the stalking case.'

Kendra was smiling like a moron at the waiter. She turned back to Elinor.

'We took our estate agent sailing round Turkey. That's how we got the mews.'

'Really?'

'You can't afford to be choosy.'

That was that, then. The waiter arrived. They both ordered linguini with clams.

'Have you seen him?'

She meant Gus.

'No.'

'Have you called him?'

'I can't.'

There were certain areas of protocol that she was not prepared to break. Not calling twice in a row was one of them.

'So forget him.'

Since her divorce, Kendra had become ruthless. She distrusted love. Elinor refused to sink so low.

'No.' she said, suddenly depressed. Talking did nothing to ease the pain.

Kendra crunched a breakstick.

'I had another dot.com.'

At great expense, Kendra had signed up with an on-line dating agency.

'Banker. European acquisitions. Charming. Tall. We were having such a nice time . . .'

Her intonation was getting dangerously high. Any minute it would come crashing down. There had been a hitch.

'Filthy mouth.'

Elinor stopped eating.

'What?'

Kendra dropped her head to the table.

'Where do you want me to fuck you?'

'What?'

'That's what he said. I was making coffee. We hadn't even kissed.'

Elinor laughed.

'What did you say?'

Kendra sighed and speared a clam.

'It would have been such a waste. I've paid so much money.'

'You slept with him.'

'Wouldn't you?'

With the excuse of errands to run, Elinor left Kendra and headed into Soho. In order to buy bras she had to make a special trip to a shop where a lady with doughy hands measured her up and stuck her head into the changing room to see whether they fitted. How does it feel, love? Can you breathe? She could buy her knickers anywhere. She tended to buy them from department stores. Predominantly white, the odd black pair, never too high cut nor too bikini brief.

There was a tiny boutique in Soho that sold lingerie, which she had passed many times but had never dared enter. Mannequins with pert bosoms in candy coloured nighties sat in armchairs in the window. She found their boldness disarming. A camera filmed you as you walked by, giving you the impression that you were being followed when you appeared on a TV screen. Elinor had been thinking about this shop for days. Five to be exact.

She found the street and passed the shop twice, turning to look in the opposite direction. It wasn't a sex shop. She was doing nothing illegal. She went in. The crimson walls and thumping music mirrored the sensation inside her head. She was the only customer in there. The girl behind the counter was wearing a corset with laces up the back. Her cleavage ballooned to her chin. It was a look Elinor could achieve if she owned a corset. She didn't. The girl gave Elinor a perfunctory once-over before returning to her telephone conversation.

'But I am a natural blonde.'

At a glance, Elinor would have said this was untrue. Fighting off an attack of self-consciousness, she sifted through the nearest rail. A rail of pink and white see-through pants with forget-me-nots stamped on the bottom. Slipping her hand inside a pair, she imagined them on. Knickers had memories. With the disposal of old knickers went old memories. She knew what else she wanted.

She owned a very old suspender belt shredded with age

and grubby white. QC had occasionally asked her to wear it but the mistress-in-suspenders cliché had put her off. It was Frida who had introduced her to the secret world beneath a woman's skirt. Bursting into her bedroom one morning, Elinor had caught her hoicking up coffee-coloured stockings over crêpy skin. It was the delicacy of the operation combined with a certain clumsy furtiveness which fascinated. What are you doing? Elinor had asked. Watch and you'll find out, said Frida with a typical lack of modesty.

The choice of suspenders didn't disappoint. Shimmering metallics, flesh tones, monotones. Elinor couldn't imagine Gus spent a lot of time thinking about suspenders. That was the point. She chose two pairs. One white, the other red with a gold trim. She bought three pairs of stockings, one with a seam up the back, and knickers in both transparencies.

'Special occasion?' said the girl at the counter as she rolled up the purchases in tissue paper.

Elinor was tempted to lie and say what? Honeymoon? Anniversary? Weekend away? Part of her expertise was to get under the skin of her clients and imagine herself as someone else. At school she had been accused of having an overly fertile imagination. She would make up answers to questions she didn't know. Theories about the origins of species, the physics of lightning and the endings of novels she hadn't read. Ignorance she saw as failure.

There had been other occasions, more recently, when she had allowed her inner world to spill into real life and cause confusion. QC had given her a 'friendship ring', a ruby set in gold, which she used to wear on her engagement finger.

Once or twice she had let the word 'fiancé' slip from her mouth. A lie.

'I hope so,' she said to the girl.

She left the shop. The sky was blue and trimmed with ticker-tape clouds. People jostled past her, talking in fast voices. She was flush with excitement. She was a woman with new underwear. She couldn't go back to chambers. Instead she wandered the streets in a trance, pretending to be content by herself, as though she were here by chance without an ulterior motive or any sense of direction.

On the corner of the street where she had come to meet Gus five days ago, she stopped and stared. There, locked to a railing, was his bicycle. She felt nervous and elated and depressed and fatigued. Brooding on whether to let him know that she was there, she considered vandalising his bike, scratching it with her key, or otherwise leaving a note. Saying what? Her eyes fixed on the windows and she counted three along. The blind was pulled. She wanted to press her face against the glass, find a crack in the blind and catch a glimpse of the body that had locked with hers. Taking a step forward, she quickly hurried back.

In the Underground, waiting for a train, she felt the weight of the world on top of her. If I lose this man, I won't be the same. I will have a scar, a deep, dark wound. Misery wavered inside. Remembering his thank-you when they said goodbye brought a strained, uncertain peace.

* * *

A small padded envelope, brown, was sitting outside the door to her flat. Nigel must have parked it there. She let herself in and smoothed the envelope between her palms, feeling the bump, wondering what it could be. She ripped it open. Green and black fluff leaked on to the floor. Poking her hand inside the envelope, she pulled out a thin plastic box. A tape. She held the envelope wide and peered inside. There was no note, no letter, the postmark told her nothing, and she didn't recognise the writing on the front of the envelope. Spidery handwriting, it was identifiably male. It had to be from Gus. She had never been sent a tape before.

In her bedroom, she fell across the bed, punched the tape into her cassette player and hit 'Play'. A female voice, craggy with heartache, began to sing. A feeling of rapture stole over her. She lay motionless, shivers down her spine, as the music filled the space that he had left behind. Hit by waves of longing, pleasure and pain, she couldn't identify the singer. The next voice, Marvin Gaye's, she knew. Seduced by his slinky promises, she believed every word. Carried on a tide of emotion, she watched the light through the window dim and drain away. Night closed in.

End of tape.

She blinked, dazed. Reaching over to switch on her bedside light, she rolled on top of her tissue-paper packages. She unwrapped them. Spreading the lingerie on the bed, she gazed at it for a while, presented with a version of herself she didn't know. She found the strangeness exciting. She got up. Slipping out of her coat, she moved to the edge of the bed. Removing her tights, she unfolded the stockings with the seams and put her arm inside them to give them shape. She unfurled the first stocking over her heel and encased the firmness of her calf. She covered her knee. Lifting her skirt to expose her thighs, she inched the stocking as far as it would go. Her freckles showed through. She traced them with her finger as he had done.

Her buzzer went. It went through her like a drill. She sat rigid, wishing that the light was off so that she could pretend to be part of the darkness and not there at all. No one rang unannounced on her bell other than upstairs Nigel, and she wasn't in the mood for Nigel's suffering. She ignored it. Whoever it was buzzed again. Perhaps it was Gus. As soon as this possibility occurred to her, she knew she would have to see who was there.

In the hall, she pressed the intercom.

'Hello?'

'It's Steve Robson.'

Elinor looked at her watch. Seven o'clock, it was well past office hours. And how did he have her home address? She remembered his satellite navigator. She had tapped it in.

'I was in the neighbourhood. I've got some paperwork.' His voice crackled up to her.

Looking down at her skirt hitched up with one leg bare and the other stockinged, she felt reluctant to let him in.

'Can you give me a second?'

She rushed back to the bedroom, took off the stocking, straightened her skirt and patted down her hair. Back in the hall, she buzzed him in. She opened the door, monitoring his footsteps, the loose change in his pockets, as he climbed the stairs. First came his head, the square brow, then the voice.

'Hope I'm not interrupting something.'

'I just got in.'

He performed a quick left–right jerk of the head and sized up her flat.

'Would you like a cup of tea?' she said.

'Never say no.'

'How do you take it?'

'Milk. Half a sugar.'

She showed him the sofa and disappeared to the kitchen. The kettle boiled slowly and she noticed that the second hand on the clock had stopped. It hovered at twelve like a dying insect. She arrived with tea and sat on the chair facing him. Steve Robson had removed the books and magazines heaped on the glass coffee table, and was spreading papers in a fan. When he leaned forward his trousers rose up, and Elinor glimpsed pink socks above his shiny black shoes.

'What sort of paperwork have you got?'

With his elbows resting on his knees and his hands cupped over his mouth as though at prayer, he took a moment to reply. Elinor hoped this boded well. He removed his hands. His eyes were steely.

'It could go through very fast. It's very important you have your agreement in principle.'

'My what?'

'Your mortgage in order.'

She had been hoping for news of the house. She buried her disappointment.

'It's all organised. I've got an inheritance kept expressly to buy somewhere. I've been in touch with my bank manager. I've got a mortgage to cover the rest.'

Steve Robson nodded.

'That puts you in a key position. Even so, I've brought round a few alternatives I'd recommend you take a look at. Building Society deals not to be sniffed at.'

They sipped their tea. She couldn't pretend any longer.

'Is there anything else?'

'No news yet. Mind if I use the toilet?'

She pointed down the hall.

'Second on your right.'

The cassette player was set on auto-reverse. The tape had started playing again. Bubbles of sound washed through the flat and made her feel watery inside. The Alsatian dog that guarded the corner shop began to bark, which meant it was eight o'clock. When the shop closed, the dog was left inside to howl. Steve arrived back with his tie flung over his shoulder as though he had been surprised by a gust of wind.

'Best be off.' He flicked back his band of silky blue. 'I'll leave the papers just in case you change your mind about choosing one of my financial options.'

She stood up.

'Thanks.'

He left.

On her way back to the living room, Elinor noticed that her bedroom door was open. The lingerie glittered from the bed as though on display. Mortified to think that Steve had seen what she could see now, she quickly folded it up and tidied it away. She felt exposed. She could have sworn she had shut the door.

Later, when she went to bed, she couldn't sleep. The dog's barking reverberated through the darkness as her mind flashed like a TV screen. Visiting the rooms of the house, she imagined what she would do in each in turn. Kitchen. Living room. Bedroom. Shed. Gus was with her. She had him by the hand and was showing him how her new life would play out in the new house. And all the while his music strummed like a soundtrack to her heart.

Greeted by birdsong, she looked at her clock. 4 a.m.

She couldn't take any more.

Stumbling into the bathroom, she cracked a pill and swallowed half. Sleep came quickly.

Chapter Thirteen

'Sorry to have been so badly out of touch.'

It wasn't a good connection. She was on the train and he was breaking up but her heart stopped. She felt as though she were being pulled out of herself, and her senses jumped to attention as every part of her told her who it was. It was the return of certainty and the knowledge that there was someone out there beside herself.

'Where are you?' he said.

That was her question.

'On the train.'

She hated talking on the phone in public places. She didn't want the world to know her story.

'Where are you going?'

'Out.'

Kendra had organised a dinner at a restaurant where four barristers – they were meeting two men she vaguely knew –

would boast of their successes and falsely toast their disappointments. She didn't want to go. She had to go. She couldn't keep her diary clear while she waited for Gus to call and tried to fathom meaning from his silence and work out what games he was or wasn't playing. There was a delay. More static.

'I've been editing. Every time I tried to call, it was three in the morning. So I didn't call.'

Nothing Elinor could do could prevent his voice from making her come alive. Already she didn't know how she could have doubted him.

'How's the film?'

'A white elephant.'

She laughed. He had her now and all her grievances, her self-control, ebbed away.

'I want to see you,' she said, hopelessly.

'I want to see you.'

'When?'

She couldn't say tonight. It went against all the rules.

'I was going to say tonight . . .'

'Yes. Tonight.'

'I'm working late.'

'I'm having dinner. The restaurant's not far from . . .'

Each waited for the other to speak.

'Do you want to come and . . . ?'

'I'll come and find you,' she said.

She had arranged to meet Kendra at chambers. She stopped in to see Derek on the way up. Derek was sitting at his desk and signing papers like a king with a fat gold pen. He didn't look up.

'How's ball-busting Annie?'

'Lucy. We've got a trial date.'

He looked up.

'You look different. What have you done to your hair?'

She was floating. Dancing inside.

'Nothing.'

'Anything to do with your fancy man?' He reached for the message pad at the side of his desk. 'Steve Robson.'

Elinor frowned.

'Did he leave a message?'

'No message. And watch yourself. You look like you'd sell your grandmother if the price was right.'

She laughed.

The restaurant was large and subterranean with the acoustics of an engine room. They had to shout to make themselves heard. They were sitting at a banquette table decorated with a daisy in a test tube. A girl tripped round selling cigarettes from a tray strapped to her neck. The men loaded up on Marlboro Lights. One of the barristers, moon faced with dimples like thumbprints, was currently at the Old Bailey. His day had been spent defending the leader of a group of Afghanis who had hijacked a plane. He had recently taken silk. Kendra said he was on the fast track to becoming a judge.

'This is a groundbreaking case.' He sparked a match. 'Sod the bloody Home Office. They're not sending him back. By the way girls, you're both looking jolly well.'

They both touched their hair. They were drinking Bellinis. Elinor looked at her watch. An hour and a half to go.

'How's Peter?' enquired the other fellow, gingery with a peppery sneeze and a signet ring which he tapped on his tooth from time to time. He was referring to QC. It was a loaded question and could mean any number of things, none of which Elinor felt prepared to tackle.

'Very well. Apparently,' she said, pointedly. 'I'd love another.'

Another round of drinks was ordered.

'It's not a question of numbers,' argued Kendra. 'It's who we're prepared to let in.'

In a tight-fitting black top with a plunging neckline, Kendra was boyishly flat chested. Elinor sometimes envied her freedom of style and movement. The way she could wave her arms about without worrying about wobbling. Not having to harness herself in every morning. Elinor was also wearing a black top with a low-cut neck. Occasionally she would catch sight of her cleavage and think how much it resembled a bottom. A diamond on a thin gold chain that she could feel, but couldn't see, nestled in her clavicle.

'My client's a university professor. He faced execution if he remained in his country. But he put a gun to the pilot's head. So you can see the problem I'm facing,' said the new silk. 'I say we order.'

Elinor left them at ten o'clock. A floater to prepare, she said, and they understood. The men were paying for dinner, their treat, which was nice. Walking fast, she felt a little drunk. Skittish and wired. The streets were unfamiliar even though she had walked down them a hundred times before. A cardboard box blew from the gutter and chased her along the pavement, causing her to run a few steps. A man tried to stop her and ask her for the time but she didn't like the look of him so said she didn't have a watch.

She rang the buzzer on Gus's building and someone buzzed her in. There was nobody in reception.

'Down here,' came the cry.

Her shoes created a fury of sound on the floor. He likes my ankles, she remembered, looking down. *I'm not surprised you wear shoes like yours with ankles like yours,* was what he had said. She opened the door.

'Hi.'

She liked his hi. The men she knew said hello. Tilted back in his chair, his shirt was crumpled, he hadn't shaved, and his hair was standing up on end. The thrill she felt was the thrill of seeing him for the first time all over again. He swivelled at the waist in a resourceful movement and reached for her hand.

'How was dinner?'

How could he be so casual? He made it sound as though their last goodbye had been this morning. She was screaming inside. She grasped his hand tight. It wasn't a feeling of security she was after, but the otherness he provided. The feeling of consequence he instilled in everything, including herself. She knew so little about him yet she yielded to him as though she knew it all.

'Wiggy.' She made him laugh.

'What did you talk about?'

'Plane hijackers seeking asylum.'

Interest flickered across his eyes.

'When am I going to see your wig?'

'You could come to court.'

'What about a private show?'

'That could be arranged.'

Pressing her leg against the arm of his chair, she did it to give herself something to do, fighting and feeding the sexual tension that drew her to him.

'What am I looking at?' She pointed at the middle screen.

It was a street scene. Paused. Locals and tourists and armed police were milling about. It looked hot and dusty.

'Border towns bring out the worst in a country.'

'Is that a line?'

'Yes.' His hand was on her thigh. 'From a movie. You're good.'

'I know.'

He slid his hand to the bottom of her skirt, and it travelled up beneath the fabric, moving cautiously, waiting for her to push it away. She didn't. Her breath was shallow and came from the top of her lungs. She tensed her thigh. At school she had been a gymnast until her bosom got her kicked off the team. Too top heavy, said the gym teacher, a sour woman with large breasts herself. His finger probed a hole in her tights.

'Am I allowed to rip these?' he said.

She buried her face in his hair. There was nothing she

wouldn't let this man do. There was nothing she would not do for him.

'Go on, then.'

Spreading his fingers, shredding the nylon, he moved inside. She gripped his shoulder, eyes straight ahead, her composure wavering. She stared at the screen. There in the left hand corner was a rangy man in a baseball cap. He looked like Gus. She squinted. He was Gus. He was in conversation with a short man in mirrored sunglasses with a desperado moustache. Gus's hands were raised in supplication, a frustrated, pleading gesture.

Elinor was about to say something when Gus's hand crept higher. His fingers found what they were looking for her and she bent to kiss him. He pulled her down so that she was sitting on his lap, her face in his neck, the picture on the screen forgotten. Deathly shadows hollowed his face.

'Have you had any sleep?'

'Do I look that bad?'

'Like a vampire.'

He tugged her tights, she stretched her legs out on either side of him and he ripped. His chair on wheels jerked back and she flew against the desk and hit the keyboard with her spine. Two strips of black nylon came away in his hands as a familiar voice began shouting behind her.

'We've paid you.'

It was Gus's voice.

'Just give it to him,' instructed a female voice in a Spanish accent.

'Shit.' Gus fumbled to pause whatever it was that Elinor had inadvertently turned on.

Curious, she twisted round, craning to see what was happening on film. Gus was arguing with the man with the moustache. The man was shouting at Gus in Spanish and waving his fist. The man put his hand on his hip. On his hip was a gun.

She turned back. 'What's happening?'

'Nothing.' He switched it off.

'What do you mean nothing? Why are you in the film?'

'The police didn't want us filming. I had to pay them. Rewarding the corrupt like that pisses me off.'

She studied his eyes.

'Did you do something illegal?'

'Everything you do is illegal. You have to pay the police to go through a green light.'

'Why won't you let me see it?'

He blew air from his mouth.

'It's dull.'

'What's dull about it?'

An arrow of unhappiness crossed his brow.

'Me fucking up on camera.'

He sounded impatient. Now that she had him here, she couldn't let him go.

'What wouldn't you do for one of your films?'

'There's . . .'

He made a hard sucking noise with his back teeth and jerked their clenched hands upright into an arm-wrestling position. Elinor realised that he couldn't answer the question because he was afraid of the answer. He couldn't admit that there was nothing he wouldn't do because that would make him corrupt.

'How can you defend someone when you know they're guilty?' He pressed their forearms together. Bones beginning to cut like blades.

She refused to dignify his question with an answer.

'That's crap. And you know it is. It's when you think your client is innocent that you can't sleep at night.'

Gus pulled away.

'I'm sorry. I've been in this room for too long. What about Frank? Did you get your verdict?'

Elinor had hoped he might have forgotten. Somehow she knew he wouldn't approve.

'He got six months. He'll be out after three.'

'For trying to see his kid. That's insane.'

She was determined not to feel injured by his outrage.

'He threatened his ex-girlfriend. She received threats, a dead rat on her doorstep.'

'From Frank?' He looked at her, his eyes swimming with disbelief.

She waited for the mood to pass.

'And I thought I knew the guy.' He seized her arms above the elbows and smiled as though he knew something she didn't. 'Now can I please take you home?'

They took a taxi. It was raining hard. The windscreen wipers were switched to double swipe to maintain visibility. The wheels roared through gutters that splashed. The driver negotiated tight corners too fast and they slid across the seat. Their mouths slipped and they gnashed teeth like fumbling adolescents.

'Wettest year since 1766,' said the driver through the slit in the glass. 'Year records began. Wife says if it stays like this we're leaving the country. She's got her heart set on Malaga. Always take the wife's advice.'

They stared at the back of his all-knowing head.

'I like taxi drivers who talk about their wives,' whispered Elinor.

His flat was cold. They went to bed. It was underneath the eaves. Beside it was a chair buried beneath a pile of clothing and alongside it a row of shoes, most of which were boots. A bit farther along was a lavatory, sink and shower. There were no dividing walls. A stepladder accessed the first floor from the ground floor. It was unlike any London home that Elinor had ever visited. She imagined herself on holiday somewhere, up a mountain perhaps, as icy wind fingered its way through the cracks. They took each other's clothes off underneath the covers.

'It's like a wind tunnel.' She shivered. 'I can feel a breeze.'

'You won't be cold for long,' he said.

They made each other warm. Drips of waxy light came from nowhere and made patterns on their bodies. It was a long slow dance.

'I've missed you,' she said.

'I missed you too.'

She had slept with four men in her life. Two of whom counted. Gus was the fourth and the intensity she felt for him had eliminated everything that came before. The longing he left her with made her want to touch her own skin when he wasn't there. His skin tasted sweet. Her left her mouth tasting salty. He made her feel sensuous, like a woman, and it didn't feel dishonest. She wasn't trying to be somebody else as she had been for QC. QC's little girl. The past, the person she had been then, was a person she had said goodbye to. Her life had started all over again.

QC was a hefty man. He creaked and lumbered and spoke from a mouth of purple-stained teeth, lunch-time's claret sour on his breath. A habitual man, he demanded routine in everything, including their lovemaking. She would start. He would finish. There had never been much laughter and she had begun to harbour secret sexual grievances, making a tally of all the things he didn't do. In the mornings, when she tore back the curtains, he would groan about the glare. He complained about most things, she had since come to realise. Gus's windows were open to the skies.

Hugging her arms around her, she tiptoed out of bed and sat on the lavatory. A draught coiled itself around her ankles and she squeezed her muscles tight so as not to make a sound. She had never peed in front of QC and he would always shut the door. Domesticity, the unthinking kind, wasn't something they had shared. Out came a trickle. She managed not to splash and she thought how ridiculous it was she should feel embarrassed in front of this man who had made her cry and call out his name.

Standing up, she brushed against the shower curtain. Concertinaed to one end of the bath, the bulk of it spilled over the edge. She took a closer look. It was transparent and covered with clear plastic pockets into which an array of postcards and photographs had been slotted. Photographs of tropical beaches, landmark buildings, famous paintings. The folds in the curtain made both sides of the cards visible. On one of the postcards was a lunar landscape. On the other side *My angel, love always, J.* Elinor couldn't miss it. The scribbled message was there for her to see. Nor could she miss the date. The postcard had been sent from Tucson, Arizona, two weeks ago. Gus had another woman.

Elinor had an abrupt physical sensation of the blood draining from her body. Her surroundings froze around her and she no longer knew what was real and what was not.

'What are you doing?' came his voice through the confusion.

She was chased back to him by the gush of the cistern. It startled her and she fell into bed and into his arms and let his hands fill the emptiness that threatened her. Slotting her feet between his, she made him gasp.

'When are you going away again?'

Crammed with questions, she could feel her heart pounding so fast she worried it might shake the mattress and he would ask her what was wrong.

'Are you trying to get rid of me?'

She leaned away so she could see him. Scared he was slipping away.

'I was going to ask you the same thing.'

'Why?'

'Every time I see you feels like the last time.'

It was the partial truth. She was hiding from him the real truth of what she had seen because she was trying to measure her sense of loss. She had no claim on him when she didn't have the facts.

'I'm terrible at making plans right now. I'm not always like this. I hate being like this. I want to make plans.'

'Do you?'

He breathed.

'I want to see you ride a horse.'

She didn't want his sympathy. She wanted to be taken seriously. At the same time she couldn't stem the pleasure that welled inside at the thought of riding with this man. He stared ahead.

'I don't want to think about going back to the States.'

'Why not?'

'Because I want to be here.'

'Good.' She collapsed on him, clinging on tight. 'I want you here.'

And then the rain became torrential. It battered down on the roof and they took refuge in each other. His body cupped around hers, his hands pressed in front, and they were hard with each other. There was deliverance in no words and she gave herself to him.

* * *

She woke up in his arms and nuzzled his skin. Soggy grey light curtained the window. She remembered the postcard and climbed quickly out of bed. Holding her bra upside down to her ribs, she tipped forward to catch her bosoms, her arms behind her as she clipped herself in.

'I like the way you do that.'

His voice was croaky. She looked over at his quiff, his beseeching eyes, the perfect shoulder, and decided that either she walked away now and never came back or else she would hold him to a date.

'I want to see you on Friday.'

She leaned over him, inhaling his furry warmth. Kissing her bruised lips, he tried to pull her in.

'Friday it is.'

She shrugged on her coat and then she ran away.

Chapter Fourteen

It was impossible to learn about the rough and tumble of what went on in a courtroom at law school. The unpredictability of witnesses, the perverse attitudes of juries, weren't disciplines that could be taught. The same ordered chaos was true of buying a property, decided Elinor. Just when she had thought her luck was in, her timing was flawless, and that everything was set to go, it had all fallen apart. Steve Robson broke the news for the second time.

'Another offer has been put in. It matches yours, which means it could be accepted.'

She had asked him to repeat it because she couldn't understand what was being said. She had redefined herself according to this house. She had handed over a hundred pounds for him to put in the offer and he had told her, off the record, that he was one hundred per cent behind her and that she was ninety-nine per cent there.

'This morning you said my offer had been accepted.' She sat uncomfortably on the chair.

'I know that. But I wasn't reckoning on the vendor registering the house with another agent. With three in fact.'

Elinor tried to gauge his tone. Did he sound sympathetic or was it all just a game? Leaning behind him, he reached for a file. He rocked forward and dropped the file on his desk. The weight of it sent a photograph in a frame spinning round and Elinor saw that it was a photograph of a young girl. Pretty, with long, toffee-coloured hair and a shy smile, the girl was Suzanne Price. Surprised, Elinor wondered why she should feel this way. She knew that Suzanne and Steve Robson were close friends. He had said so in court.

Love always, J.

It hadn't gone away.

Steve was still talking to her.

'I'm going to be straight with you.' He knitted his fingers behind his head. 'I like you. I think we've got something special and I want to make this work. What I can do is give you an indication of how much to raise your price. Next is sealed bids. That's automatic.'

Nothing Steve Robson was telling her clarified procedure. The opposite in fact. His bluff and bravado reminded her of courtroom rituals designed to generate mystique. They shared a similar vein of self-importance. The intention was to intimidate as much as illuminate. The radio was on. She hadn't noticed it before.

'What's this song?'

She began to hum the words. Leafing through multi-coloured pages, Steve ignored her.

'It's strange. I never remember the names of songs,' she continued, wanting to be distracted. 'I'm terrible with jokes. I can never remember punch lines. But I never forget names or numbers. I can remember every telephone number I've ever had.'

The song ended. Steve raised his head.

'Tell you what, I'm going to put up a few smokescreens. Get us some extra time.'

She really didn't care how he did it. It sounded hopeful.

'How much time have we got?'

Reaching for the can of Coca-Cola on his desk, he poured it into his open mouth without wetting his lips. He's scared of catching germs, thought Elinor.

'It'll be all right. You'll see.' He replaced the can, refreshed. 'I'm going to put my business head on. Trust me.'

Elinor tried to look reassured. It wasn't easy. What had appeared so simple was a Herculean task. She should have known. He offered her a lift home and she accepted gratefully. Leaning her head against the headrest, she enjoyed the purring engine like a soft caress.

In her flat, she picked up her mail. There was another small package that she would open later. She had other things on her mind. Hanging up her suit, she put on jeans, a sweater and a windbreaker. She went to spray her neck and wrists. Her perfume was missing. She wore Chanel No 5, Frida's scent that she had made her own. She had purchased a hundred millilitre bottle at the duty-free counter on the way out of the country. It lived on the shelf beside the sink in the bathroom and it vexed her that she couldn't find it because it made no sense. She would continue her search later on. Wheeling her bicycle out of her flat, she bumped it down the stairs.

'Is that you?'

She looked up to see Nigel's bald head gleaming over the landing.

'Hello, Nigel.'

He sneezed.

'I found the pump.'

His voice was snotty with catarrh.

'Can I catch up with you later?' She waved goodbye and slammed the door.

She wasn't wearing a helmet, just her Walkman. There were two of them now inside her head. The music flooded her like memories, reminding her of the quickness of his eyes, the speed of his thoughts that she couldn't see. His clever mouth. Nerves jangling, she rode fast. Approaching the street from the opposite direction, from the top end this time, she discovered a church on the corner that she hadn't known was there. Victorian Gothic with a rubbish-strewn graveyard, the ashes of a bonfire and windows boarded up, it gave the street a solemnity she liked. She no longer went to church but she believed in chants and hymns and cures, though not necessarily prayers.

The street was on a hill. Releasing the brakes, she let

herself fly and skidded to a halt outside the house. She took a moment to reacquaint herself with it. Her instincts had proven true. The house welcomed her back like an old friend and she felt instantly renewed. Stowing her bicycle between the dustbins, she sneaked through the gate at the side of the house.

It was dark. The moon's paleness, the city's glow, was her guide. She wasn't afraid. The crunch of the undergrowth ushered her in. The ground was uneven and she had to tread cautiously so as not to trip. Arriving at the shed, she pushed the door and, in the dim light, untangled the deckchairs. Dragging one of the grass-stained chairs into the garden, she erected it so as to give her a view of the house. Tall shadows slithered up the walls. Dinner table chatter punctuated by laughter spilled from a neighbour's kitchen. Gazing up at the windows of the house, she sensed them watching her as intently as she studied them.

Her parents moved house every three to five years. Her father was a man of complex talents. He spoke Arabic, could complete the *Times* crossword in under ten minutes, and knew how to fasten twenty different knots. He had spent time in Laos towards the end of the Vietnam War. Some said he was a spook. It had been Frida, in fact, who voiced this theory. Elinor had never asked her father, 'Are you a spy?' They didn't share that type of discourse. He was a man who withheld all emotions. A man who wore a tie to breakfast. His secrets would doubtless die with him.

What Elinor did know was that her parents had never sought to end their peripatetic lifestyle. They had been in pre-war Iraq in an expat enclave of Baghdad. A gated community where the windows of the houses were barred and armed security guards patrolled the streets. They had lived in Iran before the revolution, on the border with Pakistan. In truth Elinor had never felt as at home in these rented houses with their verandas and housekeepers and central air as she had at Frida's house. Which was why, as soon as she had been able to decide for herself, she had opted to stay with Frida, where she kept her horse and could invite her friends to come and stay.

Frida died the year Elinor turned twenty-one. She died at home, which was how she had wanted it. Elinor hadn't been there but had visited the day before. Captured in her face had been traces of her incendiary beauty as she drifted in and out of consciousness. Elinor hadn't stayed long. Too anguished to watch her slipping away, she had been on the verge of leaving. She was saying goodbye to the nurse when a curious thing happened. Frida had opened her eyes, smiled and then winked. At the time baffled, it was only much later that Elinor had come to realise what a brave and generous gesture it was. Frida was letting her in on the secret. Death was a comfort. It was all right to let go. It had made Elinor feel far less frightened of losing her.

And yet her death had left a void. There were still mornings when Elinor would suffer a minor existential crisis – what's it all about? – and wish she had Frida to put her straight. Despite her own demons, Frida had been able to shed light on the darkest of days. A generous woman, she had also bequeathed Elinor a comfortable inheritance. Enough to buy a home. It's for a house, she said. Now Elinor understood why it was that she had put off finding a property for so long. It was never a flat she wanted. It was this house to which she had felt an immediate and inexplicable emotional bond.

She felt the same way about Gus.

He mapped out swathes of feeling she hadn't known were there. She had tumbled out of her safe world and was experiencing life at a pitch that was fast and new. She had never felt this way before. No longer naïve, she had moved so far forward that she could never go back. She couldn't unlearn what he had taught her. She couldn't quell her passion. She wanted to talk to him now. To whisper secrets in the long grass.

Dialling his number, she got his voice mail.

She didn't leave a message.

She stood up and walked towards the back of the house. Her intention was to peer in. The kitchen window was black. She shouldered her way to the back door and jerked the handle. It was an excuse routinely heard from car thieves and joyriders. I wasn't going to nick it. Honest. All I did was try the handle.

The handle gave way, the back door opened. She was in. Why she should want to go in, she didn't know. It was as though she had lost something. She was used to creeping around in the pitch dark. Frida didn't believe in overhead lighting, and the run to the lavatory at night had been a long one. Down a hallway, the carpet of which had been threadbare, the high walls dotted with deer heads, stuffed and mounted, their antlers casting spiky shadows, their marble eyes glinting in the gloom.

In the living room, she tried one chair then the other. In the dining room she dusted the plates with her sleeve and straightened the picture of the horse on the wall. The staircase creaked as she ventured upstairs. In the bedroom that would be hers she carried the chair to the window, sat down and looked out on to the street. A car was parked beneath a yellow cone of light. The car was red. It belonged to Steve.

Terrified of being seen, Elinor ducked her head. She remained as she was, a mass of palpitations, her face squashed in her lap for sluggish minutes that went on for ever. Her mind raced as she considered what to do. Steve had every reason to be parked outside the property. She had broken in. Her act of trespassing no longer seemed daring. It was foolish. Reprehensible. She didn't know what had come over her. What would he think?

Her phone vibrated in her pocket. She slapped her thigh, slipped her hand into her pocket and pulled it out.

'Gus?'

'Steve Robson here.'

The muscles in her neck slipped into knots.

'Are you in the bath?'

'Not yet.' She laughed, sketchily, holding it together.

'I've got some good news. I've worked out how the problem with the freehold could get us that extra time.'

She had no idea what he was talking about. Keeping her head beneath the level of the window, she moved sideways like a crab to avoid the light. She sheltered behind the wall.

She could hear background noise. A listless male monotone and chiming glasses. She remembered the pub down the street and knew that *that* was where he was.

'You know me. Just trying to keep everyone happy.'

He had a knack for making her feel guilty.

'I'll do anything I have to, to get the house,' she breezed, as though talking from the comfort of her home. Not standing with her back against a wall, pursued by unfamiliar clicks and rattles, as she sought desperately to wind up the conversation before he came to find his car.

'I don't think I want a definition of that.'

She laughed again, willing him to let her go.

'Can I ring you tomorrow to discuss this?'

'I'd recommend it.'

Jamming her phone in her pocket, she bolted down the stairs. The loose floorboards alerted the world to her intrusion like a siren. She misjudged the final step – there were two stairs, not one – and wrenched a muscle in her back, as she caught herself on the banister with an outstretched arm. She eased the kitchen door shut behind her and tiptoed along the back passage, beating off the brambles that tore at her face. Inching open the gate, she peered out. A tiny blue light, his pulsing car alarm, was all she could see.

She darted into the front garden, clammy with fear. Excuses and apologies resounded so loudly through her head she was afraid they might be overheard. Straddling her bike, she didn't switch on the lights. She flew through the streets like a bat.

Chapter Fifteen

There was a chambers meeting first thing. QC arrived late. Bleary with last night's wine and insomnia, he spilt his coffee and didn't know how to mop it up. Using the napkins passed to him, he made a slushy mess. He was wearing the yellow polka-dot tie that Elinor had given him for his fifty-sixth birthday. Eyes down, she sketched a horse in her notebook. It was the only thing she ever drew. Up for discussion were the usual topics. Rent hikes, recruitment of a new senior partner, promotions, refurbishment of the clerks' room. Derek had requested porridge rather than white walls. Any objections? No one said a word. There was the upcoming chambers birthday party, five years in business, to organise. Derek's brother was in the marquee trade. Derek had suggested that they rent a marquee from him. The vote went unanimously in favour. As though Derek would agree to renting from anyone else.

Meeting over, they filed out. Elinor switched on her phone. It bleeped into action. She had two text messages. *Bring it on baby.* She checked the number. It wasn't one she knew. It didn't wipe the smile from her face. *I'll call later.* Gus didn't bother with flirtation. No euphemistic abbreviations, x's and o's. She found his directness refreshing. She had come to distrust the eroticising of e-mails and text messages sent by men she hardly knew. It was a dissembler's art. Anyone could write messages, promising the world, which delivered nothing. She wasn't impressed by doubles entendres and tricksy charm. Barristers were experts in tricksy charm.

Perhaps she had spoken too soon. Sitting on Kendra's black leather sofa with her legs folded beneath her, she felt like a bird that had fallen off a roof. Broken wings. Broken everything. I'll call later. All day these three words had circled her mind. It was eight o'clock. She hadn't heard a thing. She was trying to work out what she had missed.

'I don't know how you've survived for so long without your own place,' said Kendra, dropping her legs over the arm of the armchair. She had sinewy calves and an Alice band to keep her hair from her eyes. A bowl nested in her lap. She was peeling and popping quails' eggs.

Kendra lived in a mews house in a smart part of town. Everyone in her neighbourhood spoke English, otherwise French, as opposed to Serbian, Urdu and Turkish, the foreign tongues familiar to Elinor from the platform where she waited each day to catch her train. Kendra had been given the house as part of her separation agreement. Her marriage had lasted fifteen months. She was now trying for an annulment on the grounds of cruelty. Orlando, her ex-husband, had not entered the marriage with honourable intentions. He wasn't the husband she thought he was. He was a controlling, jealous man who had announced in their first week of marriage that he expected Kendra to give up her job and stay at home with their firstborn. A son and heir, obviously. Orlando's father was one of the ninety-two hereditary Lords to have kept his seat. A dilettantish cross-bencher, according to Kendra, who had succeeded in not falling pregnant.

They were drinking chilled Chablis. Gulping it down. Elinor's mobile phone was in her pocket. She padded it for the fifth time in as many seconds. Her destiny, possibly her sanity, was attached to it. She had reached the point where she was checking her messages obsessively. She had three numbers for messages. Her voice mail, at work and at home. It had become a full-time preoccupation.

'It wasn't important.' She drank distractedly. 'I've done everything late. I still can't drive.'

'When did you lose your virginity?' Kendra tossed her an egg.

Elinor swatted the air and caught it.

'Twelve, if you count my pony. Nineteen when I met Colin. He was in my civil law seminar group. The saddle was more memorable.'

'I lost mine to Orlando.'

Elinor didn't know this.

'You were legal at least,' said Kendra. Her face had

become pinched. 'I was fourteen. He was three years older and a friend of my cousin's. He seduced me in the back of his car. I cried. Then he went to live in Hong Kong and I didn't see him for fifteen years. When we bumped into each other at Ascot he said, "Here's my virgin bride." He told me that he had always intended marrying me. Six months later I was wearing a ring.'

'I want to say it's romantic.' Elinor sympathised.

'I don't miss the crying. Still, at least I didn't feed him poison or whack him with a cricket bat.'

They smiled encouragingly at each other. Kendra looked wounded. Elinor changed the subject.

'When you were buying this house, did your estate agent ring you day and night?'

Kendra waggled her feet.

'I told you, we took him on holiday with us. Oh and I seem to remember him being with us on New Year's Eve. We played parlour games. Yes. He slept with my sister.' She drank. 'Well, even Orlando slept with my sister.'

'No?'

'A week after the divorce. At confession, when we were children I'd tell Father Kennedy that I'd been plotting to kill her again and he'd say that sisters are put upon this earth to try us. She was the pretty one. I was the clever one.'

Elinor hadn't seen her parents in over a year.

'My mother's devoted to my father and he's devoted to his job,' she said.

'My parents are divorced but they did manage fifteen years as opposed to months.'

Exhausted by their efforts to out-suffer each other, they collapsed into silence. Elinor patted her pocket. This time Kendra saw what she was doing and swung round in her chair.

'Elinor.' She used her name like a reprimand. 'You know nothing about this man. All you know is that he likes to pick up women on planes.'

Elinor removed her guilty hand.

'I know more than that.'

'For example?'

'Do you want a list?'

'Starting with the wife and three children?'

Upset, Elinor backed down. They were as competitive as men. They sparred, which meant that too much honesty was usually a mistake, since emotions were crushed along the way. Staring at the nectarine walls, Elinor prayed to whoever was listening to put her out of her misery.

Kendra saw what she was looking at. 'You've noticed I've had the room repainted?'

Elinor remembered now that Orlando had been a minimalist. He believed in silent spaces. This was Kendra's revenge. It reminded Elinor of Mediterranean hotels with cold tiled floors she'd visited with her parents.

'Yes,' she said at which point her phone began to vibrate. The rest of the world fell away. Reaching for it in slow motion, she looked at the number on the screen. Her spirits dropped, her face dropped. She didn't pick up but collapsed against the wall of cushions. Kendra was watching her.

'Estate agent.'

'Bastard,' cried Kendra and jumped to her feet. 'Well, it's Friday night. I say we go wild, rent a video and order a curry.'

And they did. They ate chicken in coconut milk with sticky rice and watched *Notorious.* Alfred Hitchcock films were a shared passion. The crossed lines and prickly silences matched Elinor's mood. They had seen this film before. The moment when Cary Grant bounds up the stairs and seizes Ingrid Bergman, lying poisoned in bed, in his arms as the camera spins round the room was heart stopping. They rewound the scene and watched it again. Twice.

'I want to be saved,' resolved Kendra through a mouthful of food. 'Bring back chivalry.' A moment later, 'Snow!'

Running to the kitchen, they slid open the doors. Dizzy snowflakes swirled down from the sky and began to settle on bushes and pots. They stood on the patio, their shivering arms wrapped around them, stuck out their tongues and blew smoky patterns into the frozen air. Elinor thought of Gus when he was shot. It was very hot and I dreamed of snow, he said. She had reached the point when everything bore some reference to him. Possessed by something so much bigger than herself she could see no way of escape.

'Did I tell you he was shot?' she said, quietly, stamping her feet, creating footprints like dance steps.

Kendra had snow on her hair. She was hand-jiving to keep warm.

'A head injury would explain a lot.'

'In his thigh.' Elinor paused. 'Do you think it makes me a shallow person that I find him interesting because he was shot?'

'Obviously.' Kendra had begun to jig up and down. 'On the subject of macho men there was a terribly dishy gunman in the Old Bailey last week. He held up an off-licence. He shot the owner. Before he fired he said three words.'

'Stick 'em up?'

'You're dead.'

'Was he?'

'Well, yes.'

They shuddered and went inside. At eleven o'clock Steve Robson called again but Elinor wasn't in the mood. Instead she sent a text message to Gus, just as she had promised herself she wouldn't do. *I don't understand.*

Chapter Sixteen

The next day was Saturday. She went to get a bikini wax. It was an activity reserved for Saturdays, along with having her hair straightened, a labour-intensive job in which her hair was blow-dried around a cylindrical brush. Straight hair made her feel refined, all the kinks gone. Today, wrecked, she would suffer with curls. What did other people do on Saturdays? QC took his Jag to be valet cleaned and posed as a father. Kendra had lunch with her mother, squabbled with her ex-husband and shopped for shoes. Elinor didn't know what Gus did on Saturdays. She hadn't had the chance to find out.

Right now she was lying on a bed with her skirt off and her knees splayed, ankles locked together. Vivaldi's *Four Seasons* was piped from tinny speakers to enforce relaxation.

'How high do you want it?' asked the girl, who was Russian.

She was swaying in time to the music, the wooden spoon

dripping with hot wax held aloft in her hand. Up to my neck, Elinor was tempted to say. Her feeling of disassociation hadn't lifted. It was getting worse. Going through the motions of her day, she was mentally living his. She pictured Gus running for a plane weighed down with bags. She saw him laughing, happy somewhere. The last time she had been happy was with him. Now he was gone. He had left her an exile from happiness and she hated him for it. Tugging her knickers, she indicated the patch that needed removing.

'This is fine.' She closed her eyes.

The girl powdered both sides of her knicker line, applied wax with the back of the spoon and allowed a moment for it to harden. In a firm flick-of-the-wrist motion she ripped it off. The pain was gratifying and now Elinor was bare. Then came the tweezers as the girl extracted the hairs which wouldn't come out. This pain was personal. Elinor winced as she reflected on the variants of pain. There was the warm flow of blood when you broke the skin. There was the desolate chill that carved out your insides when you were left all alone. The girl displayed a thorny hair for Elinor to see.

'In Russia we have a proverb. A bad weed never dies.'

'I'll remember that.' Elinor nodded, and she would, because right now all paths to the truth were gratefully received. She was looking for signs, patterns, anything that might tell her what was going on.

Next stop was the supermarket. She didn't know what to buy. She trailed up and down the aisles with her mesh basket, identifying the exotic fruits, ogling the slabs of wet fish, fondling the fresh bread. Gus had told her that he could cook two things. Risotto and roast chicken. She knew nothing about risotto but considered looking it up in the book and purchasing the ingredients. She bypassed the cookery books. A girl was handing out free samples of an inch-high red drink. *Campari* was written on her sweatshirt. Elinor took a tumbler. The drink didn't help her decision-making but tasted sweet and medicinal and enhanced her sensation of floating. Her sound and vision were left marginally impaired.

At the check-out she joined the Baskets Only queue. This was a mistake. Normally she would take a trolley to avoid the oddballs and lonely singles who shopped with baskets. She had forgotten this tactic today. Instead she found herself behind a man who wanted to purchase a can of sweetcorn for forty-nine pence on his credit card. A woman buying eight bars of chocolate, family size, and a can of economy dog food. Elinor didn't recognise any of the items she had chosen as she lined them up on the belt. A goat's cheese. A loaf of rye bread. A red cabbage. A packet of Rich Tea biscuits. A box of Belgian chocolates. Two bottles of beer. She wondered whether perhaps someone had been shadowing her and planting foreign objects in her basket for kicks. She bought them anyway.

The check-out girl had a stutter.

'Fifteen pounds and th-th-th-th . . .' Elinor didn't prompt her. 'Thirty pence.'

They smiled at one another, relieved.

* * *

At home she unpacked her groceries and checked her messages. *Hello it's Nigel. Wondered if you fancied a glass of wine.* Waiting for the next message, Elinor was assaulted by a violent coughing fit. It came from a man's throat and masked shades of heavy breathing. He didn't leave a name. Uneasy, Elinor erased it and ate three chocolates in a row. The hard shells leaked soft fudge on to her tongue and she wondered why pleasure had to be so short-lived. She tussled with her hair: damp weather made it crazy. Picking up the new tape she had been sent, she toyed with it in the palm of her hand.

The company she kept had long influenced her taste in music. QC was an opera buff. He had taken her to see Royal Opera House performances of Pucinni's *Turandot* and *Nabucco* by Verdi. He slept through both, though later denied it. The actress loved Latin. The queen of salsa, she once dragged Elinor to a class in a church hall to learn how. It had not been a success. The actress could shake her hips like jelly. The men in the class had fought to partner her. Elinor's hips had refused to budge and the instructor had resorted to forcibly moving them. Feel the rhythm, he lisped. She didn't know how.

She was afraid of the tape. She knew the effect it would have on her. It would leave her lonely and make her world incomplete. Eating another chocolate for courage, she put it on. The music crowded the room as though Gus were there. Beginning with cautious melodies, to get under the skin, it moved up-tempo. Middle Eastern wailing pumped life into her with an urgency that bordered on sexual. Pressing every button, it made her feel weak. She upped the volume and played it loud. I want it all, sang a girl who probably knew how to get it, and made Elinor pine for what she didn't have. On the sofa, she refused to cry. She drank from the bottle of beer to remind herself of him and composed text messages that she didn't send.

What are you doing to me? Where are you?

The music died. Retreating into the calm, she tried to recover and remember what it was to feel herself again, to be content with her own company. She was joined by a sound of banging, which came from outside. She had heard it earlier but had assumed it was part of the music. It wasn't. Someone was hitting a blunt instrument against the scaffolding. It was getting louder.

'Elinor.'

She recognised the voice. Reluctantly she got to her knees, unfastened the lock on the sash window and stuck her head outside. The sudden movement sent her blood racing. White dots jitterbugged in front of her eyes.

'It's Steve Robson.'

She knew who it was. She leaned her head out farther and saw that he had a brick in his hand. The sight of him disturbed her. She didn't like him pitching up at her house unannounced.

'I rang your buzzer. Didn't you hear it?'

'No.'

Her buzzer was reliably temperamental.

'What happened yesterday? Did you get my messages?' He looked up at her like a needy child.

'I was in court,' she lied, and felt disloyal. She wanted to be alone. She didn't want to see anyone, not even Steve Robson.

'What are you doing in by yourself on a Saturday night?'

'How do you know I'm by myself?'

'Aren't you?'

She gave in. 'Well, yes.'

'The owner said he was going for a drink in his local. Thought it might be worth saying hello.'

That was all she needed to hear. Grabbing her coat, she went to meet him downstairs.

They positioned themselves at the bar. Peeling black letters spelled TAKE COURAGE across the window. A row of old men, scarves on, were staring into their pints in the corner and issuing intermittent grunts to one other.

'It doesn't look like he's here. The faster you run, the harder you fall. You ever read John Grisham?'

Steve Robson hitched up his trousers to slide more comfortably forward on his stool. They were sitting side by side. His navy trousers had a stiff crease down the front. His black leather jacket looked shiny and new and his shoes were tasselled. Called upon to identify a defining feature in him, it would be his precision, decided Elinor. She had never had a man quote John Grisham at her before.

'I prefer Scott Turow.'

She had read both and preferred neither although there was an argument in favour of Turow.

'Why's that?'

'The writing's more terse. Cleverer plots.'

'You're joking. Grisham's the master. Every jury has a leader and the verdict belongs to him.'

She rattled her ice cubes.

'Have you got a girlfriend?'

Time to establish some boundaries, she felt. Her being here with him implied an intimacy with which she wasn't entirely comfortable.

'No time. Just Suzy.'

Suzanne Price. Elinor remembered him describing their relationship as being like that of brother and sister.

'How is she?' Elinor heard herself say, as the off-limits barrier went down and her pledge not to discuss the court case was forgotten. So much had happened since. 'How's the baby?'

He nodded.

'Can't complain. I look out for them. Do my best. Like I've always done.' He drank. 'I don't know how much you know about roses.'

'Very little.'

'You've got your China roses, your cabbage roses and your damask roses. They're natives. On her birthdays, I give Suzy yellows because they're special. They're foreign.'

Something clicked.

'Was she your girlfriend?'

Steve nudged forward on his seat and a roll of flesh

pinched at the back of his neck. He throttled his pint with both hands.

'That's right.'

'I didn't know that.'

There was no reason why Elinor should have known this and yet, instinctively, she felt that she ought. It carried all sorts of implications that right now she couldn't focus on.

'You ever get sent roses?'

'Lilies,' she said, 'Are my favourites.'

'Long-stem white?'

'*Lilium Longiflorum,*' she replied, as though it were a competition.

She caught sight of his hand nearest her. A number was written in pen on his skin. An attempt had been made to rub it out but the first five digits were visible. It was her telephone number. He saw what she was staring at.

'I was about to give you a bell.'

Elinor made herself look away, uncertain as to whether to feel flattered. At school they had worn the names of their cracks, the older girls on whom they had crushes, on their hands. In court, out of desperation, she might scrawl a key word on her hand. It indicated forgetfulness, from which she didn't think he suffered, or obsessive tendencies.

'Have you got a special friend?'

Elinor nodded.

'Where's he tonight?'

'Working.'

'On a Saturday night? You tell him he's got his priorities wrong.'

'It's a passion.'

As soon as she had said this she wished she hadn't. Passion was not a word to use lightly. Perhaps it was not to be spoken at all. It revealed the suffering bound up in desire. The pounding in her head, the clamp in her gut, the squeezing of her soul. A song came on the juke-box, a song from the tape, and she was punished with electric love, with restless human magic. She shrank inside.

'I'm going on to a club. You should come.'

A rush of something dark like desire surged from deep within and, with a start, Elinor realised that she was leaning against Steve Robson. She had attached herself to the weight of his shoulder, the warmth in his veins. He was solid and helpful and where she needed him to be. He tipped his head and his glance was soft. His lips moved into a smile and his gold fillings dazzled from the cave of his mouth. Jerking herself upright, Elinor hastily drank from her glass. She hid her face.

'I don't think so.'

'You might like it.'

But she didn't like clubs. They encouraged a level of hysteria she would rather avoid. Embarrassed by her misplaced emotion, she watched a pair of legs shuffle in behind a blackboard. The blackboard was erected next to the bar, a man in a smock emerged, and the pub quiz began.

'My lords, ladies and gentlemen. Tonight is the final. Anyone caught cheating will be publicly flogged.'

'Me first,' called a camp voice.

'Question number one. When the moon is on the

opposite side of the earth from the sun, is it a full moon or a new moon?'

Turning round, Elinor was surprised to find teams of people hunched over tables with pencils and paper and competitive faces. She swivelled back.

'I'm going.'

She had forgotten why she had come.

'I don't know where he can have got to.' Steve Robson sieved the pub with his eyes. He slid off his stool, about to stand up. Elinor motioned for him to sit down.

'I'll be fine.'

'I'll be in touch,' he promised with exaggerated formality.

Outside, the moon was full. She rushed to find a cab.

At home there was a message. It was the actress. Elinor called her straight back.

'I wish you were here. How's sunny LA?'

'It's been raining for a week and the roof leaks. I've put out buckets, now the buckets leak.'

The actress didn't sound happy. She had moved to LA to be close to the magic. Rain belonged to the life she had left behind.

'I thought California was the sunshine state.'

'I've been watching a lot of daytime TV. It's sunny on the soaps.'

'Are you smoking again?'

Elinor could hear her.

'Yes.' She sounded contrite. 'Boredom. I'm sick of waiting to hear. I'm sick of playing girlfriends who die.' More smoking. 'Are you drunk?'

'It's Saturday night.'

'Why aren't you out?'

Long-distance silence washed up and down the line. Everything clenched inside and Elinor sighed as though releasing her entire self from her lungs.

'Are you still seeing him?'

The actress knew all about Gus. Elinor paused.

'I don't want to lose him.'

'What have you got to lose?'

'I don't know.'

'Well,' said the actress, taking her time, 'I think you need to find out.'

Where Kendra was blunt, the actress was perceptive. Her wisdom munificent. Elinor nodded.

'I'm nodding,' she said.

They were silent.

'Do you remember our crack books?' Elinor asked her.

It was a question that went straight to the heart. The actress laughed. Their shared past brought them closer than blood.

'I thought Kitty had been made in heaven.'

Kitty, two years their senior, was a cool blonde with a mouth like a gash who spoke perfect French. *C'est gentil,* she would dazzle them with her brilliance. Elinor's crush had been on Benedicta. A hearty horse-rider, she had the largest collection of horror books of anyone, and skin that smelled of rhubarb crumble.

'I cut the corner off her towel, her knickers, even her lacrosse stick to glue in my crack book,' the actress reminisced.

'Weren't you punished for that?'

'Dirty hair for two weeks.'

There had been a competition among the girls to see who could idolise their cracks the most. The challenge had been to construct the most lavish crack book, a scrapbook, into which went love letters, drawings, poems and bits of their cracks' things. A lock of hair scored top marks. A splinter of lacrosse stick did nearly as well. It had been worth suffering the hair-washing ban, the most demeaning form of punishment.

'Do you think they ever think of us now?' said Elinor.

'All the time.'

Elinor's twelve years at boarding school, an institution on a cliff in what had been a Victorian asylum, she likened to a sort of punishment. She had never felt happy or safe. No one but the actress and a dwindling number of other boarding school-friends understood what it meant to have survived those years.

'I miss you,' said the actress. 'Though I don't miss London. Did I tell you Dominic is moving out here?'

Dominic was the actress's boyfriend. Also an actor.

'I'm glad.'

'He's good at catching drips.'

'Send him my love.'

* * *

Elinor went to bed. She had drunk so that she wouldn't dream. She slept but not for long. She was woken by her heart racing so fast she worried she might not make it. Adrenaline churned like the rollers that crashed on the rocks beneath her school. Sweat poured, soaking her cleavage. Her night-gown was twisted like a towel between her legs. Gravity had deserted her. She was tumbling through blackness, slipping through the net. She was losing her mind. What was she scared of? Everything. She sat up and cried out loud. I don't want to be sleeping alone. I want to be with him.

She went to the window and looked outside. She could have sworn she had heard someone tap-dancing on the scaffolding planks. Up and down like Fred Astaire. There was no one there. Checking that the windows were locked, she felt her way to the kitchen and made a cup of tea. Back in bed, she sipped it slowly as every moment spent with Gus raged through her head. His absence was no longer benign, it was aggressive. He had captured her heart with such tremendous illusions that she wished she had never met him. She was trying to understand something she knew nothing about. Retreating beneath her covers, she closed her eyes to block out the light. Above the roofs a helicopter circled, pulverising the peace. The city's unrest. And now the dog began to bark.

Chapter Seventeen

'Is he here?'

It was obvious he was not. Elinor had dressed that morning with a sense of purpose. Her already pale reflection appeared bloodless and stunned, so she had rouged her cheeks, pencilled her eyes and enlivened her lips with a fiery glow. Her hair, scraped flat, frothed at the back. She tied her hair back on days when she didn't want to be noticed or feel forced to compete with her storm of red. Wearing a camel coat that skirted the ground, she had on her sternest heels, responsible for the racket in the hallway.

She was standing in Gus's edit suite. With her hands in her pockets to ground her and give them something to do, she was so strung out on nerves that it made her speech unnaturally loud. She had persisted in avoiding this moment until she could persist no longer. Rationality had deserted her. Instinct and desperation had dragged her here. It wasn't even nine o'clock.

'Oh, hello, love,' Connor greeted her in his casual Scottish lilt. He swivelled in his seat and his belly wobbled. His body had been claimed by the chair. He had peppery growth on his chin and folds beneath his eyes. Eating his breakfast, he was poring over a newspaper spread over the desk. None of the monitors had been switched on.

'He's with the lawyer.'

I am the lawyer, she was tempted to shout, struggling with a rollercoaster in her chest.

'Do you know when he'll be back?'

'Not for some time, I imagine.' Connor raised the top slice of his sandwich. A row of sausages nestled inside. 'He's been a bad boy. Broken the law. Not meant to have left the country, apparently. They'll be giving him a hard time.'

Elinor stared at Connor in a daze. He had puppy-dog eyes and a gentle manner. The facts he was informing her of were shocking and disagreeable. Running a hand across her tightly trained hair, she felt it pinch.

'I don't know about any of this.' She sounded brittle, and felt foolish.

'I don't know who did.'

Elinor hesitated.

'What's the offence?' Bracing herself for the worst, she hardly dared imagine what the worst could be. Her head was about to explode. Connor indicated with a wind-up motion of his hand that he was trying to swallow quickly. He coughed so as not to choke.

'Smuggling.'

She tried not to choke too.

'Drugs?'

'Oh, no.' He wiped grease from his cheeks with the back of his hand. 'Much more exotic than that.' He squinted at a piece of paper on the desk. 'See Code eight section one thousand two hundred and twenty-seven.'

Elinor was trying to be patient. It was excruciating. She couldn't second-guess Connor any longer. Whatever it was he was reading from, she had to see for herself. With a step, she was at the desk, a mess of pieces of A4 paper, pink Post-Its, yellow Post-Its, film magazines, men's magazines. A white document bearing the United States of America Government stamp, black, lay on top.

'Can I?' she said.

Removing the document from beneath Connor's puzzled eyes, she skimmed for facts as she had been trained to do. Connor didn't know what he was looking for. She did. She was the lawyer. It was a 'charging document'. *Mr Cox, G. R. charged with attempting to smuggle an illegal alien across the border from Nogales Sonora, Mexico, into Nogales, Arizona, on 5 February. Bail set at $10,000. Payment made of $1,000. Condition of bail provides that Mr Cox, an alien in the United States of America, shall remain at 1542 Calgary Drive, Tucson, AZ, until such a time as his trial date has been set.*

Elinor stared at Connor.

'He's jumped bail.'

In the pause that followed, she couldn't be sure but it felt like relief that fluttered through her. The weight of uncertainty lifted. She had an answer when until now all she had were questions. It gave her something on which to begin to peg the unexplained behaviour. He had other things on his mind. She wasn't going mad. She was sleeping with a man with a warrant out for his arrest. It made her head spin.

'It's probably the only thing he hasn't done.' Connor stirred his tea, visibly unimpressed by the news.

The piece of paper went limp in her hand.

'What do you mean?'

'I don't know anyone else who's caught leprosy, do you?'

'No.'

'You haven't known him very long, love.' Connor caught her dismay. 'He's not a troublemaker. He just has a tendency to get carried away and ignore all the rules.'

Searching for words to express her feelings, Elinor realised that, while she wanted to feel pity, what she felt was humiliation. She let the piece of paper float down to the desk. Her intimacy with Gus was a sham. He had lied to her. When she asked him whether he had done anything illegal, he said no. She knew so little about him that what facts he had given her she had been forced to trust. *Love always, J.* Perhaps she was a fool to have believed a word he said.

'He's only trying to make interesting work,' offered Connor. 'You can't blame him for being an adrenaline junkie.'

This she refused to accept.

'Why not? He knows what he's doing.'

Connor shrugged his saggy shoulders.

'All right. Even I don't know how he's going to get out of this one.' He pushed buttons to make lights fizz across the monitors like an electrical storm. 'I reckon he's on his own.'

Elinor was due in court. She couldn't be late. In other jobs it was possible to ring in and say, Sorry, I'm feeling poorly. I can't make it today. She didn't enjoy that privilege. She had her client's future at stake. Running down the hall, she scrambled out of her coat and into her gown. It wasn't uncommon to see barristers applying lipstick, scanning their briefs and swallowing sandwiches as they sprinted.

She found Lucy in the lobby. She was wearing a floaty dress and a silk flower in her hair as though on her way to a wedding.

'You look nice.' Elinor caught her breath as she jammed on her wig.

'All rise for the judge.'

Lucy was in the witness box. She looked demure and fragrant and not at all the type to pick fights with large men.

'Can you tell the courtroom what happened,' said Elinor.

Lucy pushed strands of hair from her face like a schoolgirl.

'I was walking home.' Even her voice was flowery. 'There were cars parked all the way along the pavement. I saw three drunken men walking towards me. "Excuse me," I said. I tried to squeeze past. "Can't you see what you're fucking doing, you fucking idiot?" one of the men shouted. I said I was sorry and kept walking. But the man carried on shouting at me. The next thing I knew I felt him grab me by the hair and swing me round and punch me on the side of my face.'

'What did you do?'

'I fought back. He punched me on the nose and blood came gushing out. I was very frightened. I punched him and wrestled him but he had me in a headlock.'

'Did you set your dog on him?'

'I thought he was going to kill me.'

'Did you set your dog on him?'

'Yes.'

Next in the witness box was the man from the pub where Lucy had fled in the wake of the assault. He said Lucy had arrived with a bloodied face and clumps of hair falling out. He said it was a disgrace for a defenceless girl to have suffered a violent attack at the hands of a man. Glancing at the jury, Elinor felt confident that she had created reasonable doubt in their minds that Lucy had set out to injure the man whose testicle had been bitten by Raj. She had acted in self-defence. The charge of aggravated assault wouldn't stick. The verdict was expected tomorrow.

Elinor returned to chambers reassured by her performance in court. She hadn't lost her mind. Her ability to think logically and construct an argument was still intact. Stopping to see Derek, she found him with a twist of Kleenex up each nostril. His cold had become worse. He hastily yanked them out.

'You just missed him,' he said, red spots burning his cheeks.

'Who?'

'Steve Robson. I told him you were in court. He didn't hang about.'

Elinor remained where she was.

'Did he leave a message?'

'No message.'

She didn't know what to tell him.

'He's my estate agent.'

'Got you, miss.'

Derek was a creature of instinct. He knew not to ask questions where information wasn't forthcoming. Not that Elinor had anything to hide. Dragging her heels as she climbed the stairs, she was perplexed. She hadn't asked Steve Robson to come to chambers, nor did she want him to. This was her world where she had a professional role that had nothing to do with him.

Her room felt close. She couldn't settle. Forcing the window open, she was greeted by a roar of traffic. She looked at her watch. Five-thirty. Gus must have finished with his lawyer by now, and then what? Where would he go? She had no sooner sat down than she was up again. On her way downstairs, she slipped into the ladies' room, splashed handfuls of water on her face and stared at her dripping reflection. Her pupils, so dilated, had consumed her irises. Fearful of being sucked into their inky void, she quickly looked away.

The curtain was a wall of dusty velvet. She sneezed. Gus turned round. He was wearing a jacket zipped up to his chin as though he had just arrived. He hadn't. He was perched on a stool, leaning over a table. The man who had been smoking a cigar at the bar the last time she was here, was seated across from him. Between them lay a backgammon board. They were in the middle of a game.

'Bad luck, mate. Double six,' said the man.

Moving his pieces too fast for anyone to see what was happening, he smashed both dice into Gus's upturned palm.

'Elinor.'

It seemed to her that Gus whistled her name. She knew it was how she would remember it later. Astonishment leaked from his brow to his gaze. His mouth twitched and his palm remained cupped as though begging for favours.

'Gus,' she said.

It killed her to admit it but the sight of him alone restored order to her universe. What she wanted to do was swear at him, tip over his backgammon board and watch the pieces scatter across the floor. She wanted to see his face twist with cruel surprise. A look that would tell her he was ruffled. That despite his appearance of calm, an ocean of doubts swept just below the surface. A dogged silence stalked the room.

'Let me get you a drink.'

Standing up too fast, he knocked over his stool, bent to pick it up and then stood with it in his hand as he leaned over and smudged her cheek with a beery kiss. It was a clumsy, nervous gesture that Elinor did nothing to make easier for him. The cigar man rumbled his displeasure at her interruption of the game. She followed Gus to the bar, questions tearing through her mind.

A wire from the mobile phone in his pocket was clipped to his jacket. It fell and dangled, severing his connection to the outside world.

'Connor said he'd seen you.'

She felt afraid. It was the fear that precedes all emotion. It was resentment that he could make her feel this way. She could smell his smoke and desperate drinking. The knot at her throat tightened. She hated confrontation. Its possible outcome frightened her.

'Why didn't you ring me?'

'I didn't want to lie.'

'So why did you?'

Watching him grapple with possibilities and throw them away, Elinor could see his brain trying to formulate what next to say. His arms were flexed, his body rigid. He flopped his head between his shoulder blades. Flooded with tenderness, she was crushed by the sight of the nape of his neck.

'It's a mess,' he said.

'I know.' She paused, seized by sudden uncertainty, by fear of rejection. 'I don't know what I'm doing here.'

Scrabbling in her pockets, all she found were her keys. Gus straightened up sharply. Willing her with eyes that shone not to walk away, he said her name and she allowed herself to be pulled in. In the protective curl of his arm she felt his breathing slow and they breathed as one. She didn't know whether the pain she felt was his pain or her pain. She didn't know what compelled her to suffer his pain or why she felt such loyalty to this man.

'I was trying to help someone,' he began to explain, and he didn't sound heroic. He sounded distant and forlorn, his usual fast-talk distilled to an echo. Staring at the bar, he slowly moved his thumb. 'The town where we were filming is a black hole. People disappear. The woman I had in my car thought she was going to be murdered. She'd found out she owed a lot of money. They had threatened to kill her. It was a last-minute thing. She was panicking. She couldn't get back to her house to find her passport. It was the middle of the night so I said I'd drive her across the border in my car. It seemed simple. But it was a mistake. I got caught and I didn't tell you, Elinor, because . . .' He looked at her. 'You're a lawyer.'

Elinor felt cold. Turning away, she focused on the row of spirit bottles hanging upside down in a waterfall of colours. Never had she felt more oppressed by her profession than now. It upset her because she had no defence. It was who she was. Stung into quiescence, she felt betrayed.

'I think so much of you. I didn't know what to tell you. You have enough of other people's problems to sort out every day, without having mine too. All weekend I wanted to call and say I can't see you because I'm stuck with a lawyer. It sounded so ridiculous. I felt like such a fucking . . .'

'Yes.' She cut in to agree with whatever insult he chose to use. The injustice of her situation was suddenly intolerable. She could see no humour, no vestige of hope. 'Why do you get yourself into these situations?' A surge of irritation unleashed the words from her mouth. 'Do you want to get shot?'

As soon as she had said this, she felt something in him shut down. The light in his eyes went out and his arm went limp. He withdrew it.

'I'm sorry,' he said, and just like that they were two separate people with separate reasons for everything standing at a bar. Sorry was a cheap goodbye. She felt as though she were being casually demolished.

'That's it, is it?'

He scratched his head.

'I don't know what to say.'

'Is her name *love always, J?*'

'What?' he said too fast, looking at her with secret eyes.

Instinctively Elinor knew that it was.

'On the postcard. I read it. *Love always, J.* Is she the woman you smuggled over the border?'

'Well, yes,' he admitted at which point the bar boy arrived and looked expectantly at them until Gus shook his head and chased him away.

Elinor buttoned up her coat. It was a struggle to make the buttons go through the holes but she was determined to succeed. All her life she had been forced to leave someone to get on a plane or a train and go somewhere else and it was what she did now. Hiding her turmoil, she lowered her eyes. Too many feelings had seeped into them. Then she turned and walked away.

'Elinor,' he called after her, but he didn't chase her because he knew he had done wrong.

* * *

Outside, she kept going, gliding through the darkness deaf to the traffic and numb to her feet. She reached the road that led to the river and soon arrived at the bridge. Remembering her Walkman in her bag, she put it on. More emotions than she knew what to do with were bound up in the tapes. She felt as infected by them as she was by him. Memories stirred, boundaries crossed, she said goodbye to the river and was drawn towards the city's lights. Associations never died.

When her parents lived in Baghdad they would go out every night, either to a party or for cocktails with friends on the terrace of the British Club. And every night she had been visited by the mosque calls that spiralled through the night. Sounds which even now took her back to lying alone in her parents' bed, the fan above her head stirring the air like the lazy swish of a tail.

She arrived at the roundabout where she knew she would find a taxi. Moored on the kerb, she had a sudden change of heart. Emboldened by nostalgia, she refused to feel sad. Gus didn't want her. She was on her own. Free to take the music wherever she pleased.

'Well, this is a surprise. A pleasant one, I hasten to add.'

QC was in his dressing gown. Racing-green towelling with his initials in gold braid on the left breast. He had been in the bath. His cheeks were flushed and his hair was combed back like a senator's. In his hand was a whisky tumbler, cut glass, no ice.

'You're wet.' It had started to rain. 'Where've you been?'

'I don't want to talk about it much.'

He closed the door behind her and helped her wriggle out of her coat. Kicking off her shoes, she pressed her aching feet into his carpet, so shaggy it crept between her toes. He rewrapped his dressing gown, revealing a flank of hairy thigh.

'Get yourself a drink. I've got to finish up. Old Bailey, Court one tomorrow. It's this spy and the MI5 business. He says we're all bugged.'

'We were bugged in Baghdad.'

QC wasn't interested.

'If you're after a nightcap, whisky's in the bottom cupboard.'

He returned to his study and she trod softly to the kitchen. Tiled red and white, it had curtains to match. She poured milk into a pan and watched the milk froth to the top. She had mixed two teaspoons of cocoa powder with two teaspoons of sugar and a dash of milk in a mug. Adding the boiling milk, she stirred vigorously and sat down at the table. Within ten minutes of being back in QC's flat she had reverted to a version of herself she had sworn she had left behind. It was a used-up model. A fake. Ashamed to be here, she had no choice. It was the only version of the truth she could live with tonight. She couldn't remember the point of her argument with Gus. All she knew was that he had forced her here. Drinking her cocoa, willing it to knock her out, she watched the kitchen blur into steaky pink.

'Are you ready?' called QC, which meant that he was.

'Coming,' she said, and then they went to bed. QC was tired and so was she but his body was familiar and that was all it was.

Chapter Eighteen

'Who's a lucky lady?' whistled Norm, his hair cut short like a soldier's, when she entered the clerks' room.

She had on the same suit as yesterday. The clerks didn't miss a trick. They knew more than was healthy and the rest they made up. All of it reeking of promiscuity. Then she noticed the flowers. Norm's remark accompanied a bouquet that he was thrusting at her. An extravagant bunch of white lilies.

'Card's inside. You must have done something right.'

Or very wrong.

Kendra was at her desk.

'Oh, I say.'

'Don't.'

'What?'

'Everything.'

'Who are they from?'

'Guess.'

Elinor had ripped open the envelope and cowered when she read the card.

'Lover man.'

'Try again.'

'Oh, God, I don't know. Peter?'

'Estate agent.'

Kendra threw back her head and roared with delight.

'Have you slept with him?'

'It's not funny. I don't want him sending me flowers.'

Kendra retained her smug expression. Laughing inside.

Elinor's desk phone rang. Still in her coat, she was staring at the bouquet and contemplating what to do with it. She picked up.

'Steve Robson for you.' Norm put him through.

'Avoiding me, are you?'

His tone was harsh in her ear. Elinor recoiled.

'Did you get the flowers?'

'Thank you. You shouldn't have.'

His persistence was exhausting.

'To apologise for the no-show. I don't know any lady who appreciates being stood up on a Saturday night.'

An atonement gift. Elinor looked at her watch.

'Did you speak to him?'

'Who?'

'The owner.'

'He hasn't accepted the other offer,' said Steve Robson in a hurry. 'And he'd rather do business with me. He knows it's in his best interests.'

His dogmatism could conjure logic from the deepest confusion, thought Elinor.

'I've got a lot of work to do.'

'I'll get back to you.'

They hung up.

'Why can't he give me any indication of what's happening with the house?' she complained to Kendra who was making googly eyes at her.

'Perhaps it's not the house he's after.'

She frowned as the ceiling shook.

'Don't'

QC had the room above theirs. He was crashing and thumping and shouting at his secretary to remind him of what he had forgotten, which these days amounted to as much as he remembered.

Elinor's memory of last night was of lying wide awake as QC's snores whistled through her like the ticking of a clock. Their sleepy embraces hadn't led anywhere. She had borrowed a pair of his Harrod's pyjamas and declined his offer of sex. What bound them together was their past. It wasn't enough for her to forsake the present. So, why are you here? QC had moaned. To see you. Oh, suit yourself, he said and rolling over, had fallen sleep.

Staring up at his stucco ceiling, Elinor had tortured herself with images of Gus driving his mystery friend across the border. She wanted to know why this incident that had taken place far away weeks ago had impacted on her life like this. She wanted to know what her reaction to his arrest would have been, had she known of it earlier. All she could summon was distant regret.

'How is he?'

Kendra, late for a conference downstairs, was standing up.

'Wanted for jumping bail.'

Kendra stared, hollow eyed.

'What?'

'In America.'

'I hope he's got a good lawyer.'

Elinor untied the ribbon on her brief.

'And I've got a neighbourly dispute gone wrong.'

Kendra smiled.

'Good luck.'

Trapped with the lilies and QC upstairs, Elinor felt besieged. Overcome by anxiety, she had to get out. Whisking past the clerks' room, she dived down the steps and on to the street. A red car streamed by, and instinctively she thought of Steve Robson. She had begun to see his car everywhere she went, like the dots that decorate dizzy spells.

She had received more untraceable text messages over the past few days. *I can see you. I can taste you. I can hear you.* Their allusions to intimacy rattled her. So did their anonymity. Someone wanted to know that she was in his thoughts and she could think of only one person whose persistence was a thorn in her side. Unless it was Gus. Why should it be Gus?

In the square adjacent to chambers was a park. Flower-beds in hibernation edged a manicured lawn overseen by a park-keeper who had his own hut. On a plinth stood a statue of a Victorian philanthropist clutching a scroll. Huddled on a bench, Elinor bundled herself inside her coat to keep out the cold. A woman in a fur was dragging a poodle in vicious strides around the park. Quickly, Munchkin, she was saying. A man in leather gloves was reading a newspaper on the other side of the square. He raised his head and smiled as though they were acquainted. Were they? Elinor's concentration was fractured. Desperate to put her thoughts in order, she didn't know where to begin.

Hazy about how long she had been sitting on the bench, she was woken from her trance by the ring of her phone. She had travelled to another galaxy and floated back again. Curiously calm, she let him leave a message.

'Elinor. It's Gus. I was hoping to speak to you. I'll call again. Later. I mean today. This afternoon. Sorry. Yes. Anyway.'

A breeze brushed her cheeks and she could breathe once more. Saving the message, she briskly left the park. Munchkin was squatting behind a bush, his mistress eyeing him intently.

She arrived in time to catch her desk phone ringing.

'Steve Robson for you,' said Norm.

Elinor lowered her head into her hands.

'I'll be straight with you. It's yours if you can make it worth my while.'

She felt his speed to be deliberate. Once the message was

out, it was no longer his. Instead the words sat between them, unclaimed by either, as Elinor allowed herself to comprehend what was on offer. Damp with dismay, she felt the heat of the courtroom when things were going badly or conversely very well. The offer was corrupt. She felt excited. He was telling her that her dream could be real and the house could be hers for a price. That price was her conscience and his fee. A sweetener. She swallowed hard.

'I'll have to think about it.'

What she didn't say was no. She hadn't intended to reach a decision so quickly, nor had she any idea of the sort of figure he had in mind. She was running away with herself.

'I'll have to call you back,' she said.

Feeling queasy, she drank three glasses of water in a row and undid her top two buttons. A bead of perspiration shimmered in her cleavage like light.

All afternoon she sat by herself as long shadows strong-armed their way into the room and she wrestled with what to do. No one could make this decision for her. In the library, she looked up two points relating to property law. She could find no record of anyone charged with aiding and abetting conspiracy to defraud for paying a bribe. Nor a criminal proceeding brought against an estate agent for accepting a bribe. Estate agents were, however, legally obliged to secure the best prices they could for their clients. They could otherwise be found guilty of breach of contract. She had no idea of the type of deal Steve Robson was cutting with the owner of the house.

On her way back to her room, she passed the clerks' room,

transporting her secret with her. She couldn't believe what she was doing. Nor could she afford to let Derek see her guilt. *What have you done, miss? You've got it written all over your face.*

Six o'clock. She was about to leave when her mobile rang. This time she was ready for it.

'It's Gus.'

She let him do the talking.

'I should never have let you go last night.' He sounded jumpy. 'You're right about me getting into scrapes. It's irresponsible. I know it is.'

'What's her name?'

He hesitated. Only for a moment.

'Juliana.'

She imagined a girl who was small and dark.

'What happened to her?'

'She was deported. They sent her straight back. She's got into the US since. She's in Tucson with her sister.'

'What happened to you?'

'They held on to me.'

She heard footsteps and imagined him rubbing his eyes, pacing the room.

'How long for?'

His footsteps died with his words.

'Can I tell you what happened?'

He sounded vulnerable. It made her feel strong.

'Yes.' She looked out of the window at a sombre sky. Black like the mood she was trying to shift.

'I still don't know why the border patrol decided to search the car. All I know is that I was tuned into a terrible local radio station. When I stopped, Bruce Springsteen was singing "Born in the USA" very loudly. They asked me to turn it down. It didn't get us off to a good start.'

Elinor allowed herself a smile.

'They asked me to get out of the car. They searched the car and found Juliana behind the seats. She was put in a patrol car and taken away. They made me put my hands on the bonnet of the car. They emptied my pockets and found my beeper. We all had them when we were filming. I tried to tell them this but they were convinced I was some sort of professional smuggler paid to bring illegal aliens over the border. It was like a bad film. I had flashlights shone in my eyes. They kept asking again and again who I worked for. No one read me my rights. Then two federal agents turned up. They were even more aggressive than the border patrol. If you tell us what's really going on here, we won't have to break your face, said one of them. He was the one who handcuffed me, said I wasn't co-operating so stamped on my thumb. He pressed my face so hard against the bonnet that I couldn't open my eyes. Eat metal, he said.'

Elinor had lost the sensation in the leg curled beneath her. She swapped legs. His words were flowing faster. A torrent of memory.

'My eyes were pink. You might have seen me rub them. It's habit. The federal agents decided I was stoned. They ripped the car apart looking for my non-existent stash of drugs then drove me into town. I was put in a cell with about thirty men. It was grim. Some of them were smoking crack and ranting. One of them was singing a song about working on a chain gang. For some reason that really got to me. I thought, now I've blown it. I'm going to end up on a chain gang. The police had arrested so many people that night that two extra night courts were set up. I didn't sleep a wink. At seven the next morning I was arraigned. I was lucky. They were entitled to hold me for twenty-four hours.'

'Did you have a lawyer?'

'A public defender. A fat guy called Rocco who wore rattlesnake boots and called me the British bum. I liked him.'

Elinor laughed.

'I hope this is in your film.'

Gus made a rueful sound.

'Connor said the same thing.'

'They gave you bail.'

'Yes. They wanted to take away my passport. Rocco entered a plea bargain and I was given bail. With the provision I didn't leave the country until my court date.'

He paused.

'But I flipped out. I felt like a released hostage. I thought, all that's going to happen at the trial is I'll get a deportation and exclusion order slapped on me so that I can't legally return to the States. I couldn't face it. I wanted to get back to deal with the film and, well, everything. The rest of the crew had already come back. So I drove to LA and caught a plane. It was probably the wrong thing to do.'

Elinor twisted in her chair. The fact was, if he had done the right thing, if he hadn't jumped bail, she would never have met him.

'When's your trial date?'

'The beginning of next month.'

'Soon.'

'Yes,' he said as their conversation petered out and they drank from the silence that swished between them. Gus seemed to be waiting for something, although she didn't know what. Advice? Admonishment? Approval? They had reached a point at which their differences dissolved and everything they knew about each other seemed to converge. Perhaps the reason they had been thrown together was in order to end up here, hanging on the phone.

'I can't see you,' she said quietly.

'I was afraid you were going to say that.'

Everything had shut down. Her emotions, responses, her sense of right and wrong. So much of life was spent waiting for the good things to happen and the bad things to pass. She guessed the secret was to know when you were equidistant from both. Then you could say yes, this is where I want to be. Now you see me completely happy.

'Can I call you? In a couple of days?' he said.

'That would be nice.'

'Thanks for listening. You're a good listener.'

'You tell a good story.'

Left with his words echoing noiselessly around her head, Elinor waited for the physical reaction to his news. She could feel it brewing like distant thunder. At school they had been trained not to cry. Tears were a sign of mental deficiency, it was said. Denial showed strength of character. Resting her head on the desk, Elinor was glad when tears burst from her eyes. They streamed down her nose and soaked her blotter, causing her inky doodles to ooze yellow and green. The tears quenched the part of her that was parched and left her exhausted but also revived.

She sat up. Clicking open her powder compact, she scrutinised her wounded face inch by inch. She mopped her eyes and concealed the redness on her nose and cheeks. Gathering herself slowly, she went quickly downstairs. Derek intercepted her.

'Have you got a minute, Miss Taylor?'

She flinched but didn't protest.

'Of course.'

Derek, sitting by himself, was playing the pen game. This involved balancing his gold pen on his forefinger and middle finger and moving them just enough for the pen to wobble without falling off. It was a test of concentration and showed formidable control.

He motioned to the chair in front of his desk.

'Take a pew.'

Elinor did as she was told.

'When I started in this game' – He caught his pen between pincer fingers – 'big Derek – he was the senior clerk – he said two things to me. He said never call in sick unless you're in your coffin and that last nail's about to go in. He said on no account offer advice to any of your guvnors unless you get a bad smell. Now all I'm saying, Miss Taylor, is I'm here to look out for all of you. That's what I'm paid to do.' He looked at her with dogged eyes. 'Do you follow?'

What right did Derek have to be so instinctive about everything?

'Yes.'

'Good. Mind if I say something else?'

She shook her head.

'You've got lipstick on your teeth.'

She smiled, relieved, and wiped her teeth with a finger.

'Gone?'

'All gone. Enough said?'

She stood up.

'Yes.'

'You take care, now.'

He picked up his pen.

On the Tube home a Japanese boy was taking photographs of himself. Crouching in front of the Underground logo, craning to reach the Tube map and advertisements for sanitary towels and weekends away on Budget Air, he was holding the camera at arm's length and baring his teeth at the flash. Elinor thought it rather sad to have to take pictures of yourself but the Japanese boy was smiling.

Chapter Nineteen

When she was staying with Frida, there had been a morning routine. Elinor would wake first, prompted by the cacophony of cockerels outside her window, go to the kitchen and prepare a pot of tea. Putting the pot on a tray with lemon suns and a jug of milk, she would take it into Frida's bedroom. There she would open Frida's curtains to let in the view of staggered lawns, mysterious trees and lake, and climb up on to Frida's bed. Frida would make a throne of her pillows, shroud her shoulders in one of her bits of Indian fabric, and together they would dissect their dreams. It had been Elinor's favourite part of the day.

Frida's gift to Elinor had been not to treat her as a child. She refused to tell her what to wear, what to eat or when to do her chores. She never once spat on her hanky and wiped her face. Instead she invited Elinor into her world and allowed her to make of it what she would. Dreams, she said, explained life. When it came to their analysis she favoured Freud over Jung. She rejected the notion that universal meanings could be applied to symbols in dreams. Dreams were about wish fulfilment. They were a means of resolving conflicts. That they created conflicts along the way was neither here nor there.

Steve Robson was sitting in Elinor's living room. He had his legs apart and his tie loosened around the neck. He looked more relaxed than she would have liked him to be. She was on her way back into the room when she was struck by the memory of last night's dream. The collision of her subconscious and real life shook her.

She had dreamed that she was dancing with Gus. They had been dancing cheek to cheek, limp with bliss. Gripping her by the hand, he spun her out across the room. When their faces met they kissed. They had kissed with concentration and for some time. Then she opened her eyes. What she discovered left her cold. It wasn't Gus who she was kissing but Steve Robson. She had woken with stomach cramps and a pit of disgust. What had disturbed her more even than the kiss was the possibility that she had been enjoying herself. Freud wasn't getting a look in.

'Ta very much.' Steve Robson took the proffered cup of tea.

He had planted himself at the same end of the sofa that Gus had chosen. Sitting some distance from him, Elinor tried to extricate herself from the physical sensation left by her dream. A hangover caused by sinful pleasures she hadn't chosen to commit.

'Think about it. Your own home after all these years. Too many years, am I right?'

He was talking too much. It occurred to Elinor that he had done this before. Extorted bribes from desperate people. Five thousand pounds was his price.

What would Frida think?

Despite Frida's disregard for the sanctity of marriage, she had never deceived her husband. Uncle Ted knew what was going on because Frida had told him. Frida believed in fair play. Paying bribes wasn't fair. And yet hadn't Frida's primary concern been that Elinor should have a home? When Elinor thought of the house's tangled garden, the afternoon light streaming through the windows, the hidden alcoves and creaking stairs, she was overwhelmed by the sentimentalities of her childhood. A physical yearning to fit herself inside the house.

'There's not a lot to think about.' Steve Robson pushed himself forward. 'I do this for the money. I'm not kinky. Mind if I use the toilet?'

'You know where it is.'

Elinor stood up and skated nervously around the room. They weren't playing a game. What he was asking her to do was to place herself in a compromising position. Was she prepared to be compromised? When she contemplated the alternative, losing the house, she felt desolate, abandoned and on her own again. That she had been offered this house was an act of fate. She couldn't surrender it now.

Steve Robson sauntered back into the room, his hands bulging in his pockets, his cheeks ruddy as though with a post-gym glow. He looked smug, thought Elinor, because he knew it was only a matter of time before she gave him what he wanted. He didn't bother sitting down.

'I'll get you the money by the end of the week,' she said.

The decision came from somewhere murky, deep within. Somewhere she wouldn't seek to go again. She wasn't a rash person and yet this was a rash decision she was choosing, deliberately, to make.

'Good girl.' He clapped his hands. 'That's what I like to hear. You're about to become a homeowner. Tell me that feels good.'

Dizzy with the effort of keeping her head, Elinor issued a smile.

'Of course,' she said.

As soon as he had gone, she vacuumed the room. She did the corners, underneath the sofa and behind the curtains. The tang of his aftershave clung to the furniture and festered in the air. She couldn't get rid of it. Running a bath, she cleaned her face. She couldn't find her moisturiser. The glass jar had been on the shelf this morning and now it was gone. Only one other person had been in the bathroom besides herself and that person was Steve Robson.

Submerging herself in hot water, she felt a wave of suspicion roll over her. She was gripped by a vast irrationality.

What would he want with a pot of Elizabeth Arden Visible Difference moisturiser? It made no sense. Its sudden disappearance made even less sense. She tried to recall having taken it with her in her make-up bag and accidentally left it somewhere. She couldn't. All that was left to her was the possibility that her estate agent was a kleptomaniac. She didn't want to think about it.

Propping her arm over the edge of the bath, elbow locked, wrist loose, she thought of Gus. Through the steam came his hand. It circled her wrist before journeying down her arm to the crook between her neck and shoulder. He had left two messages. She was luxuriating in the knowledge that he wanted her. Arching her back, her muscles throbbed.

In a towel, she checked her messages. Someone had rung while Steve Robson had been with her. She was assailed by another burst of machinegun coughing. It made her heart pound. It didn't sound accidental. It sounded rehearsed and intimate. A patter of menace. When she listened carefully, she thought she could hear the whispering of her name. Dialling 1471, she was told that the caller had withheld his number. Whoever was trying to spook her had begun to succeed.

At 4.15 on Friday afternoon, after a day spent looking at the telephone, Elinor rang her bank.

'The money's being transferred into a personal account, not a business account, is that right?' said the girl at the other end, double-checking.

'Yes.'

'This, then, is to confirm the transfer of five thousand pounds from your account, to register as debited from your account by the end of the working day.'

'Thank you.'

Elinor absorbed the finality of the click as the girl hung up. The decision had been made. The transaction completed. At once sure of her decision, providing for her future, Elinor felt removed from herself and her motivations. It was impossible to ignore the shadows of doubt that flickered at the margins of her mind.

She focused her dissipated energies by studying the brief at hand. It was the neighbourly dispute gone wrong. Another harassment case. Trying to generate some interest, she reread her guide to the Protection from Harassment Act. *A person must not pursue a course of conduct – (a) which amounts to harassment of another, and (b) which he knows or ought to know amounts to harassment of another.*

Reading her client's statement, she found herself faced with yet another misguided, angry man. His neighbours wanted a restraining order placed on him to prohibit him from harassing them. He had threatened them with a screwdriver. Bumped their car. Had tried to kill the cat. The feud had started with their cutting down of an adjoining tree. A dying sycamore. Sometimes it was hard to care.

There was a knock.

'Hello.'

'Sorry, miss.'

Norm's baby face appeared around the door.

'I was on my way up to give something to Mr Laslow. This came for you.'

He had a large package in one hand, a small package in the other. Entering her room, he handed her the small one. It had been hand delivered.

'Did you see who brought it?'

Instinctively she sensed that the news wasn't good.

'Yeah. Same chap as brought the flowers. Big bloke. Didn't leave a message.'

Norm's words had the effect of shutting off her air. Elinor was suffocating, a pillow being gently but firmly pushed down on her face. She stared at the package as though it were a bomb. Norm hovered, sensing her consternation.

'Thank you,' she said.

Tearing at the staples, she ripped her nails and lacerated her skin. She smeared the envelope with tracks of blood. She didn't look inside but held the envelope upside down and poured the contents on to her desk. Out fell one unmarked tape.

It floated up to her and she thought she might faint. Steve Robson had joined her in the room. A thin smile creased his thin lips and she saw the glint of cunning in his eyes. The idea that she had been turned on by music sent by him, not Gus, made a mockery of everything. She felt unwell.

Tossing the tape in the bin, she screwed up balls of paper and hurled them on top. She wanted the tape destroyed and to be left with no memories at all. The tape wouldn't go away. Getting up, she picked up the bin and deposited it outside on the landing. Slamming the door, she went to the window.

Her neck muscles were as taut as string. She kneaded them, dispersing the pain, as she peered outside. The gables on the front of the building obscured her view, but she knew what she was looking for. A shiny blot of red. There was no sign of it. Slumped at her desk, she drew her curls across her face, hiding herself. Hating herself. Lapsing into lethargy, there was only one thing to do. She picked up the phone.

'Hello?'

'It's Elinor.'

Her words came out at a gallop.

'Hang on, love.'

Elinor waited.

Gus came on the line. 'Hey you.' With two words he saved her.

'Did you send me a tape?'

She knew he hadn't but it was a question she had to ask.

'What tape?'

Why she had never asked this question before she didn't know.

'Can I see you?'

'What does this have to do with a tape? I'm curious.'

Hitting her desk light on and off, Elinor remembered being in the bath, watching Gus toy with the string.

'I think there's been a mix-up.'

Her voice was tight. Gus laughed.

'Someone sent you a tape and you thought it was from me? Is it rude?'

'No.'

'Do you know who sent it to you?'

'No.'

She held her breath.

'What are you doing tomorrow?' she asked.

'Seeing you.'

She felt light headed.

'Gus?' she said.

'Yes?' he said.

'Nothing.'

She died so she could come alive. He was the man she thought he was.

Kendra had a hotel on the corner of her street. Elinor went to meet her in the bar. It was blue. The walls were midnight, the carpet mid-Atlantic. Ming vases sat on shelves beneath fans of light. The corners of the room were wreathed in silvery smoke. Men in tight suits were busy lighting cigarettes for women who looked as though they came here too often. Leathery faces and straw basket hair. Thank you my darling, they spoke in champagne murmurs.

'Cocktails?' said Kendra.

Elinor picked an almond out of a silver bowl.

'That would be nice.'

Kendra squinted at the list.

'I agree it's strange to be sent tapes by your estate agent. You don't think you're overreacting?'

Elinor had announced that she would be spending the night in Kendra's guest room.

'No.'

'You think this crush is serious?'

'Yes.' She faltered, ashamed to give Kendra the real reason why she couldn't go home tonight. That the man who had sent her these ambitious love tapes, and who she feared would ring her buzzer or knock on her door, had procured five thousand pounds from her. She had bound herself to him. Kendra would be more appalled by her gullibility than anything else.

Kendra ordered Bloody Marys from the Brazilian waiter.

'They're good here. They really taste bloody. So what's on these tapes?'

'Just music.'

'What did you do? I mean, to the music?'

Elinor thought of reliving Gus's soft kisses. The eroticism of his absence in the wake of his love.

'Nothing rude.'

'I wonder what he thinks you did to the music.'

Remembering her underwear spread across the bed, Steve Robson's kind shoulder as she leant against him in the bar, her dream, Elinor saw a slowly developing picture beginning to emerge. She didn't like what she could see.

'What do you mean?'

'What I mean is he has fantasies about you. Obviously.'

Elinor choked on a nut.

They continued their evening at Kendra's flat where they made scrambled eggs. Wet and milky was how both preferred them. They ate them on toast at the table and watched the Late Night news on TV. They were bombing Baghdad again.

'What does this solve?' said Elinor, provoked by scenes of devastation exploding across the screen.

Kendra was bashing the pepper mill to make it work.

'Who said anything about a peaceful solution?' She showered her plate with black rain. 'Orlando would only ever eat eggs fried in butter. Rich and oily.'

'Eggs Florentine was QC's favourite. Rich and gluttonous.' Elinor kept her eyes trained on the murderous sky.

'Eggs Benedict.'

Elinor looked up.

'Isn't it?' Kendra backtracked.

Elinor had always got the two confused. How Kendra should know this she didn't know. She let it slide.

'What about a man who makes scrambled eggs?' she asked.

'He can cook. He likes to nurture, therefore he's kind.' Kendra handed over the pepper mill.

'If only life were so simple,' mused Elinor.

Chapter Twenty

Elinor slept badly. She woke early, scribbled a note to Kendra, *Thanks for eggs & bed & agt,* (all good things, one of their catch-phrases), and crossed town by Tube. The only other person in the train compartment was a man built like a prize fighter. He was fidgeting and twitching and muttering to himself. You've got to win. You've got to win. It was coach talk to a champ. Alarmed, Elinor considered changing carriages. Yet wouldn't that be committing the obvious mistake of making her feelings plain? What if he followed her? Instead she remained seated and studied the strip of advertisements above his head. He stood up. A giant swinging from a handrail. For a moment, Elinor feared the worst. Then the train stopped and he turned to go. Postered on his back was the self-penned message, *I AM SUGAR RAY LEONARD.* She admired his logic.

At home she found three messages. All from Steve

Robson. His voice enveloped her like a sinister secret, reminding her that she had to speak to him. She couldn't. Not now. She showered and scrubbed her skin. She believed in the authority of flannels. She shaved her legs and conditioned her hair, working fast. Propelled by a sense of urgency, she was terrified that Steve Robson would appear at her door. She was equally apprehensive about seeing Gus. Given the opportunity to prepare, she dressed in new underwear, a skirt and leather boots, her black riding boots, and a tight-fitting jacket. Unable to find her perfume, she left in a hurry.

On her bike, she hitched up her skirt. One day it would be spring. It was February, she had forgotten gloves and her fingers lost all sensation. She barely noticed. She turned into her street and was greeted by the brightly painted houses. The brilliant flashes of emerald, lemon and orange captured her mood. A streak of children descended on scooters. A woman was digging a garden with the radio on. *Last night's bombing campaign pronounced an unqualified success.*

Elinor spied a figure ahead. He was slouched against the front wall, buried in a newspaper, smoking a cigarette. It occurred to Elinor not to stop but to cycle on and prevent their worlds from colliding again. She would never survive the might-have-beens beyond.

'You're early,' she said.

Tucking his newspaper beneath his arm, Gus caught her handlebars with tight fists. Fingers overlapped. Her front tyre jammed between his knees and she quivered to a halt. The fine lines around his mouth fanned. There were spots of colour on his cheeks. His eyes were enquiring and yet for a moment his presence seemed unreal. Then came the slow warmth that told her it was him.

'Have you got a key?'

'We're breaking in.'

His face opened into a laugh.

'You take full responsibility?'

'I do.' She wrenched her wheel free from his knees. Following her up the garden path, he watched her prop her bicycle against his. She went first through the gate at the side of the house.

'I had no idea you were so intrepid.' He stepped into the holes left by her footprints as she edged a passage through nettles and briars. 'Is there anything you're afraid of?'

The question unnerved her. She continued walking.

'Pigeons,' she said without looking round. Loneliness was what she didn't say. Not knowing whether I'd see you again was what she didn't say.

'Why's that?'

'When I was about six I was woken up by a pigeon that had flown into my room. It was flapping around my head and seemed enormous. I was terrified. I haven't liked them since.'

Elinor had never told anyone this story before. The memory had lain buried, redundant, until now. They reached the back door.

'What about you?'

In the pale morning light his bones were as finely sculpted as stone. His face, framed by guttering hanging from the roof, was so handsome.

'Drowning.'

His scratchy grudge against the world. She squeezed his hand, jerked the handle. The door yawned. They were in.

'Better not,' she murmured.

Gus had hit the light. He switched it off again. They proceeded through the kitchen, which was sticky underfoot. Two oblongs of light illuminated the hallway, the panel of stained glass above the door scattering bright jewels across the floor. Gus's face glittered red and green as they passed through. Ushering him into the living room, then the dining room, she waited for his reactions. She watched him nod his head. She read his lips. *Fine horse.* He pointed to her picture on the wall. He was saying all the right things.

Clasping his wrist, she led him upstairs. Her arm felt long and slender. The weight of his wrist was her anchor. Without him she would float away. Everything she wanted she had with her now. They toured the small room with the view of the back. He pointed to the shed and gave it two thumbs-up. They stepped briefly into the middle room before landing in the big room at the front. My room, she said, delivering him into a box of dusty sunshine.

Gus leaned against the wall, eyes closed.

'It has a nice feeling,' he said.

She liked him there. Flitting past, she came so close that their clothes brushed. The floorboards had a range of moans, some high, some low. She played them like a xylophone, treading backwards and forwards. Gus was whistling something. Without warning he shot out an arm, handcuffed her wrist and yanked her in. Their feet sandwiched, hips aching, he circled her waist and they began to dance.

'What's on this tape?'

She opened her eyes.

'Just music.'

They took small steps. Claiming a corner.

'If you'd sent me a tape, what would be on it?' she said.

'Marvin Gaye.'

'Marvin Gaye is on the tape.'

'So your man has good taste.'

That stung. She stopped dancing. He stamped on her foot.

'He's not my man.'

'Who is he?'

She detected an undercurrent of jealousy. It warmed her, unexpectedly. She closed the gap between their faces.

'Someone I'd rather not know.'

Taking her hands, Gus flip-flopped so that she was pinned against the wall. She was strong but not as strong as him. They kissed, flip-flopped some more, and this time he was up against the wall. Spinning her out across the room, he made her fly. She screamed. Fingers slipped. She lost his grip and for a panicky moment was on her own before returning to the fierce loop of his arm. They danced some more to their own special rhythms. She couldn't tell where her body ended and his began.

'Having fun?'

The voice that barged into the room smashed their perfect world apart. The face that came into focus was hard and emergent. Elinor's legs threatened to give way. She hadn't heard Steve Robson come up the stairs. She didn't know how long he had been in the house or what he might have overheard.

'Steve.'

'Elinor.' He used her name against her. 'I don't remember telling you that the bit of money you paid over qualified you to show your special friend here a good time.'

He scared her. Dressed in his trademark suit and polished shoes, with every detail attended to, he was the hired enforcer. Dropping his aitches, roughening his accent. He was angry with her. Elinor wiped hair from her eyes and mouth and tried to think of what to say. She felt as though she had deceived him, personally, by being here with another man. She thought of the tapes, their covert intimacies, and felt wobbly.

'The back door was open,' she blurted, hopelessly.

'It was my idea to come in.'

Elinor stared at Gus in surprise. His mouth was smeared with her lipstick, as was his chin.

'I'm Gus. We've met before.' He offered his hand. Steve Robson's arms remained stiffly by his side. He wasn't interested in Gus's male chumminess.

'I don't recall.'

Gus returned his hands to his pockets.

'I live next door to the market. Frank introduced us. He was telling me which horse to put my money on – it was the Grand National. You stopped to say hello. You were down there looking at a property by the river.'

Impressed by Gus's handling of the situation, Elinor

hoped it might dilute the tension in the room. It didn't. The atmosphere was stifling. Steve Robson's nostrils flared and she sensed a mood change that was swift and unpleasant. He had an animal stillness. What he had beneath, she was reminded, was a capacity for violence. He spun the coins in his pocket with one hand. He bounced the keys to his car in the other.

'I don't recall.' He repeated his denial and she knew he was lying. His brazenness shocked her. That Gus thought the same was apparent in his strained jaw. She had never seen him look offended.

'I approve.' Gus nodded his head. 'Of the house. Elinor's going to be happy here.'

'She hasn't got the keys,' said Steve Robson coolly.

Elinor tried to hold her tongue. She couldn't.

'When am I going to get them?'

'I think that's a conversation for you and me to have. Don't you?'

'Let's go.' Gus took her arm. The sun had gone in and the room was chilly. 'I've seen enough.'

Steve Robson dangled his keys from a finger. Even his fingers were brawny.

'I came to lock up,' he said, which led Elinor to think he must have known the door was open. She didn't ask why.

They followed him down the stairs in silence. Gus was unhappy about being forcibly ejected from the house. Elinor couldn't watch his unhappiness without participating in it. Locked out, they proceeded to the front garden where she and Gus stopped while Steve Robson took the path in burly strides, shoving aside the front gate. The mood he left behind was spiky and malevolent.

'Is there a time on Monday that's good for you?' Elinor called after him.

He didn't look round.

'Morning? Afternoon?'

He zapped his key-ring and made his car go bleep.

'I'll be in touch.'

He made it sound like a threat. He left them without saying goodbye, his car a swoosh of red.

'What a fucking psycho,' exploded Gus as soon as he could. His male pride, everything he had suppressed, surging forth.

It had begun to rain. They had taken shelter in the porch at the front of the house. Elinor was standing with her arms across her chest. Gus was staring out at the dreary distance.

'He knows who I am. I've never liked him. And why does he smell like a girl?'

'You've met before, then?' said Elinor feebly.

'He used to hang around the market trying to get his hand on the properties down there. All the buildings are in trust. They're not for sale. He even had the balls to ask if I was interested in selling my place.'

Elinor felt miserable. It had all gone wrong. All she had wanted was to buy a house. Steve Robson's emotional thuggery distressed her. Afraid that he thought she had been leading him on in some way, she felt trapped by the inclement weather, their secret, the fury emanating from Gus.

'Of all the estate agents in this city. What made you choose him?'

Gus had turned to face her. In his eyes she had clearly done wrong.

'I didn't choose him personally,' she defended herself, unhappily. 'He answered the telephone at the office I happened to ring.'

Gus's frown deepened.

'I thought you met him in court. Wasn't he a witness?'

Elinor had forgotten she had told him this. His memory for detail threw her. The rain was splashing into the porch and on to her face and she took a step back. She didn't want to be having this conversation. She wanted it to be over so that they could be somewhere else with the memory of now banished for ever. She wanted to touch him but their physical harmony had gone. Steve Robson had seen to that.

'You're right,' she said. 'He was.'

'Then he became your estate agent?'

'Yes.'

'No connection with Frank's case?'

'No.'

She began to feel guilty, as well as upset.

'Listen. Why don't we go and have tea?' she said, just as the light was sucked from the sky and a blanket of rain sealed them in. A faint wind rocked the trees. A torrent of water sluiced off the roof and flooded the cracked red tiles leading up to the house. Gus had raindrops in his hair. A damp lock curled across his brow. She could see him thinking. He stirred restlessly.

'I'm confused. Explain to me where exactly you are vis-à-vis buying this house.'

Her heart began to hammer.

'What do you mean?'

'What have you paid him for if you haven't paid for the house?'

'I had to pay him a hundred pounds to put in my offer.'

The water on the path had become level with the step. Any moment now it would wash over the top.

'I thought you paid him that last week.'

Elinor had a scab on her coccyx. A carpet burn that until now she had been proud of. Now it was just a graze. Lining her spine against the wall, she let the rough brick chafe the injured skin.

'Do we have to talk about this?' she begged, as a presentiment of what would follow formed a fist in her gut.

'You've paid him, haven't you?' said Gus, dully, rain reflected in his eyes. 'A fee or something. To get this house for you?'

She couldn't speak.

'Unbelievable.'

Gus said this with such heartfelt disappointment he might as well have said, You've slept with him, haven't you? She draped a hand on his reluctant shoulder. He didn't respond. She let it slump by her side.

'Sorry.'

She felt his silence drum into her. She knew what he felt about bribes. She had seen him contesting the policeman's demands on film. She failed to see how the two were connected.

'You're a lawyer. You're supposed to know better,' he now accused her, as though it were his job to stake out the moral high ground and teach her right from wrong.

Elinor resented it. She didn't need a lesson in moral conduct to feel ashamed. She had always been a model of professional rectitude and personal discipline, boringly so, until now. This had been her one act of reckless, selfish behaviour. She wanted Gus to absolve her of blame.

'I didn't have a choice.'

'Of course you had a choice,' he countered, his body bristling. 'What makes you think you can trust him?'

His mood upset her.

'Why are you so angry with me?'

A flash of lightning torched the distance and the bad-tempered sky gate-crashed their argument. He surveyed the dripping landscape.

'I broke the law because of a bribe. A deal was made. The other end wasn't honoured.'

He sounded tired.

'Juliana?'

'Yes.'

Elinor felt shuddery. She didn't know whether she wanted to hear the next instalment of his wretched story.

'Her brother went missing. A few days later some men came to see her. They told her Cesar owed them fifty thousand dollars. Cesar was a driver, he was our driver, that's how I met him. She found out he'd been courieuring narcotics.'

Another clap of thunder shook the horizon and Elinor thought of the bombs over Baghdad.

'They said if she paid five thousand dollars, they'd forget the rest. She paid but the next day the men came back and demanded the rest anyway. They control the police, the politicians. You can't touch them. They said she was hiding her brother. If she didn't reveal where he was, they'd kill her. I drove her that night because she feared for her life and . . .' His voice cracked. 'Well, because . . .'

'You were sleeping with her.'

Elinor finished his story. If it wasn't the ending he had elected to tell, it was the truth. She read it in his eyes. She saw him behind the wheel of a car, hot night blowing past the windows, tyres spinning fast as he played the radio, with the girl tucked behind the seats.

Squeezing out from behind him, Elinor slithered down the path. The weather had broken. The rain had eased. The world was a new place and she was free to go. Inhaling the wet pavements, she was blown by the fast-moving clouds as she focused on the glimmer of sunshine like a glimmer of hope. The handlebars of their bicycles had intertwined. She yanked hers, sending his crashing to the ground.

Resentment smacked her hard. How dare he be self-righteous? He was angry with her because she was making the same mistake as who? His other lover. She was the one who had been betrayed. The emotional torment he had made her suffer was an unbearable weight that she had done her best to wear lightly. Until now. It all ended here. *Love always, J.* Pushing her bicycle, she walked away.

'Where are you going?'

She stopped and turned.

'Screw you.'

'What do you mean?'

'She's your holiday romance, isn't she?'

'Well, yes,' he said. His hands all over the place. 'It has nothing to do with you.'

'You've done wrong as well, you know.'

'I know,' he said. 'I know.' His voice grew louder but she didn't want to hear it. Numb with despair, she left him talking to thin air.

Chapter Twenty-one

I don't know anything any more. This was all she knew. Her mind was a sea of remembered glances, fragments of events, looping dialogue. The radio was no longer her friend. She couldn't find the music to suit her mood. All of it left her with a demented sense of loss. She fared no better with news or discussion programmes. 'The pessimism of the human condition' were the first words to greet her when she flicked it on. 'Dead babies found in an incinerator.' She tried again. It was enough to send her over the edge. She was hanging on by her fingertips. It wouldn't take much.

Trapped in a tailspin of uncertainty, she didn't know where to turn. Kendra had left town for the weekend. The actress was shooting a film in the desert. I'll be away until March thirty-first, was the message on her answering machine. If you need to reach me urgently, try the cell. Elinor had attempted to write down the scramble of numbers four times, yet each time she called she got a man's voice. Hi this is Hugh, you know what to do. Well, she didn't.

Late last night she had received another anonymous text message. *Your smell keeps me up at night.* Smell. Perfume. Steve Robson. The connection was chilling. It was also inevitable. Had she been living with this knowledge for longer than she would care to admit? Probably. Denial? She preferred to see it as desperately adhering to a belief in her judgment.

She prided herself on her judgment, her ability not only to tell but to choose right from wrong. No one said lawyers should be honest. Quite the contrary. Their job was to hide the truth in order to accommodate what was best for them. They were selfish. So was she in the courtroom. In civilian life, however, she was straight with the truth. Even Kendra fiddled her expenses. Elinor had refused to succumb to the slippery slope. Probity was the foundation for everything. Otherwise there was only darkness. Then she met Steve Robson. She had made a terrible mistake.

Kendra had received anonymous text messages for months. They all said the same thing. *I didn't even get to come.* When finally she traced them, she had found herself with the telephone number of a judge who she had dined with once or twice. *Bad luck, My Lord,* she texted back. The messages stopped.

Elinor's predicament was different. This she had instigated herself. Her belief, naïve as it might seem, was that she had been taking control of her life. For so long she had allowed others to dictate to her. She had chosen law because her form mistress had advised it. You've got the stamina, she said. What she meant was balls. She had entered into an affair with QC because he chose her. You're a fox, he said. Then she had decided to choose for herself. She chose Gus. She chose the house and with it Steve Robson. Bad choices? She was beginning to think so.

She was on a horse. If there was one thing she knew how to do, and do well, it was fly along the surface of the world in a saddle. Sunday morning. The rest of the world was in bed and the park was hers. She was on a gelding. Silent Night was his name. Slipping her hands beneath his mane, she listened to the whinnying of little girls on ponies in the paddock near by. The riding class had begun. They were learning how to canter.

'Use your knees. Use your bottoms,' sang a woman Elinor couldn't see.

Elinor was using everything she had. Cold air slammed into her face and made her pant. Mist trailed the roots of the trees so that they appeared to be floating a foot off the ground. Her horse was eager and alert. They had clip-clopped out of the stables, across the bark chips, over the slushy leaves and through the glade of ancient oaks. Here on open ground Elinor had hoped that everything would become clear.

'Go, boy,' she coaxed, dipping her head to his ears.

The horse snorted. They took off. He needed no persuading. The urge to gallop was a mutual one. Elinor rode hard. Whatever innocence she imagined herself still to possess had deserted her over the past few days. Harnessing the strength of the horse, she wondered why she had left it so long. She hadn't ridden for over a year. The beat of the hoofs on the ground, a hollow sound because the ground was wet, was a pulse of life. She was most herself on a horse. She understood horses better than she did men. The pleasure she felt transcended fear, wiped out memory, love, lust and desperate longing. There was no room for self-loathing. Riding left her strong. It was a beautiful day.

'Good boy.' She slowed to a trot, smoothing his neck.

Her horse had broken into a sweat. Steam puffed from his body. Her jodhpurs stuck to his belly and a burst of feathery breath floated before her eyes. Then she saw a car. Beyond the trees was a carpark. Strips of metallic colours interlaced the trunks. Coasting behind was a gleam of red. It was as unmissable as it was unmistakable. Thrown off balance, Elinor's rapture died. A panicky tingling muffled her head.

Pressing her knees gently into her horse's belly, she rocked forward in the saddle. The horse picked up his hoofs. She tensed her thighs and tore across the hoary earth. Her control of the horse, the height he provided, empowered her. Impulsively, she tugged the reins and steered her horse towards the trees. The car was her conscience. A bitter reminder of everything she had done wrong. She had to confront what she had seen. Something was developing behind his silence from which she couldn't flee.

In the carpark, Elinor found a gaggle of mothers with dogs straining on leads, waiting for their children to finish their class. Snatches of conversations reached Elinor's ears. Talk of fat ponies, Daphne's done it now, bloody nanny's got anorexia. She took in the parked cars. One of them was red. It was not a BMW. She frightened herself. More alarming than having her fears confirmed was the possibility that her mind was playing games with her, and that she had become possessed by paranoia. Frosty air razored her lips. The sky swooped low and left her shivering beneath her hard hat.

'Who's a beautiful boy?' cooed a metallic-haired mother, wandering over to stroke Silent Night's nose. 'Is yours in the ten o'clock?'

'No,' said Elinor.

It then occurred to her to ask.

'Was another car parked here until just a moment ago?'

The woman was gurgling at the horse.

'Sorry?'

'I was wondering if you'd noticed another car in the carpark. Red. A BMW.'

Elinor saw her answer in the woman's eyes. They fluttered like tiny birds.

'I thought it was a Mercedes. It drove in and straight out again. But yes. Definitely red.'

The totality of shock was nothing in comparison with the shudder of helplessness that came next. Nothing, not even her elevation on the horse, could protect her now. Steve Robson was stalking her. The reality had surfaced. She felt scared.

* * *

Elinor lay on her bed in the dark.

'Something's happened. Something bad.'

She had tracked the actress down to a motel on the outskirts of Las Vegas.

'It's a casino caper set in Sin City. I play a tart,' said the actress, describing her new film. 'Such a bloody cliché. At least I'm learning how to handle a gun.'

Elinor was jealous. She wished she were far away shooting at targets to earn her living.

'I've done something stupid.'

Sometimes it was easier to confess over the telephone.

'What have you ever done that was that bad?'

Elinor was tempted to take courage from this remark.

'I paid the estate agent five thousand pounds. A sort of fee to get me the house. Now I think he's stalking me.' She strung the words together, wishing they applied to someone else.

The actress fell silent.

'What?'

'I know.'

'It's so unlike you. What do you mean he's stalking you?'

'I keep seeing his car everywhere. I've been getting strange messages. Flowers. He's always turning up at the flat.'

'Are you sure you're not being paranoid? You know what men are like. QC used to come round in the middle of the night. I remember him throwing stones at the window. He certainly sent a lot of flowers.'

'That was different.'

The buzzer went. She lapsed into a whisper.

'It's the buzzer.'

'I'm not here.'

'You think it's him?'

The actress was whispering too.

'Yes.'

Then she heard her name. Her body, already stiff from the ride, became rigid. Concrete arms and legs.

'He's shouting.'

'Call the police.'

'And say what?'

'That someone's trying to break into your house.'

In the pause that followed, Elinor realised that that was what was happening. He was climbing up the scaffolding. Her chest went tight as the oxygen was sucked from the room. Darkness and emptiness swirled around her. Instinctively she rolled off the bed on to the floor, hugging the telephone to her chest like a weapon.

'I'm on the floor.'

'Jesus,' exclaimed the actress. 'Christ Almighty.'

'Don't.'

The actress's throaty gasps were making it worse. With her face pressed into the carpet, Elinor inhaled crumbs and mud and the staleness of unwashed years. She knew what she was waiting for. For the clank of metal and the sound of scuffling as he hoisted himself up. Then it happened. First a chime, then a grunt.

'He's coming up.'

'You're joking. You've got to get out of there.'

Elinor couldn't move.

'Elinor!' the actress shouted from five thousand miles away. 'Can you hear me?'

'Yes.'

'Find your mobile. Call the police. Talk to me. What's happening?'

He was getting closer. Elinor heard groans as he heaved himself up with his arms. The planks rattled as he pulled himself on to the platform level with her window. A shadow blotted the margin between curtain and window frame. He was out there.

'He's there.' Her mouth was dry like dust.

'Where?'

A sneeze erupted outside the curtains, then another sneeze. 'Sorry,' said a snuffly voice. All at once Elinor was engulfed by what felt like the brightness of day. Jumping to her feet, she dashed to the window and tore back the curtains. There, shirt-tail flapping, perspiring profusely, was Nigel, looking sheepish and blowing his nose. Torn between pity and rage, she banged her fist on the glass.

'What are you doing?'

Unbolting the lock, she threw up the sash.

'Are you trying to give me a heart attack?'

'Sorry.' Nigel clambered in. 'Lost my keys. I rang your bell. Didn't you hear me shouting?'

Words failed her.

'I thought you must be asleep.'

Elinor remembered the actress. The telephone was lying on the floor and the actress was bleating her name hysterically. *Elinor! Elinor!* Elinor picked up.

'It's only Nigel.'

'Don't do that to me,' the actress exploded. 'I thought you'd been murdered or something.'

'Don't say that. It's not funny.' The bulk of her anxiety hadn't gone away.

'I wasn't trying to be funny.'

Crunchy silence came between them.

'Sorry,' said the actress. 'I was worried. Are you going to be all right? I've got to finish learning these lines. I've got a voice session.'

'Go,' said Elinor. 'I'll be fine.'

'Let's talk tomorrow.'

They hung up.

In the kitchen she poured whisky and tried to unwind while Nigel rolled a cigarette. He had been to a gig. His clothes stank of beer and other people's sweat.

'You know the couple who have moved in downstairs?' He slurped his drink.

'Yes.'

The couple had been in the building for about a month. She was sullen and Hungarian. He was passively flirtatious. Elinor had probably said ten words to both of them.

'Drug dealers.'

Elinor let her head slump to her chest and laughed deliriously.

'What?'

'We're under surveillance.'

Elinor needed no further explanation to know what Nigel was referring to. Her knot of panic returned.

'Bit of a laugh, really.' Nigel remained oblivious to her rapidly deteriorating mood. 'We might find ourselves being roped in. I don't know. Told to prepare for a dawn raid or something.'

'Is it red?'

Carefully picking a thread of tobacco off his tongue, Nigel flicked it away.

'That's the thing. He's hardly blending in with the background, staking out the house in a car that's red, is he?'

Elinor felt whisky scorch her throat. Blurring her head.

'Was the car there now? When you came in?'

'I waved.' Nigel looked triumphant 'Why should I pretend he's not there? I'd rather have drug dealers living downstairs than an overpaid policeman in a car outside my home.'

Elinor drank to forget.

If only his version of events were true.

It was past midnight when Nigel left. The whisky bottle was empty and he had started on the rum. He had begun telling her stories that she had heard before. How he met his ex-fiancée at the recycling bins. She was doing greens, he was smashing browns.

'Nigel,' she interrupted him.

'Sorry.' He staggered to his feet and trudged upstairs. ''Night.'

Locking the door with the chain, Elinor scrambled into bed with her clothes on. The heating had gone off. It was deathly cold. Something told her that Steve Robson was still outside. The windows looked different with the knowledge he was out there but she didn't dare draw the curtains to investigate. She felt cruelly awake. Speared with intense, jabbing pains, she made a list of her mistakes. She had paid a bribe. Her actions had assumed a criminal irresponsibility. She had fallen in love with a man who had another lover for whom he was prepared to risk his life. She had told him not to call. He hadn't.

The street was quiet. Alone with the racket in her head, an onslaught of recriminations, accusations and guilt, she heard a bleep slice through the silence. It was a car alarm. Steve Robson had got out of his car and was approaching the house. Elinor heard footsteps crossing the street. She looked at her watch. Three a.m. Her buzzer went. She slid under the covers so fast it was as though someone at the other end had yanked her by her feet. Knocking over her whisky glass, she wet the bed. She hid her face beneath her hands, her breath like vomit.

'Elinor,' he yelled up at her window. 'Elinor,' he called again.

Afraid to move, Elinor imagined the black hole beneath the covers to be an extension of the fear inside her head. Only the advent of morning could deliver her from her demons. The footsteps retreated. Bleep. The engine murmured and Steve Robson left her robbed of peace. Locating a pill in her bedside drawer, she swallowed it with the dregs of her whisky and pressed her face into her pillow. *It is a burden to prove* were the last words to fade away.

Chapter Twenty-two

When eventually she stirred, she was met with a cotton-wool brain and someone else's body. Whisky and Temazepam crawled through her veins. The mattress smelt like a bar. She didn't know what time it was or how long she had been asleep. Buried alive, she couldn't think of a single reason to get up. There was a rap on the door.

'It's only Nigel.'

Depositing a foot on the floor, she prayed it wouldn't give way. Yesterday's clothes flopped like sacking as she shuffled to the door, rubbing her eyes. She undid the chain and opened the door. Nigel, in a white galabiyya and curly-toed slippers, was holding a pile of her post. She took it.

'I rang the police.'

Sirens and helmets and shiny black shoes barged into her head and made her feel weak.

'To ask them how long that man's going to be sitting outside our building.'

Elinor hung on to the door for support.

Brimming with pride, Nigel tapped his toe.

'They don't know anything about it. If he's here tonight I'm ringing the station. They promised to send someone over.'

Nigel loved a crisis. Broken boiler, faulty electrics, terse discussions with the landlord over the issue of the scaffolding, or trying to convince him not to sell. Nigel's discussions rarely led to resolution but this didn't put him off. The possibility of a prowler had visibly revved him up.

'You look terrible. Are you all right?'

'I'm going back to bed,' she said.

Closing the door, she reapplied the chain and rushed back to the safe place underneath the covers. She took her phone with her. The green eye blinked. She had a text message. *I'm on my way.* Curling into a foetal position, she was terrified of the prospect of a plan behind Steve Robson's actions. She felt afraid of his mind. Imagining police officers camped in her living room, she sank into a muddled sleep.

The buzzer went. Panic sloshed through her. Slushy light oozed through the window and her stomach rumbled. She couldn't remember when or what her last meal had been. Minutes later there were knuckles on her door.

'It's me.'

Draping the covers around her, she dragged them down

the hall. A sweater had been added to her mussed assortment of clothes. Her socks had slipped down her feet and flapped against the floor like flippers. Her hair was tangled with sleep. She couldn't stop shivering. She unbolted the locks.

'Nigel. If it's about . . .'

Overcome by joy – or was it rage? – she hugged her blanket closer.

'I brought eggs.'

It was Gus. He had a finger of oil down his cheek and wind in his hair. She saw her distress in his eyes.

'I sent a message.'

The text message. The infinite bits into which she had splintered began to mend.

'Are you all right?'

She shook her head.

'I didn't mean to upset you.'

Turning round, she retreated into the flat. She heard him hesitate before slamming the door and following her in. She flopped into bed. She couldn't see him but sensed him lingering by the door. Lifting a flap of duvet, his invitation, she made room for him to roll in so that there were two of them and she was no longer alone. They lay apart.

'I'm good at fucking things up.'

She turned to face him. Nose to nose.

'Is that what you've come to tell me?' She was tired of this game. 'Because I know that already.'

He shifted position. The mattress squeaked.

'If I'd told you the truth, would you have wanted to see me?'

'I can't answer that.'

A car rumbled to a halt outside the house. Unable to hide her fright, she shook so violently that her teeth rattled. Gus came to find her with outstretched arms and she buried her fears in his chest. Apprehensive of further revelations, more turmoil, her voice was thin.

'What else do I need to know?' she said.

'We had a fling.'

'Is that what this is?'

'No.'

She released a portion of her dread.

'It was the end of filming. We were all burnt out.'

'Were you in love with her?'

Tossed air came from his mouth. Jagged emotion.

'No.'

'Was she in love with you?'

'I don't know.' The question made him uncomfortable. 'Possibly.'

She waited. His jaw muscle quivered.

'Which is why I had to drive her. Guilt I suppose.'

Elinor studied his eyes.

'Are you going to see her again?'

'No.'

Squashing his bumpy knee between her legs, she sought reassurance so that she could share the rest.

'Steve Robson was here last night.' She mangled the words so that Robson came out like Ribson and it sounded as though he had been here at her invitation.

'What?'

'I've messed it up.'

'Going anywhere near that man is a mistake.'

'Steve Robson sent me the tapes.'

'What?'

'Anonymously.'

Gus rumpled his face.

'The man is a creep. He's also a pathological liar. He used to put For Sale signs with the name of his company in front of properties he wasn't handling, according to Frank.'

Only now did Elinor realise that despite all her efforts, her mistakes, she might not even get her house. As soon as the thought occurred to her, it became a reality. Diffusing her misery, she moved so close that all there was between them was a crush of clothes. Mingling smells.

'I've been conned. Is that what you think?'

'My honest opinion? Yes.'

'I don't know what he wants from me.'

Gus's words were warm on her face.

'I don't think he likes women. He's threatened by them. He hated Suzy seeing Frank. He made her life a misery, shouting at her. I saw him. He's a thug.'

Elinor stared at him. Hadn't she tried to establish exactly this, Steve Robson's relationship with Frank Foster, in court? That her failure to do so should have followed her here into bed on a damp afternoon defied all logic.

'What are you thinking?' Gus searched her face.

The daylight had faded and they were cocooned in gloom.

'I'm glad you're here,' she said.

And then they kissed and the rest went away.

* * *

When it was time to eat they made omelettes. QC couldn't master a soft-boiled egg. She had never seen her father switch on a kettle. She was watching Gus shave a green pyramid of chives with a fast knife. The precision of his movements fed her like passion.

'I wish we were on a desert island.'

He turned and smiled.

'I'll be back on Tuesday.'

He had a midnight train, the sleeper to Cornwall, to catch. Tomorrow would be the eighteenth anniversary of his brother's death and he was accompanying his mother to the rocks to remember him. My mother will read a line of something weepy then we'll go for a boozy lunch, he said.

He sat down beside her.

'Are you going to be all right?'

'Fine.' She tried to sound brave. 'I've got Nigel upstairs.'

She sliced her omelette and a flotilla of chives docked on her plate. She forced a hollow laugh.

'Steve Robson has been sitting outside the house so often that Nigel thinks we're under surveillance.'

'For Fuck's sake. What the hell does he want?'

That had been her question. She covered herself with her dressing gown.

'I don't know.'

He cupped her face in his hands.

'If he's harassing you, call the police.'

Nodding hopelessly at the spectre of court proceedings, the bribe, her poor judgment, she nodded.

'I wish I didn't have to go.'

'But you do,' she said.

Then he left and she felt miserable and scurried back to bed. Behind closed eyes, she thought of the waves with which he had gone to make peace and rocked herself to sleep.

Glass smashed and she sat up with a start, eyes blinking.

'Nigel?'

The glass was in her dreams. A windscreen had popped. There were shards everywhere. The sound of eruption was a fist on her door.

'Elinor.'

She zigzagged, feeling for the walls. She unbolted the door and tugged it towards her, forgetting the chain. It jerked tight as the door caught and a shiny black shoe, like a shark fin, jammed itself between the door and frame. The image was as surreal as her car-crash dreams.

'Do you think I'm a mug?'

She was as weightless as air. In the twilight of consciousness, she had been transported to another time and space. Steve Robson's eyes met hers across the chain. She tried to understand what she was looking at.

'How did you get in?'

'I've outlived my usefulness, is that it?'

A scream curled in the back of her throat.

'All I ever did was help you. It's not polite to ignore

people who are nice to you. Did no one ever tell you that?'

He jolted his foot and made the chain rattle. Her heart jumped. She stumbled over her words.

'If you don't go I'm calling the police.'

'There's no need to be like that.'

He stepped away from the door. Beneath the glare of the naked bulb on the landing, his complexion was ghoulish and his expression filled with furious despair. His fists were clenched.

'Why don't you let me in? So we can talk about this.'

Her head was unravelling. Reasoning with a man beyond reason, she had to end this madness before she was sucked in. She pushed the door, her eyes half shut.

'There's nothing to talk about. Just go.'

But he came at her, ramming the door with his shoulder. It flew back and struck her face. His mouth was so close that she picked up the scent of his skin. Chanel No. 5.

'I know what makes you tick.'

With a scream, she slammed the door, her head hot and hammering. Leaning against it, she heard him pacing outside, muttering and cursing before finally making his way downstairs, leaving her whole world turned upside down.

Chapter Twenty-three

'Thanks for meeting me,' she said, nervously.

'You know me.' He dragged over a stool with a gruff smile, and plonked down his briefcase. 'Never say no.'

Elinor had known that Brian would accept her invitation to meet if it involved a drink. They were in a pub with gold rails and pink carpets, set back from the main thoroughfare of the train station. Bing-bongs and muffled departure and arrival times warbled through the walls as harried faces flew in and out again with the hard edges gone. Jettisoned in empty glasses. Brian's daily time of departure was 6.05.

'Do you want another?'

'I'll get them,' she said.

She went to the bar. It would be her round for as long as it took to convince him to listen to what she had to say.

Back again, she waited for him to wet his mouth and light up the first of his many extra-length cigarettes.

'It's about Frank Foster. I think there could be grounds for reopening the case.'

White ash flecked Brian's bushy beard. She sensed fatigue in the sigh he failed to contain and the crows' feet that jiggled at the sides of his eyes.

'Do you remember the prosecution witness, Steve Robson?'

Brian shut his hooded eyes. He opened them again.

'I think he was responsible for threatening Miss Price with the anonymous calls and packages and letters.'

'I thought they were mates.'

Gin speeded her words.

'That's the point. Steve Robson was jealous of her relationship with Frank Foster. He tried to make her break it off. When she failed to do so, he convinced her that it was Frank Foster who was a menace by bombarding her with . . .'

Brian tugged his beard.

'How do you know all this?'

Elinor paused.

'I've seen him.'

His eyes sparkled. Now he was interested.

'Explain.' He slotted another Super King between craggy lips.

'I've been trying to buy a flat. I turned up to view a place a few weeks ago and Steve Robson was the estate agent.' She tried to sound breezy. 'To cut a long story short, since then Steve Robson has started to, well, threaten me.'

'How do you mean?'

'Sitting in his car outside my house. Sometimes all night. Sending me text messages. Getting someone else to cough into my answering machine while he was in my flat so I wouldn't think it was him.'

'Maybe he likes you. Doesn't know how to tell you.'

Brian wanted to go home.

'He repeated a line to me from one of the cards sent to Miss Price. *I know what makes you tick.* I remembered it immediately. And he stole my perfume. He wears it.'

Brian gargled his beer.

'So now he's a perv?'

Haunted by the memory of Steve's hard-boiled eyes, the whiff of her smell on him, she crunched an ice cube to make the recollection go away. Brian was weighing up the situation. She could see it in his shifting body weight. The laboured breathing.

'There're two problems here.'

Elinor nodded.

'You're talking about reopening the case to get the first conviction put aside. Now it will take longer than three months to do that, and Frank Foster's only going to serve three months, remember. Then there are new proceedings if you've got evidence to prove Steve Robson is' – he swallowed – 'stalking you. That's another can of worms.'

'I know.'

Depositing his empty glass on the table, Brian made a distracted clicking sound with his tongue.

'I don't know,' he said soberly. 'You haven't got a lot

to go on. Those DNA tests did prove positive. Frank Foster definitely sent some of those cards.'

Elinor leaned her elbows on the table.

'Not all of them. They weren't all tested. Nor do I believe he was responsible for the dead rat or the mutilated toy.'

A jingle summoned commuters to rides home. An army of suits took flight. Brian began folding up his newspaper.

'Okay. Here's what. If Steve Robson has become a nuisance, it goes without saying you've got to report him to the police. Frankly I'm surprised you've left it so long. Now if this leads to reopening Frank Foster's case, so be it. Obviously it won't be your case.' He slipped his lighter into his cigarette box. 'You'll be a witness.'

'Yes.'

They stood up together. Lulled into reflection by what had been said, they remained on opposite sides of the table for a moment. Brian offered his hand.

'Wife's birthday. Can't be late. Call me as soon as you've given a statement to the police.'

They shook hands.

'I will. And thanks.'

'Pleasure.'

Briefcase jogging, he trotted away fast.

When she got home she burrowed on the sofa, hugged a cushion to her chest and waited for Gus. He would be back late tonight. She craved his presence. Alone with the silence that rattled her bones, she waited for the dog to bark. It would be a comfort.

On her way back she had forced herself to confront another of her fears. Making a detour past her house, and it was still her house, she had discovered a For Sale sign posted outside. The name on the sign was not Brooks & Brooks but Benham & Co. The prospect of forging a friendship with another estate agent and beginning the process all over again was daunting yet she was determined to do it. Tomorrow she would ring and make an appointment to view it. She wasn't prepared to give up without a proper fight.

Checking her messages, she found only one from Kendra. 'Where are you? You weren't in chambers today. I had a heavenly weekend in the country.' She sang the last three words. Something was making her happy. Elinor considered calling to ask whether she could hide out in her flat but it would take an hour to get there and an hour back and what about Gus? She thought about ringing the actress in LA before remembering that today was her long-awaited underwater shoot. She was submerged in a tank of water in the desert pretending to drown. Elinor would have to sit it out.

Then it happened.

Perhaps this was what she had been waiting for all along. Before it gets better, it gets worse, something Frida used to say, filtered into her mind as he tapped on the window inches away from her head. Imagining him leaning in, delivering blows with his fist, she felt powerless to move. She felt in pain. She felt nothing at all. She thought of all the things she had done wrong and the lies she had told. She thought of the chaos with which she had sought to complicate her life.

Furious vibrations. He was forcing the window sash. He was about to break in. This she hadn't chosen. She was being punished for something she had not done. Self-preservation woke her from her stupor. Terror catapulted her off the sofa. On legs of elastic she ran upstairs. Banging on Nigel's door, she prayed he was in. The handle jiggled.

'I was just on my way down.' Nigel had a tea towel over his shoulder. 'I've called the police. He's been out there again. I caught him with binoculars.'

Elinor collapsed on a chair in his hall.

'I know him.'

Nigel twisted the tea towel.

'Not an ex-bloody-boyfriend?'

'Estate agent.'

'It gets worse.' Nigel hadn't lost his sense of humour.

Then the buzzer went. They heard the front door open. Meaty male voices, good evenings, what-seems-to-be-the-problems, followed by footsteps, came stomping upstairs.

'Third floor,' called Nigel, leaning over the banisters.

What followed next was a blur of stiff blue legs, helmets under arms and the smell of polished leather and disinfectant soap. For once Elinor wasn't in charge.

'My name's PC Graham. This here's my colleague PC Evans.'

When did policemen become so tall? wondered Elinor as PC Graham stooped so as not to bump his head on Nigel's attic ceiling. Both raven haired with beady eyes, they could have been brothers. Seated, PC Graham flipped open his notebook. PC Evans sat back and lined up his shoes. She looked into their faces, as bright as lamps.

'We've just been to talk to the gentleman in the car. He says you know him, Miss Taylor.'

Elinor's stomach lurched. She tasted bile. This wasn't what she wanted to hear.

'Yes,' she faltered.

'He says he's selling the building on behalf of the landlord. A Mr Singh. He's been asked to do a preliminary structural assessment. The surveyor is coming round next week. He says you've less than a month to vacate the premises. Is that correct?'

Nigel whipped the tea towel against his leg.

'I don't believe this.'

Elinor was horrified. Since when had Steve Robson been in touch with Mr Singh?

'I don't think you understand. He was trying to break into my flat.'

PC Graham maintained his neutral tone.

'As I said, Miss Taylor, I've seen the documentation which proves that the gentleman has been asked to inspect the building on behalf of Mr Singh. I've spoken to him regarding your concerns. He wishes to apologise for any fright he may have caused. Now I suggest if you wish to discuss the matter further, we go downstairs and talk it through calmly with the gentleman outside. Unless, that is, you would rather invite him in.'

'No.' Elinor jerked away from the table. 'Don't you

understand? Everything I say to him is read in the wrong way. By talking to him, I'm encouraging him.'

'Well, if you're not going to, I will,' said Nigel.

'Please,' Elinor protested, as the five thousand pounds reared itself. Her black mistake.

'I'm not trying to be funny, but you've not been involved with him, have you, Miss Taylor? He was never any sort of boyfriend?'

PC Graham was taking notes.

She resented the question.

'No.'

'He seems to think you're on pretty amicable terms.'

Nigel looked curiously at her. Elinor felt as though she were being slandered. The longer she remained silent, the stronger their suspicions.

'I don't know what he's talking about.'

'Did you purchase a property through the gentleman?'

Her heartbeat fluttered wildly.

'No.'

'Fell out over it, did you?'

'No.'

Nigel came to her defence.

'Look. Whoever he is, he should not be lurking around at night, spying on us.'

Flapping his notebook closed, PC Graham raised himself up from his chair.

'I think you all need to take a nice deep breath.' He began fastening up his big blue coat with its shiny gold buttons. 'I can see you're upset about having to leave your home. My advice is take it up with your landlord not the gentleman outside. He's only trying to do his job.'

It wasn't so much disappointment as horror that rooted Elinor to her seat. Whatever it was that Steve Robson had said to make the police officers believe him had worked. It was frightening. Nigel saw them to the door.

'You're making a mistake.'

'Thank you, sir. If you'll let us do our job. I'm sure we won't try to do yours.'

And off they creaked in their hulking shoes.

Elinor remained where she was. She couldn't move. She would wait for Gus to come and find her here. She felt small, defenceless and trapped. A hostage in her own home.

'They're all the same,' said Nigel as he uncorked a bottle of Bulgarian red and settled into a sort of post-party meditation. They had seen off the last of the guests and could now discuss their failings and foibles. 'Never on your side. I say let's sabotage the planks so that next time he falls.'

'That's attempted murder,' said Elinor quietly. Not that she hadn't had the same thought herself. Her situation was so chillingly familiar. She felt sick with disbelief. 'I've come across stalkers before.' She curled up against the armrest as Nigel joined her on the sofa. 'Only then it was someone else's nightmare, not mine.'

'So, what's the answer?'

'There isn't one. Unless I take him to court.'

'Clever man.'

'They always are.'

'Perhaps it's a good thing we're moving.'

It would never be far enough, and one day she would be coming back.

'Yes,' was all she said.

QC was in his office. Profoundly irritated by her news, he couldn't hold her gaze. Elinor tried not to feel slighted by his aloofness, the twiddling of his cuff links, taking calls from his secretary, ordering coffee. She was in her coat. She was reminded of their first encounter. Her interview. His interest in her then had been feverish. He could hardly contain his glee at the feast of nubile flesh before him. How times had changed.

'What on earth were you thinking?'

She had told him about the bribe.

'I was desperate.'

'To be what? Debarred?'

He was the father she had never had. Confrontational. Involved in her life. She wasn't sure she liked it.

'Well, you can say goodbye to the money.'

'You think I haven't?'

'Are you on drugs?'

She glared. He leaned back in his chair.

'Elinor. All I'm saying is if you do become a witness and this bribe business does come out in court, the judge won't look favourably on you or these chambers. Of course I'm unhappy about you bringing these chambers into disrepute. I'd say the same thing to any of the barristers here.'

It took a moment to sink in. But he was cancelling his

support, leaving her to fend for herself. He eased his collar away from his neck and her eyes bored in on a bruise on his neck.

'Is that a lovebite?'

'Er . . . What?' He hastily rearranged his head and neck. Too late.

'You're sleeping with Kendra.'

QC's face went floppy like a fish, and Elinor began to laugh. Only Kendra dispensed lovebites. It was her thing.

'Do you know what, Peter?' she said, suddenly liberated. 'You're the one who brings these chambers into disrepute. You seem to think it's your job to sleep with every single woman who works here. You're a married man, for Christ's sake.'

QC coloured as his expression changed. His eyes were worried because they were equals again. He cleared his throat.

'Have you filed a complaint with the police?'

The old QC had returned. The man she knew. Her friend.

'I tried to.'

'What do you mean?'

'They wouldn't take it seriously.'

'I do take it seriously.'

She began to feel emotional, as – in delayed response – the horrors of the past few days impacted on her.

'Now you know who you must go and talk to?'

She did.

'Caroline.'

'She's the expert on all this stuff. You can't let him get away with this. It's illegal. And I for one refuse to see you become a victim.

Blinking back tears, Elinor gripped the arms of her chair. QC was right. It was what she had become. Her decision made, she stood up. She had made enough mistakes and she wasn't prepared to make another.

'I'm going away.'

QC sat forward in his chair.

'Oh?'

'For a week. Perhaps longer.'

'Now listen. I really am sorry about all this business. Whatever needs doing, you must let me know.'

'I will. I'll work out what to do when I get back. And thanks, Peter.'

'I'm not going anywhere.' He offered a late smile. 'Truth is the daughter of time.'

Back at the flat, she picked up her bag. Waiting for her downstairs in the hallway, next to the packing boxes, was a bouquet. *Lilium longiflorum.* She didn't need to read the card to know who they were from. Throwing them in the bin, she forced the lilies, snapping the stems, ruining the petals. Before she did so she took a moment to rub her nose in their creamy smoothness. If only their intention were as pure as their scent. But her conscience was clear. Her life was her own. He would never win at this game.

* * *

Then they were in the sky.

'We are experiencing some turbulence. The safety-belt sign has been switched on and the captain has asked that you return to your seats.'

'I can't remember ever having felt nervous like this,' said Gus, his face lit up in vapour trails flashing off the wing. 'Thanks for being here.'

When they touched down at Phoenix Airport, Arizona, Gus would be arrested. He would be taken away to spend the following forty-eight hours in a cell. And Elinor would go quietly to their hotel and read her book by the pool and sip cold drinks and pretend to relax until it was time to go to trial. Elinor had spoken to his lawyer. You guys need to prepare yourselves mentally and emotionally, he said. He forgot financially, did he? said Gus.

He took her hand.

'If they don't kick me out . . .'

'Which they won't . . .'

'We'll go to the Red Rocks. There's one particular rock shaped like an armchair that I know fits one. We're going to make it fit two. And we'll watch the sky turn the same colour as the rocks.'

The colour of magic. It was all she wanted. Every emotion she felt was contained in the clasp of his hand. She trusted this man as much as she trusted herself that she had made the right decision. She was going to be the woman he entrusted with the responsibility of his mind.

The weight of his secrets. There were no certainties in the sky besides the clear blue of daylight and the blackness of the earth's atmosphere beyond. All she knew was that they were heading out of stormy darkness and into the sun. It was enough. The rest was as far away as yesterday.